ALLUSION

ANDI HYLDAHL

ISBN: 1541315480
ISBN-13: 978-1541315488

For my three chocolate lovers.

ALLUSION

CHAPTER ONE

A dusty, maroon pickup approaches. My pulse surges. The timing is dead on. I duck under the foliage and heft up dad's ancient binoculars, zooming in on two large hands gripping ten and two.

These hands could be the ones.

But the truck putts along the quiet street without reason to stop, leaving me empty-handed and stalking the innocent in broad daylight. I sigh and move on, waiting for the next moving target. I'll wait all day if I have to. No more secrets.

Several minutes of stillness pass. I regroup, pulling the blanket of hair off my sticky neck into a heap on top of my head. I turn away from the street and stare at the neglected house in front of me, eyeing the patchy lawn, the peeling paint, and the tired porch swing that would certainly send a sliver into unsuspecting behinds. But no one visits this house. Except for today.

I'm spending my eighteenth birthday in my front yard, lodged between two overgrown juniper bushes, chomping down the final inches of a sweaty Slim Jim. I've been waiting three hundred and sixty-four days for this.

Every June twenty-fifth, a miracle happens. An anonymous gift is left on my porch. It is the only gift I receive all year, and it is exactly what I need.

It's the reason I'm willing to get up each morning and face reality. And unlike years past, today, I will have someone to thank.

I'm going to catch him.

Assuming it's a *him*. My premise is solely based on the wrapping, or lack thereof.

The thought sends adrenaline racing through me. I hold my breath and snake my body through the shrubbery, pounce onto the grass, and do a sweep across the empty front porch. I've been out here all day and there's no way I could've missed the drop off. I resume my position in the junipers, wishing I'd brought more snacks.

Less than a handful of uninvolved cars pass, along with the time. My spirits are dropping with the sun. He's never been this late.

I absorb the hard truth I've been avoiding all day. The presents have come to an end. I'm an adult now and surprises are for kids. This year and from now on, my birthday will be like any other day. Worst of all, I'll never know who brought hope and comfort to my childhood.

I sink further into the foliage and let the sharp needles distract me from utter disappointment. I don't have time to lament. *& passionate expression of sorrow*

Nothing like a twelve-hour work shift to finish my birthday off with a bang. I've only got minutes to feed Mom and scrub up.

I walk to the front door, taking one last glance towards the deserted street. A blurry memory comes to view—a neighborhood gathering. Tables in the street, potluck, fireworks, kids. Nothing specific except the recollection of contentment.

I snap out of my trance and let go.

The leftover lasagna sizzles coming out of the microwave, and I set it on the table over Mom's placemat. I know all too well it will still be here, cold and untouched when I get home in the morning, but I sprinkle fresh parsley on top anyway.

Mom is peaceful, rocking in her red chair. The upholstered bright poppy's energy clashes against her mundane expression. She is knitting, and she is a master at it.

I flip both light switches, and the family room light turns on as well as a stream of multi-colored

Christmas lights streamed across the loft railing.

I often find my mom staring at me. I assume she's wondering what happened to her little girl. She is still absolutely beautiful in a very natural way. Her hair is a lovely chestnut color and lies straight, just below her shoulders. Her features are soft and perfectly proportioned. However, she looks too thin and she's lost any signs of normal human emotion in her face.

I squeeze her hand and whisper in her ear.

"Renee, your dinner is on the table. Anything you need? You be okay on your own tonight?"

I stopped calling her 'Mom' years ago when she started giving me that confused look, same one that I'm getting right now.

Her hum is my answer.

"I'll be back bright and early to send you off to work." At the office they allow her to do busy work like filing papers and transcribing records. It's a blessing for both of us.

I escape to my bedroom to throw on some scrubs. I give myself seconds to glance in the mirror, vowing to mold my beehive into a braid once I get to work.

I scamper down the hall, throwing my stethoscope and swimsuit into a worn backpack. But my eye catches something unusual and I freeze. The back door is propped slightly open. I hold my breath, run over, and glance between the wooden door and the screen.

Sure enough, a small brown box is resting between the doors. My hands are trembling as I pick it up. It holds a fair bit of weight, and I can tell by the rumbling inside that there is more than one object in there. I turn it over and gasp at the sight of my name, written across the front in scribbled cursive. That's a first.

I gently place the small brown box in my backpack, smiling with a renewed sense of hope. I can't rush this moment. I've waited all year for this.

ₒ nurse
₆ man is sick

CHAPTER
TWO

I hop on my bike, needing to break the speed limit in order to make it on time. Luckily my energy is soaring with the knowledge of what's resting in my backpack. I decide to keep my surfboard attached to my bike for an early morning ride after work.

I've jimmied a rack to hold my board while I bike. It's nothing more than a small, metal shoe rack zip-tied to the right side. It's less than ideal and I know I look ridiculous leaning slightly left as a counterweight, but it has been my method for years. I don't have the luxury of caring what people think.

It will take me twenty minutes to ride to work from here. Amber Waves is a nursing home nestled in a shady cove on the Yachats, Oregon, coastline.

Riding my bike to work is something I'll never tire of. The trail lies underneath fifty-foot redwoods that wind along the coastline and then wheat fields that carpet the landscape between my path and the rocky shore. Even the final hundred-meter incline is glorious, knowing the view that waits. The seclusion is rare for a nursing home, and the peace it provides is one of a kind; unless you can't find peace in changing adult diapers or draining catheter bags.

Halfway there, I zip past Carl's taco stand. Something urges me to turn around, likely my grumbling stomach. I should have left time to pack dinner. But today calls for a special treat, and this ghetto taco stand is one of the things I look forward to most after a long winter.

I pull out a dollar and fifty cents, handing it to the owner who has been here every summer since I can remember. He has long, silvery hair, sun-baked skin, and deep wrinkles lining his eyes, I assume revealing a life filled with happiness.

"The usual?" Carl asks with a smile, taking my change.

"Yes please."

I squeeze a fresh lime wedge all over the beer-battered cod and breathe in the freshly fried goodness. Carl puts extra cilantro slaw on my taco every time. He's generous like that.

I'm back on my bike, stuffing my face with one hand and leaning to one side to offset the surfboard.

All worth it.

Somehow I've made it on time but I'm not going to win any beauty contests. I walk my bike through the entrance, the nursing home aroma welcoming me. I have that smell narrowed down to stale breath, alcohol swabs, re-warmed veggies, and traces of B.O. The fact that it's a welcoming fragrance is super disturbing. I'm panicked that I smell like my old friends, which is why I've implemented an obsessive, post-shift-fumigation routine at my house, no matter what the hour.

Most of the folks are still awake and slowly wandering the halls of the facility when I arrive. They go to bed when the sun does, or when bingo is over.

My bag is stowed next to my bike and board, which are taking up half of the break room, but no one has complained in nearly two years that I've been employed here. I partially unzip and peak inside my bag, confirming my present is safe. I have to sit on my hands to keep them from ripping the box open here and now.

I say goodbye to the swing-shift crew I used to work with just a couple weeks ago while I was finishing high school. Now that I'm graduated, the night owl in me has emerged and I love my new shift.

Looking at the white board, I see that I'm paired up with Loretta tonight. She might have been a good nurse at one point, but she could really benefit from some Prozac and a couple rounds of heavy liposuction. Most CNAs hate getting paired up with her due to the extra workload she dumps on their already overflowing list of tasks. I don't complain since the night goes so much quicker.

Loretta is sitting in the corner getting report from the last shift. I try not to make eye contact but I catch myself staring at the flesh squishing out of the slots of her chair. I've loitered too long and she clucks out the first of her demands.

"Dinner then showers—you know the drill."

The squash soup dribbles out of Mr. Shroeder's lips but I catch it with the spoon, inviting it back into his mouth repeatedly until I'm positive a teaspoon has been consumed. He stares past me at the TV, grumbling incoherent answers to Alex Trebek.

"Mofofagrum," He announces, his finger up in the air, soup dripping down his chin.

"What is, mofofagrum," I correct.

Shroeder is a tall man with a large frame, even though time has caused his barrel chest to narrow and his back to cripple over. I imagine he was a shrewd businessman back in his day but when I've inquired, he utters unintelligible yet condescending half-phrases at me.

It drives him batty when I'm a smart-aleck.

I swoop in with another spoonful of the good

stuff, but Shroeder wrenches his head left and right, swatting the soup away and spattering liquid squash all across the front of me. I gasp.

To my left, Phil, the golden male-CNA on shift, cackles and continues feeding Betty, the sweetest granny in the joint. He pauses, "What is a ribosome," he says, turning his attention back to the TV. I glare at him.

"Try ribosomal RNA," I say, wiping the yellow splotches off my scrubs. Alex Trebek confirms that I'm right.

Phil turns to me. "Oh, it's on," he says, aggressively stuffing a bread roll into Betty's mouth.

Phil looks like an overgrown elf, especially when he wears those forest green scrubs. "First person to correctly answer the next question," he pauses, "gets a free pass on shower duty tonight."

"No showers?" I raise my eyebrows, glancing up at the jeopardy categories. Again, the contestant chooses DNA.

"Oh Phil," I smile, "you're on."

Alex reads, "Most of the amino acids of a protein are incorrect thanks to this type of mutation."

Phil sucks in his breath. I let him suffer for a few more seconds, spearing a broccoli for Shroeder.

"Ooh, what is…what is…" Phil smacks his hand against his forehead.

"Frameshift mutation," the contestant and I say in unison.

I don't even feel bad. It's my birthday, and believe it or not, old geezers don't like eighteen-year-old girls spraying off their naked bodies.

I spoon feed two more patients then turn the corner and sneak a peek in on one of my favorites, Miss Darby. She is struggling to get herself dressed after her shower and she motions me over.

"Lucy, you angel, come on over here and give me a hand."

Darby is the black version of Betty White, like a sweet and sassy fairy godmother.

"Hey Darb. I was hoping I'd get to see you tonight." I start untwisting her brassiere while preparing myself for the same conversation we have nearly every shift. She picks up one of the loose flaps of skin resting against her ribcage and places it into the cup of her bra.

"These used to be state of the art, you know." She looks at me with a jaunty grin. "Now they're in a state of deflate. Oh, well."

I chuckle. "You've still got it, Darb. We all know it."

"Oh don't be ridiculous. Lucy, you need to listen to me…"

"Here we go," I mumble, fastening the buttons on the front of her silk pajamas.

She shushes me while glancing in the mirror and nodding in approval. "You are the prettiest little thing I've ever laid eyes on, even though you don't fuss over yourself much. Why, if we could just trade in these scrubs for a little lipstick and them rubber shoes in for some high heels, you'd find yourself a boyfriend in no time." She pats my cheek still admiring herself in the mirror.

I shake my head and smile, taking a wide-toothed comb through her thin, salt and pepper hair. It takes three strokes to comb out her entire head.

"I've got other things to think about besides boys, Darb."

I open her top drawer and pull out her favorite fire-engine-red nail polish. I'm still swamped, but this will only take a couple of minutes, and boy, does she feel foxy with red nails.

Her fingers are cold and her knuckles look swollen from a lifetime of use. I wish I had time to massage these hands.

"Lucy girl, you're in the prime of your life. Promise me you'll have some fun. You promise me right now, young lady," she shakes an arthritic finger at me.

I finish her last nail and blow vigorously over the wet paint. I pull back the sheets on her bed, adjust the picture of her sweetheart, and rush out of there before I make promises I can't keep.

Next, I empty the garbage in each room, change bed sheets, and return all dinner trays back to the cafeteria. At last, I take the p.m. vital signs, empty catheter bags, record intakes and outputs, take blood sugars, and record the results in the computer.

Now it's late and the halls have emptied. The lights over the nurses' station have been dimmed and the only sounds are the unharmonious snorts echoing out of rooms. Glorious.

The majority of the staff has crowded into the break room to chitchat over their re-warmed frozen meals and discuss other coworkers and reality television.

My legs feel heavy and my back aches. I don't let myself count how many hours I have left or think about my soft bed. That's when I remember the present in my bag. Butterflies dance in my stomach.

I follow Phil into the break room and poor some hot chocolate mix into two Styrofoam cups followed by some hot water from the coffee pot. I scan the room, eyeing my backpack.

The gift will have to wait until I have privacy. I want the moment to be perfect. Glancing left and right, I slip out of the room.

No one ever asks where I'm going.

CHAPTER THREE

I don't have a lot of friends. It's easier that way.

My best friend makes up for the low numbers. We're like Edward and Bella, minus the blood sucking and romance. And then add some wrinkles and Ensure.

Truth is, we get each other.

I make my way down to another beige hall that I haven't visited yet tonight, walking slowly as to not splash the hot cocoa. The passage looks sleepy but I notice a soft light glowing from the end.

The residents in this wing are the most independent of the bunch although they still have a daily check up, three prepared meals per day, and prescribed meds delivered by a nurse.

Each individual room in this hall has a small bathroom with a toilet, sink, and shower. Besides that, they look exactly the same as the others with call lights above each door and individual names plated at eye level to the exterior.

I've made it to the very last room. The door is shut but light is escaping through the crack at the bottom. Just as I'm about to give the door a light kick, it cracks open.

Arthur is fully dressed in some khakis and a button-up red and navy-plaid shirt. His white hair stands up from his head in a sort of mad-scientist way and he is sporting some unintentionally hip reading glasses.

His walker is in between us, blocking the entrance of the door. He smiles warmly at me and peeks his head through the crack.

"I heard you coming." He sends me a welcoming smile and pushes the door open all the way. I love that his voice sounds like Winnie the Pooh.

I often wonder if he was sent to me by an angel, as a consolation prize for the crappy lot in life I've been given.

Arthur has been around ever since I started working here, two years ago. His diabetes started demanding insulin injections several times a day, which eventually required some supervision. I personally assume that he was forced here by a family member, since I know him to be the independent, stubborn type that would prefer to do things on his own.

I have a testimony of diabetes. Best thing that's ever happened to me, probably worst thing that's happened to him. I cherish the relationship we've developed, especially considering I have very few.

"Seriously, Art, when do you ever sleep?" I whisper loudly as he moves his walker out of the way.

"Well, I'll have plenty of time to sleep when I'm dead, now won't I? Come on in here and make yourself comfortable, Lucy Loo."

He leaves the door open and slowly makes his way back to the office chair behind his desk.

I plop down in the green checked armchair across from him, finally able to relax and sip my warm beverage.

His room looks the same as it always does. In the far corner lies a small twin sized mattress, the provided sea foam green linens unwrinkled, the crisp hospital corners exact. Three pairs of shoes are neatly lined up in a row along the closet floor, and above them, a modestly sized wardrobe consisting mostly of khakis and plaids. An aged black and white photo in a thin silver frame rests on his nightstand. It's all very simple and tidy, at least on this side of the room.

On the opposite wall stands a sturdy oak desk. I can't even see the top of it due to the landfill of books and papers. All sorts of nonsense is scribbled in no legible order on loose papers littering every square inch of the desk. I can barely decipher some coordinates and equations but nothing that makes any sense to me or any normally educated human. I know he was a genetics professor back in his day, but he still studies "to keep his brain from going to mush."

When Art finally makes it back to his desk, he lets go of his walker and falls back into the plush chair. It is a luxurious, tufted, brown-leather swivel that doesn't match the surrounding nursing home décor in the least.

He has very few pictures and trinkets from home, but I often find him staring at the black and white picture of his deceased Mother.

Most of the time he lets me do the talking, but from what I've gathered, he has very little family. Just another thing we seem to have in common.

Gingerly, he tiptoes the chair around to face me. "So glad you came, Lucy. Extra chocolate?" He glances down to his cup.

"Two packets," I say slyly.

He chuckles and his thick-rimmed glasses slide down his peaked nose.

I know he is old, but his eyes reveal the clarity and sharpness of his mind.

"How were the waves today?" He asks with enthusiasm.

"Actually, I didn't surf."

Art raises a suspicious eyebrow and lowers his voice. "Did ya catch him?"

"No, but I will. Next year. If there is a next year."

Arthur studies me for a minute before he reaches around towards his desk and lifts up a stack of papers. I watch as he reveals a shiny gold box with a red ribbon tied around it.

"This is for you." He hands the gift over like it's nothing out of the ordinary.

For a few seconds, I wonder if I'm going to start crying like an old sap.

I bite my lip to try to disperse my emotions. "Arthur, I didn't tell you it was my birthday."

A large smile is sprawled across his face. "Eighteen is a big one. Now open 'er up!"

I close my eyes in disbelief and find myself smiling like a little kid. The ribbon unravels with one pull, and I open the box.

I gasp and pull out an antique ring like nothing I've ever seen before. The oval gemstone has swirls of blues and greens with an inexplicable and mesmerizing depth in the center.

"Arthur!" I thank and scold him simultaneously. "Oh my goodness. It's amazing. I've never…I don't even know what to say." I sit there gaping, my mouth wide enough to fit my fist inside.

"Abalone," he interrupts. "The stone is called

abalone. It's actually a type of shell. The Native Americans believe it to be sacred and use it to carry messages to heaven. I thought of you immediately when I saw it."

I'm overwhelmed by his thoughtfulness, and all I can do is shake my head in gratitude for several seconds.

I pick up the ring and try it on all my fingers before finding a permanent home for it on my right ring finger. I'm never taking it off.

I reach for his hand and hold it for a minute, cherishing the feeling of being cherished. But since Art is a no-nonsense kind of guy, a two second hand embrace is all he gives me before he turns towards his desk and buries his head in whatever it was he was studying before I entered.

I hug the ring against my chest and peek over his shoulder at a detailed sketch of what I imagine to be a cell and neurons. He takes his pen and points to a space between two nerve cells.

"What's this?" He looks up to me with raised eyebrows.

Please. This is child's play.

"That would be a synapse." I shoot him a *give me a real question* kind of look.

"And what is its purpose, ya wiseacre?"

"It's the junction where signals pass between the nerve cells…"

He sits patiently, obviously expecting me to

expound.

"Impulses pass by diffusion of a neurotransmitter." I go on. "If the neurotransmitter is damaged or blocked it can lead to severe memory loss, disorientation and slew of other destitute conditions." I exhale somberly.

Art pauses thoughtfully and looks up at me. "Would you rather we discuss heteroplasmic point mutations? I just read an astounding article on the transfer RNA gene this morning."

Just as I am about to gladly agree, a call light goes off down the hall. I sigh. Time to leave my happy place.

Before I leave, I poke Art's fingertip and get a blood sample for the glucometer. The machine sucks in the blood and after a few seconds it beeps and displays the results.

130.

I guess I won't feel too guilty for sneaking the extra chocolate in his cocoa.

As I leave Art's room, I see him slowly reading the insulin sliding scale. He looks relieved when he realizes he's off the hook tonight. One of these days he's going to have to relax and leave the meds to us.

I glance down at my watch. Yet again, I've nearly conquered another twelve-hour shift. Every time, night after night, it seems like an impossible feat.

As I ride home, the sun is just starting to peek over the tree-topped mountains. I am exhausted, groggy, and can barely send the signal from my brain to make my legs push the pedals. What I can feel is the unfamiliar sensation of the ring around my finger. I don't remember the last time someone gave me a gift—in person at least. At this thought, I pedal faster.

It's time. It's finally time. I know exactly where I'm going to open my gift. The sudden adrenaline rush is fierce, helping clear the fog in my tired head.

As I ride, I think of the last nine gifts, and how they seemed to be the exact thing that I needed at that time.

For example, when I switched from middle to high school, the boundaries of my house no longer qualified me to ride the school bus. I walked more than a mile each morning and was often late making sure Mom got off to work on time. That summer, a beautiful baby blue bike was sitting on my porch. It wasn't just any bike. It was fabulous, with several gears and a basket to hold my books. It remains my main mode of transportation.

After one abnormally frigid year, a luxurious and heavy fur blanket was rolled up with a giant bow tied around it. It was a lifesaver in my drafty house.

At last, I arrive on the empty beach, throwing my bike down and whipping the bag off my shoulders. What could it possibly be? Money? Gift cards? I know, keys to a car. I throw my head back and chortle. I can't take it a second longer and I rip into the brown box and throw the lid open.

My heart drops as I stare at the thing I've been waiting all year for. It's not even close to anything I expected. I exhale through pursed lips.

Four assorted chocolates lined in individual gold-aluminum wrappers are neatly nestled in the box. They look expertly crafted, each hand-dipped with a smooth chocolate coating and elegant swirls on top.

I'm stunned, trying to wrap my mind around this.

Chocolates.

Chocolate.

Chocolate? With each word I slip into a deeper sadness, even though chocolate usually brings me way more joy than it ought to.

From an intellectual standpoint, there must be a reason I need chocolate right now, on my eighteenth birthday. Never mind college or a car. I don't need a boyfriend. I don't need my own life.

My gaze is frozen on the crashing waves just feet in front of me. The splashes of blues blur together with the early sunlight into a bleary storm as tears well up in my eyes. I'm mad at myself for having such high expectations.

My disappointment is replaced by a sudden epiphany that pauses the storm: *this gift is from somebody else*. It's obvious. For one thing, it was stashed in a different location. Second of all, it had my name written on top. My mystery gifts have never had writing. I can feel my body relaxing from its tense state at this realization.

But then where's my real present? And who could these chocolates be from?

Well, there's Ryan... the awkward but not completely unattractive band geek who asked me to prom. He avoided me for a couple weeks after I turned him down, but I still caught him staring at me all hour during psychology. I might have gone if I wasn't forced to choose between buying a boutonniere or milk that week, or if I didn't have to go through the hassle of borrowing a dress. I should have tried harder.

It could have been Judy, Mom's co-worker who is always checking in on me. I'm not sure how she could have found out it was my birthday, but it's a possibility.

I glance at my watch. My board sits next to me, dislodged from my bike during the excitement. I can't find the energy to surf. But going home now means trying to stay awake for another hour before sending mom off to work.

I glide my finger across the smooth yellow surface, feeling the deep notches in a row on the underside of the board.

The notches on my board are evidence, deep scores representing each year he's been gone. Time and responsibility have stolen away my innocence and now I stare at the fixed reminders of my fate.

Ten lines, ten pleas, ten years, depicting my

solitude. With each new tally, the fairytale memories I once carried vanish, one by one, swallowed up into the thirsty ocean. And now I wonder if they were indeed fairytales, composed by my wishful subconscious.

I fall back into the cool, soft sand and tug my locket around so that it rests on my chest. I stroke its smooth, circular surface between my fingers, sensing its weight in my palm. For ten years it hasn't left its place around my neck. It has become a part of me, and feeling its presence has become as instinctive as breathing.

I slide my nail between the grooves and the locket opens with little resistance, its clasp overused and barely catching these days. The faded picture is reflecting against the sun, but my dark eyes still find his. They are full of kindness and wisdom, but I also see secrets, hidden beneath the tangible depths. I move down and study the dimple claiming his right cheek and trace my own with my finger. Thank goodness I didn't get his nose.

Often I imagine how he would look now, and if we'd still be out exploring the ocean together. The concrete memories I'd once had are cloudy and, to my frustration, tangled with my prior teenaged musings of him.

"Tomorrow we'll surf, Dad." My words are carried away with the steady Oregon winds.

I reach for the box of chocolates and bring them

up to my nose, taking in a whiff of sweet, dark cocoa.

Breakfast is served.

I remove the polka dotted tissue paper resting on top and snatch one out of the box, looking for any indication of which candy shop these came from, but they are unmarked. Just as I'm about to pop the first one in my mouth without a second thought, my eye catches something subtle. I draw my hand back and inspect the top of the morsel. Drizzled on top in the same color as the whole, is what looks like a cursive E. I turn it around and view a number 3. I glance towards the other chocolates, and sure enough, I find a 1, 2, and 4, lightly drizzled across their tops in melted chocolate.

Am I supposed to eat these in order? "You're not the boss of me," I mutter to the chocolate. I keep hold of number three and am ready to find out what's inside this bad boy. Hazelnut? Carmel? Mint?

I pause for a second wishing for once I could be a rebel. 3 is now back in its gold wrapper and I take number 1.

"You win," I whisper, popping the whole thing in.

The milk chocolate is smooth and silky and melts on my tongue. I bite into the center and strong almond cream hits my taste buds and oozes out of its chocolate shell. At first it's sweet and silky, but after a minute, I'm left with an unpleasant metallic aftertaste.

"Pathetic excuse for chocolate," I mutter, smacking my lips. Started out so promising. Makes me wonder if these are homemade. Number 2 has a lot of ground to make up. I sit up and reach for the box but am forced to pause.

With no warning, the world starts spinning. I close my eyes and when I open them back up, I see two of everything. I put one hand out in front of me and count eight blurry fingers. My head feels light and my eyelids heavy, in fact, I don't think I can keep my eyes open a second longer. I manage to grab the box but my exhaustion is so severe now, I crash land on top of my surfboard. Black spots are closing in on my vision one by one, until all light is consumed.

The last thing I remember seeing is the cursive writing.

CHAPTER FOUR

I've got to stop the twirling. I crack my eyes open and realize I'm sitting up in a chair, spinning round and around. I look down and see two short legs, barely hanging over the edge of the seat. There is laughing and squealing, but I don't see anyone else. As I spin, I catch a glimpse of a drawing taped to the wall… a ballerina. I pass it over and over again and discern my name written on the bottom left corner in amateur manuscript. I see books, shaggy orange carpet, and blurry, colorful Christmas lights.

I'm in my loft.

Suddenly, two arms on either side of the chair bring the spinning to a stop. Dad kneels in front of me, his face inches from mine. He's smiling at me like he has a million times. I want to touch him, but I don't have any control, so I watch.

Short silver whiskers cover his face, and dark circles cradle his eyes. I don't remember him this used up and exhausted.

As he stands up, he touches my nose then turns away, straightening things on his desk.

"What's that, Dad?" My voice is innocent and lively.

"It's my plane ticket, sweetie. Want to hold it for me?"

My heart aches at the sound of his voice but my subconscious doesn't allow me time to mourn.

"Okay…but I wish you didn't have to go." My little voice is distraught.

"Oh, my Lucy, me too." He bends back down and takes me in his arms, hugging me tight for much longer than a typical hug. When he releases, I see the onset of tears in his eyes. He hides them from the little one, but not from me.

"Let's practice your reading." He tries on a brave voice. "Why don't you read to me what's on that ticket."

I take it, eager to make him proud.

"Truman Lichty, June 25, flig…flig…

"Flight," Dad corrects.

"Flight 2107. Depar…departure: 1147 pm, POR to HNL.

"Really good, Luce. Read it one more time."

I read it to him again, this time without any help.

"You are the brightest, kindest, most beautiful eight year-old in the whole wide world. Which reminds me…"

He reaches into his pocket and pulls out a small box wrapped in pink paper with a real red tulip on top.

I squeal in delight and reach for the gift, nearly falling off the chair. Dad holds it away and pushes me back onto the seat.

"Ha. Hold your horses, little missy. Let's talk for a minute first. I know things have been…things have been a little crazy lately. But don't think for a second I forgot my baby's birthday." He continues to hold the gift out of grasp.

"Luce, I need you to promise me something."

My eighteen-year old ears hear the burden he carries in his voice.

The girl interrupts him. "Dad, when's Mom going to get better?"

Dad turns toward the window. The sky is black, and heavy raindrops are sliding down the windowpane.

An eerie déjà vu creeps into my mind as the torrent falls harder, forcefully beating on the roof like an orchestra of wet static.

I remember this moment, and now I recognize it as the moment I was ushered into adulthood. He might as well have wrapped up the heaviest burden he could have found and handed that to me.

Dad's voice is shaky. He brushes a stray blond hair out of my face. "While I'm gone on this trip, you get to be the queen of this castle. Mom isn't going to remember when you need to go to school, or when you need to go to bed, or when you might be hungry. You know what? She might not even remember when *she's* hungry."

"That's so weird, Dad." I sound amused, almost like it's a game and when the timer runs out, everything will be back to normal.

"And so that's why you get to be the queen. You get to be in charge of yourself and help Mom out, too. Do you think you can do that for me?"

"Yeah. But you didn't tell me when she's getting better."

Dad takes a deep breath and stares into my eyes, in a way that forces me to believe every word he says.

"I don't know, but I won't give up until she's better. And I want you to promise me that you won't give up either. Do you promise?"

He teasingly brings the present closer, dangling it in front of me like bait. I take a swipe at it, but he pulls it away again. He tickles me and won't hand it over until I succumb to his request.

"I promise!" I scream and explode out of the chair, jumping into his arms. He catches me and hands over the present, then starts swinging me around in circles until I'm too dizzy to stand on my own. Afterwards, he hugs me hard, then kisses my forehead.

I'm still giggling wildly as I tear open the paper.

The eight year old doesn't know what's in that box yet, but I do, and I watch patiently as it's unwrapped. I turn around once and glance at Dad. He's standing by the door holding his plane ticket, rubbing his tired eyes. But now I watch him through a mature lens, and I see him fiercely wiping troubled tears off his cheeks, carefully hiding his emotions from an eight-year old girl. He turns away when he sees me watching, and places his ticket in an old Bible on the shelf.

I carry on with my gift. The lid is pulled off and out of the box slides a shiny gold locket. Its round surface is perfectly smooth. The clasp is new and tight. It takes a few minutes before I figure out how to open it. At last, my fingers press against the right notches, a motion that will become as familiar to me as breathing.

I'm excited to see the picture in its original form, before time faded away the details, but things become hazy. I look into the locket but instead of the picture all I see are a few words floating around in the fog, and I can't decipher them. I turn around and realize Dad is gone. I look over the railing just in time to see the front door close; its sound, solemn and permanent, echoes loudly in my mind.

Over and over I hear the latch locking. The sound upsets me. Things are spinning now and the haze is thick. I curl up in a fetal position and start sobbing.

He was only supposed to be gone for a week. I wish I could protect the little girl from the heartache that will come in the next few weeks, and ultimately, years.

After some time, the rain stops. I wipe my eyes, put on my new necklace and feel a little braver.

*

The boisterous crash from a wave jerks me awake but my head is still in a cloud. My body is cold despite the warm sun. The ocean has stretched, wetting my feet with every current. I sit up, gathering my bearings, and notice that the beach is speckled with more visitors. My bike and board are still sprawled on the sand next to me, along with three chocolates, protected by the shade of my bag.

I squint at my watch and my heart leaps. Panic engrosses my logic. "Excuse me, could you tell me what time it is?" I ask a visitor.

"Four-thirty."

My watch wasn't lying. I shove everything into my bag, throw my board on the rack, and tear out of there, guilt consuming my emotions. I can't believe I passed out on the beach for eight hours.

I didn't feed mom breakfast or send her off to

work. If Judy came to get her and saw she wasn't ready, she might have assumed she was taking the day off, leaving mom home alone all day.

I pedal harder, noticing the deep shade of pink on the tops of my forearms—a souvenir from the early summer sun.

When I reach my house, I ransack every room, calling her name. In the kitchen, I find a piece of dry toast on the table, two mouse bites eaten from one corner. Judy has been here. Looks like she fed Mom and took her to work.

I plop down on the couch and exhale, relieved and embarrassed, confused at why I feel so well rested.

CHAPTER FIVE

I was four when we moved here from Perth. Old enough to secure a thick accent, and young enough to easily lose it, along with memories of my Australian heritage. Both of my parents are purebred Australian, which I guess makes me one too, but their separate absences leave me confused about where my place is in the world.

For a short while, I felt the cultural differences at school, but I soon realized my reclusiveness wasn't because of my background or even because I'm an awkward only child. There are too many secrets hidden behind my walls.

My home is unique. Nothing about it fits the personalities of the two people it houses. I have a hard time imagining it ever did.

I only remember Mom in her current state. Perhaps if she had died when my Dad had, I'd remember some good things. I feel guilty wishing for those memories of her, but I want them back so badly.

The imaginative touches in this house are the only remnants of my real Mom, before she turned into the empty, transparent version of herself.

It hasn't been touched in over a decade, but in a weird way, its bohemian-eclectic vibe has kept it from looking dated. Wacky is always wacky.

From the outside, it's just another modest house on the block. The inside, on the other hand, is a masterful work of unpredictable creative comfort.

In the family room where mom spends most of her time rocking, cheerful golden curtains with a border of fuzzy ball fringe hang floor to ceiling next to four large picture windows, allowing streams of early morning light to enter from several directions. Overstuffed vintage pillows in various shapes and colors sit on fat cushions of a velvety-teal tufted sofa.

A vintage persimmon-painted piano stands in the corner with a thick layer of dust. Several strings of fishing wire are strung down from the loft supporting dozens of ornamental snowflakes, frozen in time.

Above a reclaimed-wood mantle hang two

vintage surfboards, one sea foam green and the other bright tangerine. There used to be three, but the yellow one is attached to my bike out back.

I've taken down all the old family photos to avoid more confusion. There is one that I saved of my parents on their wedding day. It sits on my nightstand.

My thoughts are interrupted by the cheerful ring of Judy's voice. I've got to think of a way to repay her for this one. Occasionally Judy drops off a treat for us and checks in on me. I always reassure her that we're just fine and that she has done enough, but I don't know what I'd do without her help.

"Lucy!" She sings. I sheepishly turn the corner, facing her. "Good morning, sunshine," she greets, looking amused by my bedhead. "I guess I should say good afternoon."

"Judy, I feel terrible. I fell asleep on the beach and—"

"Oh, good for you," she says, patting my cheek. "You deserve a morning to yourself every once in a while. As long as there wasn't any hanky panky involved, I don't want to hear a word more."

"Oh no. No funny business. It was just me, sawing logs on the beach."

Judy looks like a happy housewife that's been beamed here directly from an eighties sit-com. The bushy blonde hair, the heavy red lipstick, the unnatural blush—I love it all.

"Speaking of, this weekend is our office retreat. We are escaping up to Portland for some 'team-building fun.'" She punctuates the air with finger quotes. "I would love to bring Miss Renee with me. Do you think you'd let me steal her until Sunday?" She goes on in more of a whisper now, "I'm guessing you could use a weekend to yourself." She winks at me and puts an arm around Mom.

I don't remember the last time I was alone for an extended period. Wait, that's because it's never happened. *Two days of only worrying about myself and doing whatever I want.* I think I might do a cartwheel.

"Sheesh, Judy. That's so nice. I don't know though. Might not be the best idea. Renee, do you feel up for it?"

Mom shrugs and Judy cuts in, "she does. It wouldn't be the same without her. I'll pull up at six o'clock tomorrow morning. You, go do something fun." It's more of a demand than a request.

Once Judy leaves, I start dinner for Renee. Knowing she'll be gone tomorrow, I bypass tonight's baked potato and skip to tomorrow's menu knowing it's her favorite. I'm more in the mood for pancakes and bacon but it's dinnertime after all. I want to make something she'll eat.

We munch on our antioxidant-rich salads full of kale, blackberries, sunflower seeds and avocado with a light lemon vinaigrette drizzled over top. I used to make this in desperate hopes of these super star foods healing her memory, but now I only make it because I know she'll eat it.

My cooking repertoire has come a long way. After years of PB&Js, cheap mystery meat weenies, and ramen noodles, I eventually came to my senses and started checking out cookbooks from my local library. One of my most prized possessions is a cookbook that was waiting for me on my front porch on a birthday several years ago. My childhood was filled full of nitrites and preservatives, but I suppose that was better than starving. Despite being on a rigid budget, food is one thing I'll spend a few extra bucks on these days. Cooking for Mom is one of the only ways I can show her some kind of kindness, some kind of love.

Nearly every night we sit across from each other at the table as mother and daughter, but in reality we are nothing more than two strangers.

As I nibble on a curly piece of kale, I glance up to the window in the loft, and an intimate memory dances into my mind. I see raindrops, I feel kisses, and I hear words. They are Dad's words, and they come across as plea. "Never give up trying."

For a few minutes time stands still as I relive pieces of this morning's vivid dream. Suddenly, I am desperate to write down every detail that I can remember.

When I look up, Mom's chair is empty. Her plate remains mostly untouched. I look around the corner and see her thin arms resting on her chair. Looks like her retreat has already started.

I run to the drawer and pull out an old notebook from school. My pen doesn't leave the paper for quite some time as I frantically jot down every detail that I can remember. Partway through the dream, I am overcome with guilt as I realize I'm not keeping my end of the promise. In many ways, I've stopped trying. I'm only surviving.

I'm not in the mood to finish writing right now. I take a break and thumb through the stack of mail Judy dropped on the counter.

I hesitate when I see a letter from the University of Oregon, but ultimately decide to open it.

Attn: Lucy Lichty

Miss Lichty,

As president of U of O's scholarship program, this will be the final time I reach out to you. Please confirm that you will accept the full tuition scholarship starting this fall, September 2nd. If I don't hear from you in two weeks, your position will be filled. We would be thrilled to have you as part of our student body, and look forward to the great things you will accomplish here.

Sincerely, Laura Jorgenson

U of O Recruiter

I close my eyes and bang my head down on the

letter. It smells like hot copiers and wood. A high school teacher demanded I apply for a scholarship, even though I admitted I wouldn't be attending. I pick up my pen and start scribbling angry words in my notebook.

Dear Miss Jorgenson,

Thank you so much for your interest in my attendance. I will happily accept your offer. All I need for you to do is move your university to my tiny town or duplicate me so I can continue watching my Mother while I attend. You have two weeks to clone a human.

Lucy Lichty

I crumple up both letters and throw them across the room. They miss the trashcan by a couple of feet. Hopelessness is about to tip me over the edge of human stability.

I'm convinced that work is therapeutic. Keeping busy occupies the spaces in my brain that remind me I'm a lonely mess and that my goals are unattainable. Twelve-hour shifts mean I have three to four days off per week. I pick up extra shifts whenever I can, but I'm already in overtime this week. I have the next three days off. And two of them are completely off, without responsibilities at home. I also have no money, no connections, and no agenda.

I crawl up into the loft and linger before grabbing a book off the shelf. I'm not in the mood to muse over Dad's chemistry books tonight. I turn on the Christmas lights and curl up on the sheepskin rug lying on top of the shaggy carpet. I've nearly memorized every book we own, but I need something to take my mind off my hopeless future.

The beautiful passages of *Pride and Prejudice* occupy my mind until well after two in the morning. I wouldn't consider myself boy hungry; I'm much too realistic. But something about Mr. Darcy gets me all hot and tingly.

I place the book back on the shelf without saving the page I was on. I need a change of scenery and, unfortunately, I'm still wide-awake. That's the predicament with working night shift.

As I tiptoe down the spiraled staircase, I realize that the TV is on. The bright light is blaring in the black room. I see Mom's silhouette in the chair. She breathes heavily in a listless pattern. Just as I'm about to wake her and escort her to her bedroom, I pause and stare at the screen.

We don't have cable. Just a stack of ancient videotapes I haven't bothered watching in years. I wonder where she found this one.

The colors are muddled, but I see a stunning young woman in a lace wedding dress, standing under a pink flowering tree. The glow of the late afternoon sun gently illuminates her face as she delicately smells her bouquet. Her lips are full and un-painted; her long brunette locks loosely spiral down her back in a timeless way. A youthful pink flush colors her cheeks and brown freckles dot the top of the nose.

She looks up and across the orchard and her countenance changes. Now she wears an expression of excitement, longing, and trust.

My father meets her under the tree. He wears an apricot tie and light grey suit with sprigs of stephanotis as a boutonniere. He looks nervous at first but his eyes make it obvious that the only emotion he truly has room for is infinite love for the woman in front of him. I watch as he takes her hands into his own. They finally look sustained simply through the power of touch. I can tell how much he loves her just by the joyful look on his face, a strict contrast to the tired man in my dream last night.

They begin stating their vows. Dad repeats after the minister, "For better, for worse... for richer, for poorer... in sickness and in health..."

At this moment, the tape starts skipping. Images flicker haphazardly, and within seconds static consumes the screen. I run up to the VHS player and rewind. I hear Dad again, "For richer, for poorer...in sickness and in health..."

Static. I let it search for a signal for several minutes before I sigh and push the off button.

I flip on the hall light and guide Mom to her bed and tuck her in. When her eyes are closed, it's easier to believe that she's the beautiful woman in that video, full of love and emotion.

I grab the notebook I was writing in earlier and carry it to my room. I pick up my backpack as well and dump the contents out onto my bed. Three chocolates roll out, tumbling onto the floor. I stop right where I'm standing and look around suspiciously, eyeing the place like it's a crime scene.

My foot nearly squashes a rogue chocolate into the carpet. I pick up the straggler, number 3, and gather its mates.

Back in their assigned places they go. I leave the box on my window seat far from my bed, as if they are armed grenades. I slouch into my unmade sheets and stare at the little mysteries from across my room, recalling the metallic aftertaste and trying to avoid the possibility that my dizzy episode correlates with the sweet chocolate birthday present. The questions chafe my mind until I allow them to be heard. Did someone drug me? Who are these chocolates from?

Eventually, I decide to blame it on sleep deprivation, though my heart tells me otherwise.

I pick up my notebook and continue scribing my dream. I've got to figure out how much of this dream is real and how much of it was concocted by my entranced mind. I pause for a minute finding it curious that Dad had me read and repeat his flight information.

2107. The flight number is stained in my mind, but I'm skeptical that they are legit. I dive deeper into my dream and catch a vague scene, one where Dad very calculatedly looks at me before placing the ticket inside the old Bible.

My heart starts thumping as I throw down my notebook and leap out of bed, hurdling my scampering limbs through the dark house and up to the loft.

I flip one light switch and the colorful Christmas bulbs give me just enough light to find the dusty black book, wedged in the corner right where Dad left it. In ten years, I haven't paid any attention to this book, always choosing fictional heroes over ancient prophets. Reverently, I wipe the dust off the cover and start thumbing through the thin pages.

The pages fly through the Old Testament and soon after, the book willingly falls open near the center. An airy, quarter sheet of paper is stuck into the index. It's a plane ticket. Four small yet bold numbers, identical to the saturated symbols that imprinted my mind earlier, are the first to steal my attention. "2107" vouches for my dream, and I feel an eerie wisp of chills prickle the pores of my neck and creep down my arms. A bizarre nostalgia washes over me, and I can't decide if I should flee or continue.

I remove the ticket from the Bible, nearly closing and losing its resting place for good, but a highlighted verse hidden behind the ticket draws my attention and I lay the book back down. Something deep within me prompts me to read, so I whisper the highlighted words into the stillness.

John 8:32

And ye shall know the truth, and the truth shall make you free.

Chills have now run up and down every square inch of my skin. I take some quick glances around, imagining unseen eyes watching me from the shadows. This room holds more secrets than I'm comfortable with. I lurk back down to my bedroom with the ticket in hand and close the door.

The overpowering urge to curl up in a ball and bury myself under my covers wins. I feel violated, puzzled, scared, but most of all, intrigued. I feel my hot, heavy breaths filling up the small, entrapped area under my blanket.

It's close to three in the morning now. It would be smart to get some sleep and make sense of things in the calm of the morning. Instead, I throw the covers off and walk across the room. I take chocolate number 2 and put it in my mouth. Perhaps it will tell me the truth that someone would like me to know.

CHAPTER SIX

Thick, salted caramel oozes out with every anxious chew. I take my time, studying the flavors and waiting for something bizarre to transpire.

Down the hatch it goes, though some caramel lingers behind still stuck to my teeth. I stand motionless next to my nightstand, waiting. I hear my kitty clock noisily ticking in the distance. I double check my vision and am dissatisfied by the clarity.

For a split second I feel that my initial accusation was dramatic. Perhaps there is no reason to correlate chocolate number one with the recent revelation.

I kneel down and pull some pajamas out of my bottom drawer. When I stand up, a relentless vertigo collapses me down to my hands and knees.

It's like my equilibrium has been drop kicked across the room. My tongue is dry and fuzzy and feels like a heavy foreign object in my mouth. At last, the familiar metallic taste seeps into my taste buds and masks my other senses.

I try and crawl to my bed, but I can't find my legs to take me there. Gravity slips away and I'm floating, flying up towards my chandelier. The light gets brighter and brighter. A faint smell of smoke fills my nostrils. The burning bulbs in the chandelier are painfully bright. Even when I give in and close my eyes, I still see the light.

*

The bright fire flickers in the breeze, just inches in front of me. Mom waves out the match and I smell the smoke fumes from the extinguished flame. One, two, three, four, five candles.

I'm sitting cross-legged on a large blue blanket. I study the foreign faces of each person sitting around me, their voices joined in a birthday melody, but I only recognize my parents. Their youthful faces are turned towards me with the same look of exuberance.

Behind the guests sprawls a large green grassy area with swings. A little to the left lies a shallow pond filled with large white geese, and to my right, a winding walking path with cheerful zinnias and ranunculus stretching their necks every which way along the border of the path.

Directly in front of my nose stands the most gorgeous three-tiered cake frosted princess-pink. I take a dramatic breath in and blow all five candles out. The strangers cheer. Mom kisses my cheek.

A boy comes running back from the swings, a large golden dog chasing at his feet.

"Luce! I told you to wait for me. Aw, man! Why is your cake pink?" His thick eyebrows furrow and his chubby, round face is scowling at me.

I stick my tongue out at him. "Hey, Mom. Mom!" I call. "Light up my candles again. Christopher didn't get to see."

Christopher. Christopher Summers. I remember that kid.

Mom lights up the candles again and Christopher and I blow them out together. Again, the strangers cheer. The golden dog brushes past me and its giant tongue takes a robust lick right on top of the perfect confection. The top tier plops off and lands upside down on the blanket, the frosting a gooey mess.

"Howie!" Christopher scolds his dog. A mustached man talking to Dad chases the mutt away.

"Oh well. Guess that's mine!" Christopher announces. He grabs the upside down layer with one hand and shoves it into his mouth, leaving nothing behind except a pink beard.

After we've eaten our weight in birthday cake, Dad walks up the path holding a brand new sparkling-pink bike in his arms.

I squeal in delight and run to him, throwing my arms around his legs, jumping up and down in an elated frenzy. He promises me he'll teach me to ride once the party is over.

The guests leave one by one until finally it's just the three of us left. The sun is setting in the sky and orange and pink hues dust the horizon.

I hug Mom and thank her for the party. She picks me up and spins me around and around. Her white cotton sundress is twirling out like a princess's. I look up and the sun is behind her face, the glowing backlight illuminating her flowing locks. She is beaming and giggling along with me. She looks full of magic, almost like a fairy delivering peace and happiness to the rest of us.

Dad has more patience than a resident on Ritalin. He trots along side of me for nearly a mile until I get the hang of no training wheels. At last, he lets go. I hear him cheering from behind me. I trust him. I continue pedaling one leg after the other; my pink high-top Chuck Taylors push left and right. My heart is racing and I'm gloating over my new independence.

Just a few yards in front of me, the path ends and the pond begins. The geese are honking. I start panicking. My legs feel numb and I start screaming.

I hear Dad running behind me. Just in time, he snatches me by the back of my jumper. He picks me up and holds me to his chest as my bike skids into the bushes. "That's my girl," he pants. I hear his heart thudding like a galloping horse. "Tomorrow, we'll work on stopping. Oh, and I forgot to give you one thing."

He reaches into his deep pocket and pulls out a horn. He squeezes it and it honks like a boisterous duck. I giggle at the silly sound and squeeze it over and over as he sets me down and tightens it onto my handlebars. The geese in the pond get curious and start honking back. I hug his leg and squeeze that horn a hundred times, giggling wildly after each squeeze.

So this is what a perfect birthday looks like.

CHAPTER
SEVEN

An obnoxious car alarm jars me awake but I'm not ready to leave the bliss of my dream. Over and over it honks, eventually bringing me to my feet. My back is sore from sleeping on the floor. Someone is frantically knocking on the front door. I run clumsily out to the entryway, flipping on the porch lights. It's Judy. I unlock the door and pull it open.

"Help me, Luce!" She shrieks over the honking, throwing her keys at me as if they are a poisonous reptile. I aim the remote at the car and press the red button.

Silence.

"I swear I tried that!" She pants. "Idiot car. Your neighbors are gonna egg your house tonight—you know that, right?"

"Judy…is it morning?" I rub my eyes and try to clear the fog in my head.

"Six o'clock my dear. I'll go get your Mama up."

"Agh, sorry. I meant to have her ready to go. Guess I forgot to set my alarm."

Judy would make an excellent nurse. She's kind, compassionate, and has a way of getting the job done.

Twenty minutes later, her car disappears around the corner, gifting me with forty-eight hours of absolute freedom. I know exactly what I'm going to do first.

The past four hours of deep REM reaffirmed what I assumed. I know that this dream was a piece of my reality. I'm anxious to escape my home, still creeped out that someone dropped the tripped-out chocolates off at my house. I don't know who it is, and I don't know what they want me to know. I need fresh air to give me a fresh perspective.

Into my backpack, I throw my wallet, a light jacket, a water bottle, and an apple. My hand hovers over my swimsuit for two seconds before I throw it in, just in case I need a break from my investigating. With extra care, I wrap a dishtowel around the box containing the two remaining chocolates and pack them in with the other necessities. I tuck the plane ticket inside my notebook and throw that in as well.

After running a brush through my blonde waves,

I change into an airy white blouse and some faded jean shorts.

I exit my house and breathe in the freshness of a crisp, silent morning. Now I'm ready to soar down the road like a bird that has just received its wings for the first time, and I must admit I feel good, like I've finally had enough sleep.

The sharp morning air is cutting, but it wakes up all of my hibernating senses. As I ride past the ocean, the waves crash boisterously against the shore. Seagulls circle the swells and dive down for their breakfast.

At last, I pedal up to the gates of Amber Waves. The parking lot is full of cars from the doctors, nurses, managers, accountants, social workers, physical therapists, cooks, occupational therapists and many others that I get to miss during my nightshift solace.

Art's room is several halls away from the front entrance. Without my badge, I can't enter from the back. Today, I'm a visitor, but I have purpose. I'll have to follow the visitor rules and deal with the staff questioning my early morning appearance.

Luckily, there is so much hustle and bustling occurring with the a.m. activities that I nearly make it all the way to my destination without a single hitch. Joel, a kitchen aide hands me Art's breakfast tray just as I'm about to knock on his door. It's pretty apparent that Joel has worked an all-nighter.

He doesn't take notice that I'm in street clothes. "Take that in for me?" He mumbles and walks away. I'm guessing he also didn't notice that this tray isn't a diabetic tray and that there are two Ensure shakes next to a Belgian waffle. At the end of a twelve-hour night shift, even a truly intelligent person has the IQ of a toddler.

I gladly take Art's breakfast tray and tap on the door.

There aren't any signs of stirring. The idea of him actually sleeping seems ridiculous. Art is part vampire. I knock a little harder and wait.

Still, silence. Now I'm starting to get worried.

"Art?" I say before cracking the door open and peaking inside.

I nearly jump a foot in the air when a hand from behind taps my shoulder.

I turn around and see my co-worker.

"Nicole!" I gasp. "You scared me. I was just looking for Art and got worried when he didn't come." I slide the waffle back to the center of the tray and try to wipe the guilty look off my face.

"Lucy, what are you doing here?" Her tone is more surprised than anything. "This is the last place I'd be on my day off."

"Right, yeah, me too." I stammer. "I just…I just have to finish some online education. You know how it sneaks right up on you."

Amber takes the breakfast tray from me. "Art

isn't here today. He's checked out for the next two days, actually."

"Really? Where did he go? Who picked him up?" I start firing questions without a valid permit.

Amber laughs but suspicion hides under the surface of her expression. "I really don't know. I wasn't here when he left."

"Okay, no big deal." I shrug my shoulders pretending like his absence doesn't ruin my entire day. "I just had something to show him," I say and pat my backpack. Amber raises an eyebrow.

"A math problem. He was helping me with some trig. Yeah. Hypotenuses and other…functions. But I'll just uh…" I motion to the computers at the nurses station and disappear out of her line of fire. I roll my eyes at my pathetic attempt to lie.

After logging in, I unzip my bag and peak inside, making sure my two remaining chocolates are still in their package. My stomach is growling and I could really go for something sweet. These edible mysteries have quickly become one of my most valuable belongings. Obviously I'll have to settle for vending machine chocolate.

My online education has been done for weeks. Biking back to my empty home will answer zero of my questions, and I'm not swallowing number three until I figure out what the first two dreams were trying to tell me. I bite my lip in frustration, wishing Art was here to help me decipher my latest gift, or on the other hand, concur that I'm delusional.

The empty blue screen glows in front of me for several minutes, and I feel the weight of every emotion churning in my mind. I drop my forehead and rest it on the desk. I can't believe this is how I'm spending my precious alone time. I stare down at the black Chuck Taylors on my feet and a flashback of my pink high tops floods my memory. The dream starts back-playing in my mind. Small flashes of the pedaling, the twirling, the pink cake, the dog, the boy. I pause and perk up.

Christopher Summers.

My fingers are typing swiftly in a browser search box. I've never stalked anyone before. This could be fun. I type his name in and add a comma and "Oregon" afterwards.

Pages and pages of links show up, but the second one down catches my eye: a news article from University of Oregon. I click and am redirected to an article from the University's tribune.

Christopher Summers of Eugene, Oregon, expected to break cross-country school records this fall. Last year, the six foot-three sophomore was teasing the state front- runners with his long stride and seemingly endless stamina, quickly becoming a weapon in the hands of head coach Leval Saunders.

I enlarge the thumbnail picture, doubting that

this could be the chubby chump I used to call my best friend.

Before I can get a good look, my nurse supervisor Barbara and the chief physician stroll into the nurses' station and stop right behind the back of my chair. I catch the last half of their conversation about this afternoon's meetings at headquarters. I manage to open a new window and login to my employee page just in time for them to turn around and see me pretending to scroll through the completed tasks page.

"Lucy!" Barbara says, and pats my back. "Good for you. Looks like you've got all your online updates completed as usual." Barbara is a picture of nursing perfection with her starched white jacket, perfect red lipstick, slicked back auburn hair, and of course, her compassionate disposition. We call her Florence Nightingale behind her back and sometimes to her face. She continues, "Dr. Beck, this is Lucy, one of our finest CNAs. In fact, Lucy, wait right here one minute. I have something for you. I didn't realize you'd be here today so this is a fun surprise."

She skips off to her office leaving me alone and staring up awkwardly at the bald physician.

"Sounds like you've got your hands full today," I say, trying to fill the silence.

"Sure do. Just have to finish making my rounds here and then I'm meeting with corporate over in

Eugene."

"Eugene?" I lightly gasp, thinking of the cross-country star.

The doc raises his wiry gray eyebrows. "You have family in Eugene or something?"

I don't know if what I'm about to say is out of desperation or boredom.

"Yes, actually. I was planning on riding the bus up there today to help out my grandmother." I pause and wait for his response, half expecting my nose to start growing.

Barbara interrupts my charade and hands me an envelope. She straightens up, looking around as if she's about to make a public announcement. "Lucy, you have been officially chosen as one of the employees of the year! Your hard work is paying off, my dear."

"Oh Barbara. Really? That's…that's really nice. I'm honored. Thank you," I say and graciously take the envelope.

Barb decides to go in for a side-hug while I peak inside the envelope. My eyes get wide as I count five, twenty-dollar bills inside a sappy card with a long inspirational message in cursive italics. "We'll put your plaque up next week. Way to go girl!"

Before I can adequately thank her, she rushes off to an unanswered call light.

Dr. Beck smiles. "It wouldn't be any trouble if you would like to catch a ride with me. I'd love to help out the employee of the month." He winks. "I'll be leaving here in about fifteen minutes. Meet me out front."

He leaves me just enough time to sneak the chocolates into Art's room and hide them inside a loafer, but not enough time to second guess my hasty whim to hitchhike across the state.

John Lennon serenades us in the immaculate, massive pickup truck where I'm riding shotgun. Dr. Beck munches on pre-shelled sunflower seeds. I let the uncomfortable silence linger much longer than what's socially acceptable in hopes of getting my thoughts in order.

I realize that I've bummed a ride with a complete stranger and am currently freeloading my way to see another stranger. This second stranger may or may not actually exist in Eugene. It's a total shot in the dark.

All right, someone lock me up in a padded cell. Just drop me off at the psych ward.

Let's try this again. I'm in an incredibly posh and safe vehicle, with a respectable physician, hoping to locate a childhood friend who absolutely did exist at one point, in order to set facts straight from my latest dream. I never get to leave the house and visit a college city, and a little white lie plus some modest freeloading is acceptable in this situation.

There, that's better.

Doc decides to break the silence, and I can't

blame him.

"So, you going to college?" He leans back in his seat and drums his thumbs against the steering wheel.

How could I go to college if I'm working at a nursing home that is at least two hours away from any forms of university life? I need to squander this bitterness.

"Nope. Just working. Hopefully one day," I fib.

"Well, if you move over to Eugene and live with your Grandma, you could transfer to the Eugene facility and get half tuition at the U of Oregon. They've got a great RN program."

I smile and nod politely.

"Or heck, maybe nursing isn't what you want to do. You've got your whole life ahead of you. What are your dreams?"

And for a minute, because I've already dug myself so deep into this pretentious pit of pretends, I feign that I actually do have my whole life ahead of me, free to go anywhere, be anyone, and do anything I've ever wanted. Filling the silence will be easy.

"Well, since I'm a bit of a genetics nerd, I'd love to follow a route in that direction, but I wouldn't want to leave chemistry out," I say. "My dad, he was a scientist. A chemist, actually. Following in his footsteps would be a dream."

"Is that so?" The doc replies. "What parts of

chemistry and genetics are you interested in?"

"Lately I've been studying gene abnormalities, genome sequencing, and brain chemicals—you know, acetylcholine, norepinephrine, serotonin." I pause feeling self-conscious, but his smile is encouraging.

"So you're interested in nerve cell communication," he replies. "Or lack thereof, I presume. Any direct interest in Alzheimers?"

I flit around his question. "I'm fascinated by physiology as well. Specifically on the cellular level in the brain, like neurodegeneration, synaptic plasticity, mitochondrial dysfunction. I've studied that plenty but I'd be more interested in the other side of that: the exercising and rebuilding nerve cells, or finding clean substances to break away amyloid plaque without damaging existing cells. You know, studying the hopefuls instead of the hopeless. Most of the books just cover what we already know. I imagine that college could provide the resources to find ways to discover and test the effects of—new ideas."

"Lucy," the doc says boldly. I look over and see a glimmer in his eye. "Don't let anything get in the way of your education, all right? We need you."

I pause and am tempted to get honest with this man I just met. And because I'm already so far out on a limb today, I jump.

"Do you have family, Dr. Beck?"

"You bet, I'm a family man. Have three kids and a wonderful wife." I nod.

"Would you give up some of your dreams to keep them comfortable and safe?"

He takes his eyes off the road for two seconds to steal a glance at me. He stares back at the road in a thoughtful way before he answers.

"For me, family always comes first. You put other things in front of your loved ones, and you risk jeopardizing happiness. Regret is a heavy burden I wouldn't want to live with." I nod again, already expecting this answer and reaffirming my own decisions.

"However," he suddenly continues with the power of a minister giving a sermon, "sometimes doing hard things and struggling together is what makes you stronger. Sacrifice can't be one-sided for happiness to thrive. Everybody has to be willing to give."

Silence fills the chambers of the truck while we both process. The bag of sunflower seeds is nearly empty.

We turn off the freeway just under two hours into our journey.

"So where am I taking you?"

I'm a little caught off guard and remember that I'm supposed to know where my fake Grandma lives. "Uh, do you know where the University of Oregon is? She just lives in a neighborhood over there."

"Yep, that's not far from the facility. I'm only planning on being here for a couple of hours, but I'll give you my number if you want a ride back home late this afternoon."

He hands me a business card before dropping me off at a charming red brick home a few streets away from the university. Considerately he waits and watches as I try and wave him away and motion to the back of the house. Eventually, I crouch behind a boxwood before he finally backs out of the driveway and takes off.

As soon as his truck is out of sight, I sprint out of the yard like a guilty juvenile delinquent and start walking toward the school. I glance back at the house only once to make sure no one is suspicious, and for the first time, notice a sign on the window.

Shining Stars Preschool

Looks like Grandma teaches preschool. I am the worst liar there ever was. I bury my face in my hands and my emotions play Russian roulette. The outcome results in several giggles escaping.

Despite my pathetic behavior, I feel the surge of an unknown emotion tingling inside my chest.

Drastically changing my routine has presented a new light in my personality that has been buried. I'm stepping outside of the box I've been trapped in for eighteen years.

CHAPTER EIGHT

Towering rows of saturated, leafy trees line a path toward the campus. A giant yellow *O* represents on the top a red brick building.

Jumping in that truck was a desperate attempt to escape my world, and finding Christopher Summers doesn't seem like the next logical step in finding answers to my dreams. But without Art's expertise and advice, I'm stuck and unwilling to sit around waiting. I'm not sure why Christopher was in my dream or what information he can possibly offer, but I'm here, and there's no harm in pretending to be Lucy Lichty, college girl, for an afternoon.

The grounds are still and quiet. The summer-student crowd seems sparse, which gives me the courage to walk under the giant brick archway, up to the impressive wall of glass doors, and walk right in.

My attention is immediately drawn up to the rows of floor levels overlooking the ground I stand on. Tall white columns reach up to the ceiling. The enormous wall of windows in the front overlooks the luscious green grounds.

Round wooden tables and chairs are scattered throughout the main floor with a handful of students studying in various corners. Worn in couches overlook the balconies on each floor and bored studiers have a bird's eye view of the prey that walks in.

About three floors above, a girl in a bright green school t-shirt stands with her arms resting on the railing. She stares down this way and when I meet her eyes, she offers an enthusiastic wave. I look around and eventually give her back a half-hearted gesture, curious if I'm the one she's actually waving at.

I walk further into the building and find a sprawling room with several couches and beanbags. Two boys in the far corner are conversing in a foreign language without looking up from their phones. I turn back around and take a right into another hallway. I'm relieved see the word *Admissions* above a group of booths with glass windows. I make my way over there and walk past each booth hoping to find some kind of life form who can point me in the direction of a map. Light is coming from the very last booth. I walk over and peek in front of it. An older lady is in front of the window, bouncing gently up and down. I get a better look and realize she's sitting on a yoga ball. When she notices me, she pauses the bobbing and smiles.

"Good morning. May I help you?"

"I'm actually not a student here," I confess. "I'm just having a look around if that's okay. But this place is huge, do you have any sort of map I could have?"

Without getting up, she pivots around on her ball and opens up the bottom file drawer behind her, pulling out a two-sided map with the university's logo on top. "The Ducks," I read. I hold out my hand but instead of handing it to me, she picks up her phone. "Yes, Jamie, extension four," is all she says before hanging up.

A few seconds later, the friendly girl in the Oregon t-shirt from a few floors above takes my limp hand and starts shaking it with gusto. Now I can see the knee high green and white striped socks she is sporting.

"Hi there! I'm Jamie, a student ambassador, and I'm here for your tour!" Jamie is a whole head shorter than me but her energy would make it nearly impossible to overlook her presence.

I retract my hand and reach for the map. "Oh, hi.

I'm really just fine with a map, but thank you, that's very nice of you."

"I've got golf cart access! You can't say no to that! We can zip around and visit anywhere you want to see. I'm full of historical facts, sporting stats, department info—you name it."

"Maybe next time, thank you. I need to get some exercise anyway," I say.

The lady on the yoga ball raises two eyebrows and looks at Jamie. "Looks like you've got a taker for the running tour."

"Running tour?" I question.

Jamie explains, "Oh, you bet! Three days per week we offer a running tour here on campus. Today isn't one of those days, but you're in luck, I know the route! The purpose of the tour is to emphasize this area's running pedigree. After all, Eugene is called Tracktown USA!"

Jamie starts jogging in place. "We'll go at the pace of a ten-minute mile. That shouldn't be a problem for you by the looks of ya, but we'll make stops to point out the various landmarks. It's about three point seven miles total. The best part is that the tour ends with a victory lap around the historic Hayward Field! Oh you're just going to love it."

"Hayward Field. Is that where the track and cross country athletes train?" I ask.

"The best of the best!" she replies with two thumbs up.

This could work to my advantage, and besides, the admissions lady seems to be holding the map hostage until I agree to a tour.

I didn't come prepared in the best jogging attire. I throw my shoes into my backpack and then tighten the bag's buckles around my waist and chest. I feel like a barefoot hippie.

The dark, lush grass feels like velvet under my toes. Trees are sprouted up all over the place, and fuzzy, lime moss garnishes their trunks. We pass many original red brick buildings, expertly preserved from well over a century ago.

Jamie's incessant questioning between coughing out facts leaves no time to take in the beauty from a serene perspective.

I'm about to see if she wants to play the quiet game but I can't sneak in a word between her chatter. "Tell me your name and where you're from and everything else! You're just going to love it here—I know it. Quack!"

The quack was unnecessary but she has managed to bring a smile to my face. This girl has some serious school spirit. I hope she rubs off on me a little. I have to hand it to her because this running tour is genius. I feel healthy and alive and completely entertained by the history and architecture.

What this place lacks in coastline, it makes up for in running trails and beautifully wooded hiking areas. The longer the tour goes on, the more I can picture myself here. I try not to let my logical self squander the thought.

At last, we reach the outskirts of Hayward Field. From a distance, I mistake it for the football stadium because of its enormity.

Jamie is nearly out of breath by now, and I'm downright shocked. Her bottomless pit of enthusiasm is closing in, but between strides she still chokes out a few more facts like it's her final duty.

"Hayward Field is the Carnegie Hall for track and field athletes. We've held more Olympic trials here than anyone anywhere else. Just wait till we make it inside…. You won't believe it…. You will love it." She bends down with her hands on both of her knees and puts her head between her legs.

"Quack," I say, and pat her moist back encouragingly.

At last, in silence, we jog side by side and enter the field.

My eyes grow wide in amazement and I have to stop and do a slow motion three-sixty to take it all in. Flocks of athletes populate various corners of the field. A group of ten or so slim females stretch near the middle. Pole-vaulters are actively flinging themselves nearly twenty feet in the air. Sprinters with legs thicker than my waist practice their takeoffs, and impeccably toned ladies in spandex leotards jump over hurdles that look taller than

Jamie.

I can't believe I'm running on this track that so many legends have trained on.

From a distance, I hear the pitter-patter of hoofs behind me, almost like a group of trotting Clydesdales. Jamie turns around to take a glance and her jaw drops.

"Step aside, Lucy, step aside," she manages to whisper, and directs me to the side of the track without breaking her stare.

I turn around to see what the fuss is, and immediately try and divert my eyes away from the flesh, but I can't. There seems to be a magnetic pull from the human eye to any naked and exposed human appendage, no matter its condition.

A dozen or so nearly naked men are trotting in unison. Their ribs show through their bare, long torsos and the muscles on their legs look like they've been super glued into place. Occasionally one turns and spits into the grass but their pace looks effortless. They are like a pack of emaciated wolves but strong and impressive all at once. It's very confusing, and I'm still staring.

Behind them, a fat man in a shiny tracksuit follows close behind in a golf cart. "Pace! Pace! Stride! Stride!" He yells out, glancing from the runners to his stopwatch.

I turn to Jamie in question, and she continues to stare and mutter under her breath. "I just wanna bite one of those drumsticks or nibble on a hamstring." Her nostrils are flaring.

Now I'm really confused. "Are you talking about?" I nod towards the skinny fellows who are quickly approaching, but Jamie doesn't pay any attention to me. Finally, she musters an intro for the fellows.

"Lucy, feast your eyes on the heartthrobs of Oregon. Meet the men's cross country team."

I giggle and watch as the men draw nearer. The coach barks out orders and suddenly, they increase their speed and start sprinting around the track on what I imagine to be their final leg. Their heads drop, strides widen, and arms pump fiercely. Now I can hear grunts and exhales.

We watch as one breaks ahead of the pack. He is taller than the rest and makes winning look like a piece of cake. He draws closer and closer to us, a decent distance ahead of the others now. His body language portrays an uncertain smugness, and for some ridiculous reason, I hope he trips.

He zips past us, and at the last millisecond, his eyes dart over to me, allowing me to catch a still frame of his face. Out of all of the characteristics I could have noticed, I only take in one thing: the frolicking mischief in his eyes. And like a familiar sense of deja-vu, my dream from last night fast-forwards thirteen years and I know I've found him. Christopher Summers. The realization is intoxicating.

I tell myself to keep breathing but the air feels expired. I'm panting harder than the sprinting runners. Fate has made our encounter much simpler than I'd expected, and I haven't planned anything past locating him.

The rest of the pack finally rushes past us, and a waft of sweaty air helps me catch my breath. Christopher is only a few yards from the end but he makes a sudden U-turn and sprints away from his finish line.

"What the—?" Jamie mutters.

I watch helplessly as he trots towards us like a prized pony on display. My nerves are raw, but I can't help thinking what a showboat he is, a direct contrast to my desire to be invisible most of the time.

His stride slows and at last he comes to a halt directly in front of me. Without a word, he squints and stares thoughtfully—first at my face, and eventually up and down my whole body.

The coach comes rolling over in on his golf cart. "Summers! You were ten yards away from breaking your record! Ten yards, you idiot!" His double chin jiggles like an engorged turkey.

Christopher doesn't take notice. When he's finished examining me, he takes another step closer, and I gasp lightly. I've never been this close to a boy—except when I had to dance with Dan Rogers at the eighth grade dance, which doesn't count—let alone a full-grown and nearly naked one.

I take a step back, to which he steps forward.

"Lucy?" His voice is low and unapologetic. "Lucy Lichty? I can't believe it." He smiles and shakes his head. "Don't you know who I am?"

Jamie finally catches her breath and pipes in. "Yeah, Lucy, you should know who this is. He's kind of a big deal. This amazing specimen is Toph Summers, the record-breaking champ who is going to put this school in the history books. Toph, will you sign my shirt? I have a marker in my fanny pack. Don't go anywhere. I've been trying to catch you for months now. Wait just one second."

While she fishes through her affects, I quickly decide it's best to fake my intentions.

"Toph?" I ask dumbly.

"Yeah, from Yachats. We were buddies. Come on, you have to remember." I feel a twinge of guilt at the sound of his disappointment.

"Christopher?" I ask innocently as he nods. "I...I can't believe it's you. You're so grown up and so..." I try not to stare at him the way he did at me.

"So what?" He grins.

I look away and laugh. "You look really great." My voice forges confidence. "Do you need to finish your—lap?" I gesture to the fuming coach, now pacing at the finish line.

"We'll finish with you!" Jamie yelps, but not

before holding the magic marker and bending down in front of the celebrity.

Christopher shakes his head and chuckles as he graffitis the back of Jamie's shirt with his John Hancock.

The three of us are a sight as we run the remaining quarter of a lap. I try to muffle my heavy breathing and by the sound of things, Jamie is trying to do the same thing, but her face is turning redder by the second. Mine is too, but only because Christopher keeps stealing glances at me.

The finish line is anticlimactic but at least I can try and breathe again. Jamie gives me a scripted farewell speech and hands me a university information pamphlet. Christopher is a little ways away getting an earful the whole field can hear. The coach is leaning forward, his face pink and sweaty, his arms waving angrily in the air. Christopher listens intently but looks unstressed and somewhat entertained.

As I try and read his body language, Jamie goes in for a tight hug, making me promise to come see her again. She hands me the marker and encourages me to get some autographs. I watch her walk away, as she ungracefully attempts to get a good look at the signature on her back.

I can still hear the coach lecturing, even though he's inches form Christopher's ear. Clearly, now isn't the time to sit my subject down and ask him what he remembers about my fifth birthday party. In fact, now that I'm here and right next to him, I'm feeling the ridiculousness of my presence. My fight or flight instinct sprouts wings and I'm desperate to escape this situation. If I hurry, I can get to a phone and catch a ride home with Dr. Beck. Maybe Art will be back sooner than they said.

I try and slip away into the crowd of female athletes, but my wussy set of quadriceps give me away.

"Lucy!" Christopher calls out, interrupting his personal lecture.

I keep walking, trying to get lost in the herd of spandex, but someone grabs my arm.

"Where you going?" I turn around and lock eyes with the boy in my dreams. His familiar face gifts me with the warmth and happiness of a different life. The mischief in his eyes transports me to a playful memory. A lemonade stand on a late summer afternoon…dragonflies and dandelions…adults enjoying drinks on the patio, and Christopher trying to weasel extra nickels out of customers.

"Lucy," he repeats, bringing me back to this decade. His freckles and double chin have been replaced with stubbly whiskers and a strong jaw line. A stubborn cowlick in back sticks straight up just like it used to, reminding me of his stubborn six year old self.

"Oh, hey." I turn around and face him. "I didn't want to interrupt anything over there. I already made you miss setting a record."

"Could we catch up over dinner sometime?" He gently holds my wrist captive until I answer.

"I'm actually just here for the day today. I've got to get back to…" My voice trails off. To nothing, really.

"Five o'clock?" He suggests.

I nod, and mentally watch the doc in his truck, driving away without me. The thought of being stranded rattles my nerves. I'll make it a priority to find when the last bus back to Yachats departs tonight.

"Where can I pick you up?" He leans in, studying my face and I'm reminded of his lack of personal boundaries.

My fake grandma's house isn't going to cut it this time. I think fast. "Why don't I just meet you at your place and we can go from there. Unless you don't live close—"

"That works, I live on campus. I'll text you the address. What's your phone number?"

"I don't have a phone." I find the marker Jamie was using and offer it to him, still looking through my bag for a scrap of paper. He takes the marker and tattoos his address onto the underside of my forearm in the worst handwriting I've ever seen.

"Dude, that's permanent marker," I scold.

"Now you'll never forget where I live," he smirks. "And if you could bring your Aussie accent with you tonight, that would be great," he adds before running off.

I laugh, surprised he remembers this detail from years earlier. But his comment reminds me that every part of me has changed drastically since our last play date. I wonder if time has been good to him. By the looks of things, it has.

In raising myself, the bare necessities of human survival were my focus, and this alone was often more than I could manage. I was writing grocery lists and paying utility bills at nine. I had to teach myself how to tie my shoes, register for school, and buy new jeans when they got too small. I had made a budgeting spreadsheet to keep us out of the red at twelve. The middle school nurse gave me my first tampon and a pamphlet to take home and read.

My life hasn't allowed me to indulge in making my physical appearance a priority, and up 'til this moment, I haven't given it much thought or action. The sun highlights my hair, I wear very little make up, Mom's old clothes and thrift store finds fill my drawers, I've never even had my ears pierced.

I've got an entire afternoon and five twenty-dollar bills in my back pocket. This may never happen again.

I pull out the map from the admissions office and study it for a minute. A few paces away, a dark girl with a friendly face reaches past her toes, stretching her hamstrings in the cool grass. I stroll over and crouch down beside her. "Excuse me, could you tell me which one of these bus routes will get me closest to a shopping center?"

She glances to my map. "Food or clothes?" She asks.

"Both, preferably."

"Yeah, I'd go with D. You'll still have a little ways to walk but this area has the most what you're looking for."

I thank her and start toward a bus stop, but not before taking one more glance in Christopher's direction. He is back with the pack stretching his tight, spindly limbs. The sun's rays seem to bounce off his white skin. Hope fills my spirit and I'm looking forward to reminiscing in the happy moments of my past, and even more so, rekindling a friendship.

The campus bus is relatively quiet. Only once did a large, linebacker-looking guy ask me for my number. Even if I was attracted to him, it's a bad idea on so many poignant levels. If I brought a boy back to the house, mom would jump off a cliff. I run a tight ship in there. Once I rearranged the pillows, and she didn't know whose house she was in. Getting her back to her comfortable routine was a big ordeal, and I learned my lesson.

I'm getting really good at dismissing the male

spectators, but it doesn't mean I like to do it. Sometimes I just want to tape a *no soliciting* sign to my back.

I ride the route as far as it will take me. The campus bus driver points me in the right direction, and estimates my walk to be under a mile. I'm sure I could find a public bus, but it will likely take just as long.

I pass apartment after apartment. At last, the first commercial building I walk past is *Luxe Nails and Spa*. I slip off my shoes and glance down at my feet. Grass and dirt stain the sides and bottoms. My dry heels are callused and my dirty toenails look like I've been living in a barn for the past decade.

I peek my head in the salon, and a small Vietnamese man welcomes me. Without a single word of English, he manages to make me feel comfortable and welcome. There is just one other woman in here who is currently getting some one-inch red nails glued into place.

The man takes my backpack and gestures to my hands and feet, raising his eyebrows. I take off my shoes and point to my toenails, to which he replies, "Mm, yah," agreeing that my feet are the worst offenders.

Before I know it, I'm sitting in an oversized spa chair with my feet soaking in a bubbling tub of hot water. The nice man hands me a remote. I push a button and the chair starts massaging my back. I can't believe I'm doing this. I hope Mom is having fun on her retreat.

My first pedicure is a soaring success. My feet have been scrubbed, massaged, peeled and painted. I stare at the shiny lacquer on my fancy red toes as they dry under a heat lamp.

"How much?" I ask the kind man when I'm all finished.

"Firty. Firty dollar."

I give him a little extra for a tip and then walk back to the chair where I left my shoes, and begin loosening the laces.

"Du'ng lai! No!" The man shouts, waving his arms at me. He races across the salon, jabbering in long Vietnamese sentences and comes back holding a pair of disposable foam flip-flops.

"Oh, thanks," I say as he personally shimmies the foam piece in between my toes. His doting nature is suffocating my loner disposition. All of this forced relaxation is making me uncomfortable, but I ignore the uneasiness in my stomach and decide to fill it with something new and tasty.

Around the corner, a gourmet creamery is summoning me, and I waltz in sporting my flimsy flip-flops with the dignity of a salon diva. When I exit, my arms are cradling a bowl of ice cream that's bigger than my head. Rocky road with added brownie chunks and a mountain of whipped cream fits the bill for a perfect lunch.

A stretch of sunshine lures me to a warm section of grass where I swing off my backpack and place my naughty lunch on a flat piece of sod. I snatch the bright cherry off the top and twist the long stem between my fingers before plucking off the fruit with my teeth. This day has been full of surprises, but this moment might very well be the proverbial cherry on top. Even if tonight goes swimmingly with Christopher, it can't beat this.

The cherry is sweet and sour and the perfect palate cleanser for the gallon of heavy cream and sugar I'm about to overindulge in.

Today, things have fallen into place, even with my lack of planning. I feel the world working its magic to assist me in finding out my purpose for this outing. Even so, I'm working hard to block out the creeping homesickness that wants to bus me back to my comfort zone. Everyone has that place they think of when they are homesick—a cozy bed, a bubbly bath, a warm reading nook. Mine is my own corner of the ocean, and I can't help but think about what a perfect day it would have been to surf the day away. But then, I wouldn't have gained any real impressions of college, and Christopher Summers would have remained a child, trapped in my dream.

Another bite of ice cream pushes my wistful ocean thoughts away. I've got planning to do for tonight, specifically, finding out if there's a reason my subconscious brought Christopher Summers into my life, and I need to find this out without appearing to be a psychopath. Maybe I shouldn't tell him mental illness runs in my family.

CHAPTER NINE

I missed the bus. I've already walked a mile or so and I still have a couple more to go. Unless I hitchhike or sprout wings, I'm going to be late for the first and only date of my life. With each step, I hear the remaining coins jingling in my pocket. I'm flustered that I spent my entire wad so frivolously. I stare at my perfectly manicured pigs and the lovely new sandals decorating my feet. Until now, my foot wardrobe has consisted of second-hand tennies and dollar flip-flops, not unlike the disposable ones I wore throughout my shopping spree. These new beauties are brown leather, with straps that crisscross and buckle around my ankle. They give me about an inch of height that I don't really need, but it can't hurt. My remaining cash was used to purchase a tube of mascara, a travel sized deodorant, and a single use mini toothbrush, all of which I already made use of.

I'm nearly always punctual. Thinking about how late I'm going to be compels me to start trotting down the sidewalk. Eventually it turns into a full-blown run. I've already clocked three point seven miles today, and I'm no cross-country star. If Christopher didn't shower, our smells might cancel each other out.

After another five minutes my pace is really slowing to more of a speed walk. I start to recognize where I am. I see a few students walking and I know I'm getting closer.

I hear wheels racing up from behind me, so I scoot to the edge of the sidewalk. Just as I expect him to pass, a long-boarder hops off his board and turns to me.

"You in a hurry?" He asks.

I do a quick analysis. He's wearing a backpack, must be a student. Has a friendly face. Not bad looking at all. I can't deny that my 'no soliciting' sign would come in handy.

"Oh, hi," I stammer. "Yeah. Running a little late."

"Want a ride?" He motions to his board.

"Oh, on that? Nah," I say.

"Where are you going?"

I glance at the underside of my arm. He reads it along with me.

"Burlington Hall? That's right on my way. I'll take it slow, I promise. Hop on."

It's a day of firsts. I hop on that long board with the good-looking stranger. He doesn't ask me any questions, just tells me to hold on to his legs. He steps on behind me and we roll down the sidewalk, the wind blowing through my hair. I hold on tight and sway with his movements, surprised at how secure I feel. Just minutes later he stops us in front of a sign that says Burlington Hall. I step off and turn around to thank him. He smiles and nods and then takes back off down the path.

All right, sign me up for college.

I jog up three flights of stairs of what I imagine to be very nice in terms of dorms. Each level consists of a long, thin hallway with the dorm doors on one side and a half wall open to the outside world on the other. I pause and walk to the open aired view, looking out towards the street. I take in a therapeutic breath and exhale, preparing for this moment. Number 304 is right in front of me. I double-check the writing on my arm.

A few guys from the dorm next door exit their room and walk this direction. Their long skinny bodies look familiar even with shirts on. I knock on the door in front of me and try to ignore the uncomfortable stares they deliver as they shuffle their way down the stairs. I've never felt more like *the new girl* in my life.

The door opens and I find Christopher standing in the doorway. Before he can say anything I interrupt.

"Hey, are girls allowed up here?" I whisper all flustered. "I'm sorry I don't know much about college and dorms. I just got some really weird looks from some guys next door. Maybe I should…" I gesture down the stairs. Christopher leans out the door and glances down the hall. I notice for the first time just how tall he is. His head barely clears the doorway.

"A couple of nerds gave you a weird look?" he says without question in his voice. "Huh. Did one have a Yoda shirt on?"

I shrug. "Maybe."

Christopher walks past me and leans out over the open wall looking down onto the grass. He looks around and then cups his hands around his mouth. "Jarvis!" He hollers. "Jarvis! Larsen! Barton!" He bellows. I'm confused and walk over to see who he's calling. "Boys! Run up here for a second."

To my horror, the three oglers start trotting back this way like trained poodles. "No, no, that's not necessary," I beg, but their master has already called.

Within seconds, all three are up the stairs and lined up, facing us like soldiers. Christopher fists bumps each of them and then interrogates. "Did you guys give Lucy here a weird look?"

"No, it's fine, they didn't do anything," I say under my breath, completely mortified. When we were younger I'd sit on his head until he apologized for embarrassing me. That won't be happening anymore.

"Guys, this is Lucy, an old friend. She's thinking about coming to school here, so don't mess it up, all right? No stalking her or sketching creepy pictures of her, okay?" He turns to me. "These are the new freshmen. Girls are allowed up here—they've just never seen anyone as pretty as you before. They can't help themselves."

I might die. "Okay, I'm going to leave now." I give the freshmen a disconcerted wave and scamper down the staircase, totally lost on which direction to go.

"Lucy!" Christopher, the king of Burlington Hall calls after me. "Lucy! Wait up, I'm comin'!"

His words seize my memory and in an instant I'm six again, waiting for that stinker to catch up. I hear his agitated young voice again and again, "Wait up, Luce. Wait up!"

Some things don't change. I shake my head in annoyance but laugh off the flashback. Despite his being a couple years older, I was always the one he was chasing after.

He catches up quickly and we stroll towards the car lot.

"You forgot to bring your Aussie accent," he says when he's finally reached me.

"You forgot to not be irritating." I've forgotten what it feels like to use such blunt words, but it felt strangely natural coming out.

He snorts out a chuckle and asks, "The freshmen? You're mad about the freshmen? Oh, come on, It's summer. There are almost no girls here. It was the least I could do to let them stare you down a little more."

I roll my eyes. He points ahead to an old beat up white pick up and opens the passenger door for me. I sit down and look around quickly as he walks around. In the back is an Oregon-green duffle bag. Surrounding it are three different pairs of well-worn running shoes littering the floor. A couple of loose fast food wrappers are scrunched up and in the crack of my seat.

What a pig. He hops in and adjusts the rear view mirror.

"All right, Christopher Summers. Where are we going?" I take off my backpack and place it down by my feet. He buckles himself in and looks over at me.

"Don't call me that."

"What? Your name?"

"It's Toph. I haven't gone by Christopher in ages. The only person who still calls me that is my mom. Christopher!" he squawks out in an obnoxious old lady screech.

"Your mother sounds nothing like that, Christopher Summers," I say.

"Hey, I'll start calling you Mom if you keep it up," he threatens.

"Fine."

Silence fills the truck for several seconds. There is so much to say but my mind feels paralyzed in the moment. Shallow conversation wasn't in my plans but the words I need seem stuck behind a barrier. I start to wonder if a decade of living is too much to catch up on.

Toph leans over to me and takes in a deep breath. "You smell so good," he says casually, shifting down gears and reminding me of the seven different perfumes I sampled during my afternoon adventure. I probably smell like a Russian cab driver. But then again, anything smells good next to his stinky gym shoe air freshener.

"Oh, it's just some perfume I sampled earlier."

"Well, it smells good on you."

"You smell better too," I say, instantly regretting my choice of words.

"I smell better?" he croaks out, in a put-on state of awe. "You're implying I smelled bad?"

"No," I hang on to the word as long as possible. "Not bad. Everybody likes sweaty, wild boy smell."

He shakes his head but looks amused. "For your info, I could bottle up my sweat and sell it in the student store."

I laugh, and it feels freeing. "I should be so lucky to go out with such a legend."

He nods in agreement.

"Do you like Thai food?" he asks, pulling into a gas station.

"So, so, so much."

"Good. One sec." He hops out of the car and disappears through the front doors without another word. I'm wondering what business he's got here. Drinks? Candy? Restroom? But that's when I peer out my window and see the neon sign stuck next to the beer ads. "Thai Me Now, open 10am-9pm, located to the left of the restrooms."

"Please, no," I groan.

We drive away a couple minutes later with a sack overstuffed with gas station Thai take-out cartons resting on top of the gym bag in back. Warm smells of ginger, soy and old socks infuse our senses.

"Tell me you've eaten here before," Toph says as he carries on to our destination. I take a look at him and recognize the 'dinner's a'comin'' expression on his face. He's like an eager puppy hopping around as his food bowl gets filled.

"Nope. The only Thai I've ever had was cooked up in my own kitchen."

"Really? You Aussies think you've got it all figured out. You're going to be in authentic food heaven, Lucy." He licks his lips. "But then again, Renee's got mad cooking skills."

I take notice of his use of present tense, cluing me in that he may not know the extent of my mom's condition.

I wouldn't classify my cooking skills as homegrown, but my Mom must have had something to do with it, especially since a first grader remembered her as a culinary wizard from way back in the day. He's already helping me remember.

We pull in to a dirt parking lot already stuffed with cars and mosey our way over a large and flat grassy area encircled by trees. We follow behind a group of girls with long tresses and minimal clothing. Toph glances ahead at them. "Those shorts make me want to pick the wedgie I don't even have." He carries a large blanket in one arm and the food in the other.

"Where are we?" I ask, following the group in front of us. Suddenly, guitar strings resonate over a monster speaker system and a crowd starts cheering. I peek around the ladies in front of us and see a large amphitheater down the hill with dozens of grassy tiers built up from it to accommodate hundreds of viewers. It's about a quarter filled with people our age.

"We call it music in the park. Most of the time it's really great. Bands rooted from our university get to play here every weekend. Some are still hoping to make it big, but most of the time it's just for fun.

I'm not promising much tonight," he continues. "In the summer when enrollment is down, it's just a step above karaoke."

We hop down a few tiers so that we're still toward the back. Toph spreads the blanket out on the grass and sets down the grub. I glance down at the quilt just before sitting and notice that it's made from a bunch of old, soft t-shirts in every different color. I see a fluorescent orange one that says *Summers Family Reunion* with the picture of a badly animated sunset underneath.

"Hey! I remember this shirt. You used to wear it all the time. Right up until the ketchup squirted out of your hotdog and all down the front of you." I take a closer glance and see a light pink streak that's been scrubbed away.

"Do you remember everything?" he asks, shoving a forkful of dripping pad thai into his mouth. He tosses me a plastic fork.

"No. Everything's just sort of coming back now that you're here, in the flesh," I admit, grabbing a veggie roll and dipping it in a dark orange peanuty sauce. "To tell you the truth, I haven't thought of you in over a decade. Not until yesterday at least."

He stares at me for a long second before crunching into a fried shrimp. "Ouch."

"Sorry, I didn't mean for that to come out harsh. Wait, don't eat that!" I cry out as he pops another shrimp in his mouth. "You're allergic to fish!"

Toph sneers through an overstuffed mouth. "Haven't thought of me in over a decade? Luce, your pants are on fire. Only a seasoned stalker would know my allergies."

"No, but seriously, why are you still eating that?" I ask.

"Not allergic, I was faking it. My mom makes some nasty seafood." I think of him as a chubby juvenile, pretending that his airway is closing in. Poor Mrs. Summers.

"Don't be disappointed but I really haven't been stalking you all these years," I continue. "It's just weird how being with you tonight is unlocking little… gifts… of remembrance that have been camping out all these years deep in my brain."

"So happy for you," he says sarcastically with a hint of bitterness. "Just so you know, I didn't block you out as easily as you seemed to get rid of me." He talks with his mouth full of seafood and spears the last two prawns onto his fork.

"Really?" I ask.

"Yeah, really. I used to think about you all the time. Every day we were out in the world together," he pauses and runs a hand through his chestnut hair, "catching crabs, looking for treasure, trying to light ants on fire," he grins and I swear it has a chain reaction. "I mean, most of my happy childhood memories are with you. Then suddenly I moved away and never saw or heard from you ever again. It was almost like…you died." He keeps his tone casual but looks away, and I can tell that he has been largely impacted.

A slight breeze shifts through the trees and the rustling leaves noisily interrupt our background music. Toph throws the last empty carton into the sack. "It's weird that our parents haven't stayed in touch. They were even closer than we were."

I shiver, now comprehending that Mr. and Mrs. Summers must have chosen to shield their son from a sad story. I remain speechless, lost in my thoughts.

"You look cold. I wish I had a jacket to give you," he says, studying me. "Here," he pulls the t-shirt quilt up around my shoulders. I guess he's learned some manners despite the mischief running wild through his veins.

"Thanks," I manage to whisper. "I think," I pause and wonder if it's the right time to divulge my family history, "there's a definite reason your absence wasn't the first thing on my mind."

The artist who is singing has a bluesy swing to her voice and she's performing an acoustic arrangement of a familiar tune. Toph shifts his weight and leans over, resting his elbows on his knees. "Oh?" He asks. "Well it'd better be a good one."

I expel the air within me and try to dig up the courage that has been dormant for far too long. The sun's evening shadows are casting an orange hue on

Toph's face. I can't help but stare at his face for longer than I should. He is really attractive.

"What time is it?" I gasp suddenly, reaching for the watch in my backpack.

Toph beats me to it and pulls out his phone. "It's early. Man, Truman must have you on a tight leash. I can't blame the guy though. You are," he pauses, hunting for the right words, "you are trouble." His eyes glimmer as though he knows me better than I know myself.

I raise an eyebrow. "I'm going to be in trouble if you don't drop me off in twenty minutes. I've got to make it back to Yachats tonight and the last bus leaves…" but Toph only hears his own ideas.

"What's your phone number? I'll talk to Truman myself. He'll bend your curfew a bit, just you wait," he says with swanky confidence. "He's always liked me."

I turn to Toph and gently take the phone out of his hands.

There are very few people in my life I've trusted my story with. Mostly because I chose to keep the world a safe distance away, but also because I don't know how they will react, and I'm not sure what response I'm looking for. In this moment, I have no idea how Toph will process this, and the thought of it makes my heart flutter wildly in my chest.

My inner voice is yelling. Isn't this why I'm here? Keeping this from him could be like throwing away a gift before even looking inside. It would be like forgetting about my bizarre and remarkable dreams, and discarding the curious chocolates that brought me here.

I find the courage in the familiar warmth of Toph's eyes.

"Toph, my dad is gone. He passed away around the time that you moved."

I watch the color drain from his face. He remains as still as a stone statue except for several forceful blinks. I can almost see the information being processed in his brain, as it's rejected and re-sent for submittal. When he doesn't find understanding, he starts shaking his head back and forth, hoping to gain some insight; but his eyes remain full of confusion and anguish.

"Lucy, I'm devastated for you," he manages to whisper. He takes my hand in both of his. They are warm and comforting. "I don't…I don't understand. How could I not know about this?"

"I don't know," I shrug. "I guess I thought you knew. Maybe your parents thought it would be best for you to start fresh in a new city. No one likes to be weighed down by tragedy."

Toph's back straightens and his arms become rigid. "Wait, you think my parents knew about this?" His voice has more heat than a dragon's.

"Don't be angry. Honestly, they may not know. There was a funeral, but I don't remember who came. I don't remember much. I was hoping you could help me remember...the good things. And you are."

Toph can't quit shaking his head. "I would have been there for you. I could have helped you, distracted you." He starts fervidly twisting a tuft of his hair round and round his fingers, reminding me of his boyhood mannerisms. He always twisted his hair when he felt anxious, eventually creating an awkward bald spot on the front of his hairline. His mom ended up shaving his head to rid him of the habit.

I lightly take his spiraling fingers and hold them still. "It's all right. I'm okay."

With great hesitation, he asks the inevitable. "Lucy, will you tell me what happened?"

I nod and take a deep breath. "Dad had a business trip in Perth to tie up some loose ends and answer questions about his past *Chemcore* projects. From what I've gathered, that's who he worked for during our time in Australia. En route, he had a one day layover in Hawaii so he decided to go out surfing." I look at Toph, who is breathing in every word I say as if it's life-preserving oxygen. "He always drilled me about safety, you know, about never going to the ocean alone." I bite my bottom lip and close my eyes for a breath. "He didn't follow his own rules. Tide was high at that time, and a storm was on its way. You know that's a bad combination. There was a powerful riptide—" I shrug, hoping I've said enough.

Toph closes his eyes for a long period, letting it sink in. The warm touch of his hand seems to have a healing power over my grief.

"Sorry, I wish we had more time to talk," I mutter, "but the last bus leaves at seven. Would you mind taking me to the hub?"

"You're planning on riding the bus home?" He asks, coming back to reality. I nod. "No way. I'll drive you. But I'm not letting you go yet. We need to go do something crazy fun so I can see you laugh and smile again." I blush and look down. "Will you let me keep you?"

For the second time in my life, I feel like someone has taken a piece of my burden and carried it on his own shoulders. I think of Art and now Toph, and I'm grateful for my secret keepers.

"It's a long way to Yachats," I say.

"I know." His eyes sparkle with excitement.

It doesn't take him long to devise an artful detour to our evening.

"There's just one hitch," he says as we march our way back to his truck. "We're going to need to find you a swimsuit."

"Got one," I say, patting my backpack.

"Really?"

"I surf on my days off," I explain.

"Alone?"

"No," I lie.

He explains his plan as we run back to his place to grab his swim trunks.

I head into his bathroom to change and find some tighty-whities wedged in the corner of the vanity, blocking the door from closing. I grimace and look around for something to scoot them away with. The bathroom is bare with not even a bar of soap to be found. I look across the hall to one of the bedrooms. The door is wide open and I behold a red light saber mounted on the wall. I borrow the weapon and use its point to fling the underpants out of my way. I hold my breath and dress as quickly as possible, trying not to let the college boy smell absorb through my skin. Once I'm in my suit, I throw my same clothes back on over top.

I find Toph dressed in a dark and slim, double breasted navy suit, waiting for me outside. He looks straight out of magazine, his tall, lean figure the perfect mannequin for fashion. Even his eyes match the deep hues of navy. He invites me to stare, but I'm mean and decide not to succumb to his wishes.

"Do you have a plan B if this one tanks?" I ask as we drive.

"Don't need one," he says. "This is my lucky suit."

"You look really nice," I offer the flattery, but then remember the wedged underpants. "Boxers or briefs?" I ask with my nose slightly turned up.

"Seriously?" He asks incredulously. "Neither."

"Ew," I laugh. "You're gross. I had to fling your underpants out of my way so I could get dressed."

"Oh, sorry, Mom," he retorts.

"FYI, in case you ever have a real girl over sometime, you're going to want to check your bathroom first."

"Thanks for the tip. And what exactly do you mean by real girl?"

"You know, like a girlfriend or someone you're trying to impress."

Toph rolls his eyes.

We drive up a winding path and park under the portico of the ritziest hotel I've ever laid eyes on. A sultry light gleams out of the tall building. I can't tell if we're inside or outside due to the light marble flooring extending out from the gold-lined front doors and the heavy crystal chandeliers decorating the patio.

A valet in a familiar navy suit takes our car. "Follow big daddy," Toph mutters and swipes a shiny gold luggage cart while no one is looking. A black Beemer pulls up and Toph swoops in as smooth as a greased weasel. From a short distance I hear him welcome the silvery couple in a charming manner. He proceeds to pile their luggage up onto his commandeered cart. He then directs them where to park and shoos them away before the real valet gets back.

I slouch behind the luggage and midget-walk along side while he bustles the cart in and beelines it through the open elevator doors. Luck finds us, and we are alone. The entire elevator wall is polka-dotted with buttons, and Toph pushes the top right circle. I hold my breath and wait for what seems like an eternity as the elevator door closes, shutting out the lobby.

Up we fly, higher and higher, silent and eager. After we pass floor nine, Toph does an ugly victory leap in the air and immediately starts stripping down to his swim-trunks, which are well hidden under his suave suit. I pick his beautiful suit coat off the floor and hang it on a borrowed hanger that was on the luggage cart.

Suddenly, the elevator dings and the doors swing open on floor seventeen. Toph stares ahead at a gaping gaggle of middle-aged women who immediately quit their babbling and drop their jaws. Toph stands bare-chested with his pants down around his ankles, and offers a wave. I reassume my position hiding behind the luggage.

"Ladies, care to join us?" Toph invites. The women's expressions turn from shock to chagrin, now looking like an angry group of livid mother chickens, ready to peck away at the elevator creep. Time is up and the elevator doors close out the red lipstick and glaring eyes.

I'm nervously cackling behind the luggage cart

and hanging up the remaining components of Toph's suit. He kicks off the offending pants, leaving him in his swim-trunks and a wide smile across his face.

The elevator dings again and the doors open, inviting us to step out onto the deck of the last floor, twenty-one. Toph takes his suit and then sends the luggage unaccompanied back down to the lobby with a smug smirk.

I step onto the hickory floors and am greeted by a warm, soft wind against my face, compelling me to take in breaths of chlorine and fresh wood. We walk around a corner and are presented with a view that makes all this transgressing worthwhile. The entire top floor we stand on is an open deck, with only glass railings enclosing us in, leaving us feeling like we are standing in the bright starry sky. The entire city is glowing around us.

Just ahead, five separate bubbling, green hot tubs lie flush with the ground, the steam hissing and floating up into the night. Standing at the very front of the deck is a twenty-foot screen, currently playing a sultry scene of a 007 flick. A small wood hut is on the opposite side of the elevator, festooned with dangling globe lights hung around the pitches of the roof. Cocktail glasses with crystallized sugar around the rims are lined up along the shelf of the bar, waiting to be filled.

Only a handful of people are currently occupying

floor twenty-one, and their dark shadows are on the opposite side of the deck leaving me feeling like we are all alone.

Toph leads me over to an unoccupied pool and is already sprawled out and tranquilized amidst the bubbles before I even have time to undress.

"Don't look," I say as he watches me shed my top layers. He doesn't obey, so I'm forced to leave my clothes in a heap and hop in as fast as possible, extinguishing any extra staring time.

"I didn't know you were on the eighties Olympic swim team," Toph declares, referring to my one-piece women's Speedo that I stole out of my mom's drawer years ago.

"Always a jerk," I say and splash a wall of water into his face.

Toph laughs and wipes his eyes. "I'm pretty sure you're the only person in the world who could make that look good."

I'm glad it's dark because I feel my cheeks flush.

We are able to catch up on high school calamities and some of his basic family happenings before another couple joins us in our pool.

"Let's talk in an Aussie accent," Toph whispers in my ear, far too excited. The seemingly pleasant middle-aged couple politely greets us and sinks down into the tub.

"G'day mates!" Toph says in a terrible and thick accent. I have to turn away to hide my laughter.

"Where are the likes of ya from?" He continues, fading from Aussie to Irish. "We come from the land down undah."

The man leans forward, squinting. His mustache moves thoughtfully from left to right before he leans back and elbows his wife. "May, doesn't he look just like that kid we were reading about in the paper? That running whiz? Seh..sah..suh..Summers!" He croaks out, splashing the pool with his hand. "Isn't your last name Summers?"

Toph glances over at me, looking like a kid whose hand got caught in the cookie jar. I decide to spare him some grief and take over.

"Sweetie," I say in my old Aussie way. "I'm getting a bit hot and bothered. Mind if we take a step out?"

Toph doesn't follow my lead. He just stares at me and mutters, "So hot."

"Have a lovely evening," I say, dragging the wet legend out.

We ride down the fancy elevator dripping wet and howling with laughter. "You're famous!" I yell at him.

We snatch our own keys from the valet station, leaving two puddles on the marble floor before running out into the dark night to recollect the truck.

Before we cruise onto the freeway, Toph pulls into a fast food drive-through, ordering three tacos and a side of tots. He tosses over one of the tacos, and we start stuffing our faces for a second time. I worry about it not getting along with the Thai, but as I pop in another tot, everything seems right in the world.

We roll both windows down and take the freeway back to Yachats, airing out our wet bodies and singing Queen's greatest hits at the top of our lungs. About a half hour in, my teeth are chattering like a frostbite victim. Toph pulls over without saying a word. I wait as he gets out of the truck and walks over to my side. He opens my door and leans in, reaching for something in the back of the truck. His body is right next to mine, and through the chlorine, I can smell a delicious woodsy pine and feel the heat of his breath on my neck. I hope he can't feel the pound of my heart.

He snags the blanket we sat on during dinner and wraps my whole body up, reminding me of how my dad used to tuck me in at night. I haven't had that thought in years, and those warm and safe feelings flood my being.

Now that our sing-along is over, Toph gives me a CliffsNotes version of his dating history. It might have been the full version, but either way it was short. Before he has a chance to question me, I distract him by querying about his running career. Since running is his life, it's a safe and easy conversation, and I love hearing the passion he carries in his voice.

We take the exit into Yachats, and for the first time, the truck is filled with silence. The low rumble of the engine is calm, but the air inside is still charged from our discussions.

"Turn right here," I say, breaking the hush.

"I remember." His voice is low and thoughtful as he drives half the speed limit down the familiar streets.

I'm impressed as he pulls into the driveway of my dark home without any guidance.

"I'll walk you in," he says and gets out of the truck. Since Mom isn't home until tomorrow, I let him.

I take the hidden key out from under the mat and open the door, flipping on the lights as we walk in.

"It's exactly the same!" Toph affirms, his voice full of nostalgia. "So many good memories here."

I bite my bottom lip and nod, suddenly overwhelmed by the new pieces Toph has helped me recapture. He glances down at me. "You okay?"

"Yeah, yeah, I'm good. Thanks so much for today." I try to dilute my emotions. "It was just what I needed. I'm so glad we ran into each other."

"Yeah, it's crazy. Me too." Toph is leaning up against the side of the doorframe in his swimsuit and green tee, his hair swooped back in a wild, wind-blown fashion. "So, tell me you're coming to

U of O this fall."

"Ooh." I rub my eyes. "I want to. That would be, yeah," I sigh. "Honestly though, it might not work out for me, Toph." I look up at him and he has that recognizable, naïve look in his eyes.

"You have to, Luce. I'll talk you into it—just you wait."

I laugh and change the subject. "I'm worried about you driving home this late." I glance at the clock and realize it's well past midnight.

"Nah, I'll be fine." He reaches for my hand I give it to him. His big, warm palm encompasses my fingers and he tugs me forward, forcing me into a hug. "I've missed you, Luce," he says barely loud enough for me to hear. My ear is pressed against his chest and I can hear the deep rumble from his voice and the steady beat of his strong heart. He pulls away, but I'm not ready to leave.

"Tell Renee hi from me."

"I will," I lie.

He waves and I slowly shut the door, already feeling colder in his absence.

As I lie in bed, I remember my chocolates buried in the toe of Art's loafer. I won't need them. I've collected enough happy memories to help me sleep, at least for tonight.

CHAPTER TEN

I had a good night's sleep. And that's where the good ended.

The incessant creaking is the only sound breaking the eerie silence. Back and forth she rocks, filling the air with an uncomfortable force. The feeling is comparable to the nervous energy and hush in a room that precedes something terrible, but in this case, I can only hope the worst is over.

I blame myself, knowing deep down that sending her was a selfish and irresponsible move. Now I'm paying the consequences. A step forward for me, ten steps backwards for us. The darkness I feel now is a stark contrast to the magic I was floating in just yesterday.

Things didn't go well at the retreat, and with regret, Judy dropped Mom off early. Getting her into that chair took everything I have in me, and as she rigidly rocks with every muscle strained and her face in a painful pinch, I have nothing left to give. My mental and physical reserves are all used up, leaving my spirit drained and damaged.

Now I hide out of her view, prisoner in my house, anxiously waiting for something to set her off again. Even the breaths I take stand as weapons against me, so I hold my breath and wait a few more minutes for the rocking to slow.

When her exhales are evenly puffed intervals, I start breathing again and take a look at the damage. Every object now seems to be a traitor to Mom's lost inner peace, and I'm the only one around to fix it.

I creep past the kitchen and don't bother picking the food up off the floor. I need to start in her bedroom, where she won't hear me. The late afternoon sun doesn't provide much light, so I work in the shadows.

Every piece of clothing mom owns is flung about her room. The carpet is buried and drawers are left wide open in an uncharacteristically chaotic state. I see one spot of bare carpet in the corner, flashing me back to hours earlier, just after Judy dropped mom off. This is the spot mom lay unclothed, screaming in the fetal position. Rocking back and forth in a miserable and confused state, she was unable to recognize where she was, unable to find a familiar piece of clothing to cover herself in.

Seeing her this broken rocked me and left my mind numb. In the nursing home, I would have thought of something clever to get this task completed, but my own mother, now completely lost of her self and sinking deeper into this disease was too hard to process.

There was one last shirt in the back of her drawer left to try, the one she's wearing now. At the time I didn't understand why she agreed to wear it. I was just relieved. After all the trouble she had given me, she took the stretched out grey t-shirt and hugged it, eventually letting me help her slip it over her head.

It was Dad's.

I sit wilted on the floor, looking at the overwhelming mess around me. Hot tears stream down my face, but I press forward, picking up the clothes one piece after another, hoping I can find some love in serving someone who doesn't love me back.

The last remaining pair of socks is eventually picked up, and at last her room looks exactly the way it has for a decade. I even go as far as arranging her sock drawer the way she usually has it, whites in the front and the colors in back. As I push a black dotted pair to the very back, my hand catches on the ruffled end of a notebook paper that seems to be stuck to the very back of the drawer. I pull the crinkled sheet out and unfold it.

It's composed to Renee. Following her name are a few paragraphs scribbled in man-cursive and I recognize Dad's writing immediately. I start skimming through the lines, fully aware of the intimacy within meant for just the two of them.

No date is listed, and from what I can tell, there was no specific occasion. Just a random love note, and one that my mom couldn't part with. I reread one of the lines.

I will love you even after I take my last breath.

I shudder as a morbid thought crosses into my mind: It's almost as if Dad knew he was going to die.

I try and shake off the idea, but the passage from John shines brighter than a light bulb in my head, one without an off switch.

"I'm ready for the truth," I say under my breath.

It's time to do some research, and I'm going to need some help from Art. My next shift isn't until tomorrow night. If I can get Mom to bed early tonight, I might be able to slip out to the nursing home.

After gently replacing the note, I start on the next room, this time with increased motivation. As I pick the cold, soggy broccoli off the floor, I hear the foreign curse words that fired out of Mom's mouth just hours ago. Every action she took was uncharacteristic and hurtful. So much anger and confusion targeted straight at me.

The house is getting dark, and I tiptoe in to peek at Mom. This afternoon's chaos wore her down, enabling her to finally release some emotional pain and loosen the reins of her fury. And for a minute, I stop and stare at her face, trying to see past today's actions and her usual, indifferent mannerisms.

Is she still in there, crying for help, wondering if I've given up on her? Does she realize she's stuck in a maze with no finish in sight? My heart is heavy at the thought of a piece of her, still trying to break through her fog with no cheering squad around. I need to keep my end of the promise to Dad. She's still in there somewhere, even though it may never be manifested outwardly to me.

I dim the lights and take one of the thick, nubby blankets she crocheted to cover up her bare legs. Then I quietly lie on the velvet couch, watching her rock, gingerly enjoying the peace that comes after the storm.

Seconds later, a deafening knock on the front door echoes throughout every corner of our house. My heart jumps out of my chest and my entire body lurches upright. I hold my breath and panic, glancing from Mom to the door, praying she doesn't wake up.

I run to the door, eager to silence the intruder, but whoever it is persistently knocks again, this time with more vigor.

I bite my bottom lip in horror, all the while Mom starts stirring.

I'm still holding my breath, somehow believing this will mute my actions. I crack the door open, ready to bark at the person who is trying to make my life miserable.

A familiar face greets mine and for just a second, our eyes lock. These are the same eyes I left less than twenty-four hours ago, yet it seems like it's been ages. These eyes took me away from my life of entrapment and introduced me to another world. I should wrap my arms around him in a delighted embrace. Instead, my survival instincts take over.

I can see him take in a breath to greet me, and wildly I wave my arms in front of his face and shake my head to silence him. Then I mutely close the door and glance back at Mom. She's rubbing her forehead, but her eyes are still closed. I only have a few seconds. I crack the door back open, and poor Toph's face is baffled, but I don't have time to coddle him.

"Back door," I mouth and point to the side of the house. "Go."

I don't wait around to see his reaction, and I know there's a chance he might take off. I sneak to the back of the house and open the creaky door. His tall figure is there waiting for me, and I feel relieved. This time, he doesn't try to say a word, just waits for me to give him instructions.

"Don't make a peep," I whisper under my breath and shove him into my room, shutting the door behind me.

I glide back out to the front room and find Mom sitting upright in her chair.

"Who was at the door?" She croaks out in a sleepy voice.

"Neighbor. Needed to borrow something. I sent him away." I quickly glance around the room and everything looks just as it should. I'm hoping Renee doesn't have to relive the events from earlier today.

"Are you hungry, Renee? How about a bowl of cereal or something?"

Renee stands up slowly. "I would just like to be in my room, thank you. Very tired."

I escort her through the hall and past the kitchen, hoping she can't smell the boy I'm hiding in my bedroom.

I anxiously watch her eyes graze over her bedroom as we enter. She seems satisfied with its normalcy and makes her way straight to her empty queen-sized bed. I skip into her bathroom and put some toothpaste on her toothbrush and soak a cloth with hot water for her face, but when I return to her bedside, her eyes are already closed. I sigh another breath of relief and return her items to the bathroom before turning the lights out and shutting her door.

When I race back to my bedroom, I find Toph standing on top of my bed, fiddling with the smoke detector that has been broken and dangling from my ceiling for months. He twists it back into place and then wipes his hands off as if to say, "all in a good day's work." But he remains mute.

"Hi," I say happily, finally able to take in his existence here in my house. I want him to wrap his lanky arms around me and tell me I did good today, tell me everything is okay, but he appears puzzled over my actions and stays back a bit.

"Can we start over?" I ask blithely, keeping my voice down.

Toph takes a step closer. "Is Renee going to come in here and slap me silly, or what?"

"Let's go outside, but not out this back door. It's too creaky…follow me."

I lead Toph through the still house and grab my backpack with my notebook in it. Toph stops at the kitchen table and takes a look at Renee's untouched dinner plate before grabbing half a baked potato and dipping it in the sour cream, cramming the whole thing in his mouth.

We still have a decent amount of sunlight, and Toph walks next to me, loudly chomping in my ear.

"You came all the way out here," I say, my voice soft and still surprised. "How come?"

Toph swallows, but then holds up his finger like he remembers something. I watch him run the few yards back to his truck and open the door. A huge, golden retriever plops out, swiftly wagging his tail back and forth, meagerly walking towards me.

"Oh, Howie!" I exclaim, rushing towards the pooch. "I've missed you!" Howie licks me right across the cheek. "Oh, you're such an old fart now," I moan, rubbing his back.

"So you do know how to properly greet people," Toph scoffs, sneering at me. He puts an old chewed up tennis ball in his pocket. "He wanted to take a drive with me today."

I ignore his cynicism. "I'm so glad. I've missed him," I say, patting Howie's soft golden fur.

Howie walks in between the two of us. I take in a breath. "I'm sorry about that," I say, motioning back towards the house. It's been a weird and hard day." I let the words linger in the air without an explanation. "But I've missed you too." I reach up to the top of his hair and playfully pet his head, thoroughly messing up his hair. "And I'm glad you're here."

Toph shakes his head but smiles.

"Why are you here?" I ask gently.

"Whoa, whoa whoa, you think you get to ask the questions after you gagged me and tied me up in your closet?"

I laugh but realize that soon, I may not have

many secrets left from Christopher. I can hear the ocean waves now with each nearing step. I glance over at him and my instincts beg me to let go.

"I have a lot of secrets," I mutter. I can feel Toph's eyes on me as we walk. "I don't usually like to drag people down."

Together we take a left turn in between two pine trees and our feet hit soft sand. We both turn our faces toward the ocean in front of us and inhale the salty air. The wind blows into us and large waves crash right at the shore, serenading our silence.

I notice Toph staring at the sign, perhaps bringing new meaning to him now.

Beware of Sharks and Riptides
No Lifeguard

Without saying a word, we sit down next to each other with Howie at our feet.

"You shouldn't have to be alone—in that dark place," Toph replies.

I nod, trying to understand how telling him is going to change my situation. I don't want to be that girl, stuck back in Yachats that he feels bad for. But the concerned look in his eyes presses me forward.

Before I even speak, one tear escapes my eye and slides down my cheek. I try and hide it, but Toph catches it with his finger. Today has softened my emotions.

"Please. I hate seeing you in pain," Toph begs.

"I'm not sad, I'm just…I'm grateful for you," I say, and he squeezes my hand encouragingly.

I breathe in deeply, preparing myself for some soul purging. I let go of his hand and stand up, taking a few steps towards the water, gathering my thoughts. Howie follows at my heels.

I turn back around and sit down again, facing Toph's welcoming face.

"Renee is sick," I divulge. "Renee is really sick, and has been for a long time." Toph remains silent, eagerly listening. I carry on, closing my eyes.

"She's mentally sick, something similar to early on-set Alzheimer's. At first it was just small, funny things…she couldn't remember our address, she let go of any rules she'd made, she forgot things we had done just the day before. But it quickly progressed to her being anxious all the time, in denial about my dad, and really moody and withdrawn. She let go of all of her ties and friends. Before I knew it, she quit feeding and dressing herself. She can, but she doesn't think to do it. She forgets my dad died and asks for him daily. She doesn't realize I've grown up. I have to help her stick to the same routine, day after day, or she completely loses it."

I press my lips together. "I don't mind helping her. I just hate how she looks at me, like I'm a stranger." My voice quivers. Toph slowly breaths out through a small airway with his lips pursed together.

"So, now I have to keep my house exactly the way it always has been. I have to keep all visitors out, or it sends her into an anxious fit. I have to stay at home and take care of her, feed her, dress her, or nobody else will."

Toph's eyes are glassy. He takes my hand again. We sit in silence for a minute before he finally speaks.

"How long, Luce? How long have you been taking care of her on your own?"

"She got sick a week before my dad died."

Toph now closes his eyes, and I can feel him taking on the weight of my burden though it's not his to carry.

"Stop," I say. "It's okay. This is my life; I've lived it long enough to handle it on my own. There isn't much anyone can…"

"What about Christmases? Birthdays? Were you all alone?" he interrupts.

I shrug, and it breaks him. "Don't you have family in Australia who could take care of you?" I shake my head.

"I'm fine now. I can take care of myself and Renee."

"What about a nursing home? Doesn't she qualify to stay in one?"

Deep down I know Toph is looking out for me, but he just hit a dangling, abused nerve.

"Would you, Toph? Would you send your mom to a nursing home at forty-five? Would you stick her in with the other seniles, without a single grey hair on her head, her skin still soft, her back still straight and strong? Would you take her away from everything familiar? Send her deeper into her disease? Forget about your only remaining family member on this earth?" I start silently weeping, turning my head away. Toph scoots closer and wraps his arms around me, letting me sob.

"You are the most selfless and brave human I know." He whispers into my ear and continues to hold me tight.

I sniff. "There's a tiny piece of me that still believes she's in there somewhere. I promised my dad I wouldn't give up."

Toph nods, but it seems his mind is racing. After a minute, he pulls the dingy yellow tennis ball out of his pocket and launches it down the shoreline, sending Howie hobbling after it.

"Can I ask you something, Luce?"

I nod. I'm in such a vulnerable state I would tell him nearly anything.

"One thing…" he trails off in thought but then picks back up. "One thing you said yesterday. I haven't been able to stop thinking about it."

I should keep my mouth shut more.

"You said you hadn't thought about me in over a decade," he scoffs with a level of disdain in his voice. "But then you added, 'until yesterday.'"

He glances at me quizzically. "Yesterday when we ran into each other on the track, it wasn't coincidence."

It's definitely not a question, but he's waiting for my answer.

I shake my head. "Not coincidence, but maybe fate."

Toph drops his head in confusion. "What made you think of me? Why did you come find me?"

"How deep into this do you want to get? The road to my craziness is a long way away from normal human life," I half joke.

"I've got record breaking stamina," he says, chucking the ball again. Howie's eyes follow after it, but he walks to me and collapses on my lap with his tongue out.

"You asked for it," I say, still unsure this is a good idea. "Well, I had a dream about you, the night before I found you. Howie was there too. We were at a park, and it was my fifth birthday."

Toph nods. "Your dad bought you a wicked awesome bike. I was so jealous. I always wished I was an only child."

I roll my eyes.

"That doesn't seem too out of the ordinary, Luce."

"Well, I don't believe it was random that I dreamed that. I think I was…" I pause trying to think of the right word, but I can't think of it so I just come out with it. "Drugged."

"What?" Toph blasts, his eyebrows drawn together in an angry line.

"Relax, it's not what you think," I say, tugging down on his arm.

"Ever since my dad passed away, someone has been looking out for me. Every year, on the night of my birthday, long after the sun goes down, there is a package left on my doorstep. It's always something I need. This year, it was chocolate. Four chocolates, actually," I clarify. "I've eaten two so far. They seem to have some crazy affect on my memory, sending me into a deep dream. When I wake up, I have these crazy detailed memories about past events that have actually happened."

Toph is shaking his head back and forth in a disturbed manner. "You're telling me that some stranger left you chocolate that messes with your head, and you've willingly taken more than one?"

He is standing up now, pacing the beach.

I stand up in defense. "It's not a stranger. This person has been my only source of hope and comfort for years. I trust them. Obviously there's something I'm supposed to know. They led me to you, didn't they?"

Toph is grumbling under his breath. "I don't like this." Eventually he walks back to me and crouches down. "Tell me more about these dreams."

I take him through my recollection up in the loft; the spinning, the laughing, the crying, even the odd eye contact with Dad and the plane ticket I found, proving my dream was real.

"I even have it here. The ticket, I mean." I reach into my bag, pull out my journal and find the ticket, wedged in between two pages. I hand it over to Toph. He studies it as I continue.

"At the very end of my dream, I open up this locket," I grab hold of the necklace around my neck, swinging the charm left and right. "Only, this picture wasn't there. It was some jumbled words I couldn't make out."

At this statement, I take off the locket for the first time since I was little. I unscrew the metal plates that envelop Dad's picture. At last, the hollow top piece comes loose. I remove the protective plastic over the image I've spent a decade staring at. I place my thumb on Dad's face and slide his picture to the side.

I gasp sharply. Sure enough, behind it are the words I saw in my dream. But this time, they aren't cloudy.

*Chance favors
the prepared mind.
-Louis Pasteur*

My hands are trembling as I look back and forth

between the picture and the quote. Eventually I turn to Toph and start talking a million miles an hour now. "There was also a scripture meant for me to see, a passage in John…something about how I will know the truth and it will make me free." My limbs feel numb as all the blood is pumping inside my fluttering heart.

"I need to prepare my mind…I need to figure out the truth. Toph, I want to be free. I don't even know what's real or where to start." I beg him to steady my sanity.

His face holds a look of astonishment as he looks back and forth between my locket and the ticket.

I can envision the wheels turning in his head by the look in his eye. "This ticket is photocopied," he announces, waving the paper in the air. It's been printed on normal printer paper." He continues talking mostly to himself, trying to make sense.

"He wanted to make sure you saw it. Made a copy of it for you to see, years later…" He trails off, studying the ticket harder now.

Suddenly he breaks the silence. "You told me he was going on a business trip to Perth, correct?"

I nod.

"Luce, this is a one way ticket to HNL…Honolulu. There isn't a connecting flight to Australia. From what I can see, there is no return flight either. It looks like he wasn't ever planning on making it to Perth."

"That can't be right. There is no explanation for that. Why would he go to Hawaii one week after my Mom was diagnosed, if it wasn't absolutely mandatory for work?"

A devastating thought implodes the beliefs I held onto for years. "You don't think...you don't think he did this on purpose?" My chest is rapidly rising and falling in panic.

"Before he left, my dad hugged me as though it was his last time. I saw the tears on his face in my dream." I start to get choked up. "Was it all too much for him? Did he end his life when he realized my mom's was over? Was I not enough for him?" I cry angrily.

Toph shakes his head. "Not Truman. I won't believe that," he says firmly. And the confidence in his voice lifts me up, and I want to believe him. Dad's reassuring words back him up. *I won't ever give up trying.*

Toph bites his lip. "There's one other thing I should tell you."

I raise my eyebrows.

"This morning, I went to my parents' house to drop off my laundry."

I roll my eyes but can't hide a grin.

"I told my dad that I ran into you. He started getting really flustered and tried to change the subject. I kept pushing, asking him about Truman. I told him I knew that he had passed. Then I asked if

127

he knew."

He takes a big breath and turns to me. "I wasn't going to tell you all this, I just thought it would upset you. But there's something really sketchy going on."

"What did he say?" I prod.

"He denied it. Said he didn't know. Pretended to act upset for a few minutes before escaping out of the room."

I shrug. "He was probably telling the truth," I say.

"There's something else you should know—the reason we moved out to Eugene," Toph pauses. "Lucy, my dad is the chief of police. There is no way he wouldn't know about Truman's death. He's hiding something."

CHAPTER ELEVEN

The waves are now just noisy black tides pushing toward us in the night. The full moon casts a glow over Toph's face, and I'm pleased I can still make out his features. We sit in silence now, trying to make sense of any of the pieces we've gathered.

At last, Toph breaks the hush. "Do you remember much of his funeral?" he asks delicately.

I shake my head. "Not much. I know it was in my home. I don't think I fully comprehended what had happened. Obviously my mom didn't provide much solace. She hadn't completely lost herself at that point, but she was already gone to me. I remember locking myself in the bathroom to avoid the sad stares from strangers."

Toph fidgets before asking his next question. "Were you able to say goodbye to him, see his body before he was buried?"

I look up at him, wondering why he would ask. "His injuries were too substantial. It was closed casket. They wouldn't let me see him."

Toph fidgets even more. "So, they were able to recover his body, and send it here for the funeral?"

His hard questions are starting to grate away my bravery. "I assume so."

"Did anyone see it? His body?" His voice is low and placid.

His questions hush me to silence.

"Luce, what if…" He trails off, hoping I'll finish the sentence for him.

I shake my head, unwilling to help him out. He's stubborn enough to continue.

"What if the casket was empty?"

"Impossible," I say soberly. "There's no way he would have coherently left me alone all these years to suffer on my own."

"The gifts," Toph continues. "He could have been the one who left the gifts for you."

Again, I'm angry. Angry that he thinks this is a possibility, angry that it really could be.

Toph reads my body language. "You're probably right. I'm sorry to even bring it up. But one way or another, your dad was in on this." He holds the plane ticket up. I grab it and stick it back in my journal, safely zipping my backpack around it. This conversation is making me dizzy.

"Ugh, I hate that you have to drive all the way home in the dark again," I say looking up at the black sky, trying to break the tense conversation.

"What—are you kicking me out?" He frowns. "I pushed too hard, I'm sorry. I'm just trying to come up with every possible scenario."

"No," I sigh. "I know you are, and I'm grateful. It's just so much for me to take in all at once. I need some time to process."

"Are you going to be okay? I hate leaving you right now, with no answers. I've got a crazy week with practices before the season opener. I'm going to be worried about you."

"I'm fine," I insist. "In fact, I've got a friend who can help me. I think he'll be able to really get to the bottom of the chocolates," I say, trying to reassure him.

Instead, his body goes rigid. "Friend? Who?" His jealous tone makes me smile.

"Easy, he's a senior citizen," I say. "His name is Art. He's the only person I've ever opened up to, besides you, and he's basically a wizard. He'll be able help me in some way, I'm sure." I hold up my ring. "He is the one that gave me this."

Toph grabs my hand. "Looks more like a cheap sea shell than a ring," he mumbles, and I slug him in the gut.

"Look," Toph says. "I'm glad you and Farty Arty have a special bond. I just want you to promise me something."

I bat my eyes at him and smile.

"Don't take any more of that chocolate until we can find out what's in it, and what it's doing to you."

"I'll have Art look at it first. He'll probably want to dissect it himself," I say.

Right then Howie meanders back from the darkness and shakes his wet fur, dousing our faces with stinky, dog infused water.

"Howie" I scream, standing up and running out of his range.

Toph snickers and chases after me. "Oh, did the widdle puppy get you all wet?"

I push him away, but he picks up my entire body effortlessly, holding me in his arms like a baby, and makes his way into the cold, dark swells.

"Don't you dare," I shriek as he wades deeper and deeper. I push and fight against his chest but there's no use. I glance up at his face just inches from mine, and he looks positively impish, and I fully recognize that look.

By now he's up to his waist in the ocean, and I'm clawing onto him like a kitten, avoiding the waves that are trying to reach up and slosh my behind. The noisy crash of waves becomes quieter as we move away from the shore, and the only sounds are our own breaths in the silent, dark night.

"You know you're going down with me," I state as he manually removes my arms from around his neck. Before I even have time to take a breath he swings my body back and forth and hurls me into the cold wetness. I scream before the cutting chill takes my breath away and my entire body is immersed. His arms find me and pull me back up against his chest.

I shiver and scowl at him, finally getting my bearings enough to push his head down into the water, and he lets me. When he comes back up he flips his hair to the side and his white teeth glow under his smile. He takes my hand and we swim out a little further, so that our bodies rise and fall effortlessly with each swell.

"You deserved that," he announces, wiping the drips of water off my face with his thumb. "For pretending you didn't know me on the track."

I tip my head back and laugh, and a wave tries to take me away with it. Toph pulls me back, bringing me close to his chest. I turn my head and rest my chin on his shoulder, but again he pulls me closer so that my cheek is up against his. I feel his short whiskers against my face and the galloping beat of his heart against mine. His warm breath tickles my ear as he whispers, "I just needed to see you smile again."

Then he takes me by the shoulders and pulls back, studying my eyes. I look up into his and find happiness, my own happiness. At this moment, the little boy I used to see fully transforms, and I realize that I want him. I look at the curve of his strong jaw line and follow up to his soft lips. He licks the salt off them, still studying me.

"Do you like me, Luce?" he asks and stares into my eyes. "Or am I just a piece of this puzzle?" His eyes sparkle eagerly. "Either way, I won't leave you. I'll help you through this. I just need to know."

I smile, and let my hand graze over his whiskers and move through his smooth, dripping hair. "I really like you, Toph." And for a minute, I feel like the air has been knocked out of me, as I consider kissing the boy of my dreams. Toph brushes a wet strand of hair out of my eyes and takes my face in his warm hands. Our lips inch closer and closer, but a distant sound of panting suddenly breaks our focus. At that moment, something sharp scratches the back of my leg and my heart nearly beats out of my chest as I see a shadow swimming up behind me.

A yelp escapes from the intruder's mouth, and fuzzy wet paws scratch against my back. Howie howls for help, his panting old body exhausted from his swim. Together, we rescue the old mutt, carrying his heavy, wet body back to shore. I can't help but giggle for several minutes while Toph cusses him out.

We jog back to the house with our teeth

chattering, and I help Toph load Howie into the back seat. Toph wraps him up in a towel, leaving his long pooch muzzle the only visible part of him.

I shut Toph's door behind him, and talk to him through the window. "Hope your heater works."

"We'll be fine," he smiles, trying to appear tough. "How can I get a hold of you this week?"

"I can call you from work tomorrow night?"

He grabs my arm through the window and pens his phone number on top of my hand. "Don't forget," he says and squeezes my hand for a lingering minute before backing out of the driveway.

I watch him drive away down the narrow, dark street. For a few minutes, I swoon in the bliss of romance and the nearness of my first kiss. Butterflies dance in my stomach as I brood over when I can see him next.

When I enter my house, sensibility washes away the enchantment as several realizations hit me like a brick wall.

My dreams are disabled by circumstance, unless I find the truth. I need to find what will set me free, and I have a feeling it has to do with Mom. She is the only thing keeping me tied down, because her safety and comfort will always be my main focus. I know that her demise or being institutionalized will not and cannot be the thing that sets me free; it's simply not an option. But I still don't know what will.

And then there's Dad. I know Toph is right—he must have played a role in these chocolates, but deep down inside, I can't truly imagine he is out there somewhere, walking on this earth, breathing in the same air as me.

A heavy rush of chills races up my arms. I close my curtains and bury my whole self under the covers, hiding from unanswered questions.

If Dad wants me to be prepared, then I will be.

CHAPTER TWELVE

Everyone complains about Mondays, but I'm more chipper than a young spring chicken this morning. Mondays mean that Mom is back to her job at the office, and she seems glad to be back to her routine.

I never really miss the nursing home, but today I'm overly anxious to see Art.

Yet again, I enter the building in my street clothes, hiding myself behind the early morning ruckus of busy staff. Nobody stops me today, and I look left and right before knocking on room 309.

I hear his voice and crack the door open. I lean in and find him in his fancy leather chair. When he sees me his face lights up.

"Lucy! Where have you been? You had me

thinking you escaped this place for good." Art is wearing a red and grey-checkered shirt. His hair is standing up like a wild turkey as usual.

The door shuts behind me and I jet to his side. I take his aged hand and squeeze it, and he rests his other one on top of mine, patting the abalone ring.

"Where were *you* is the question," I say. "I came to visit you just a couple days ago and you were MIA."

Art turns his nose up. "Oh, those clowns made me go to the hospital and take all sorts of tests. It took all rotten day."

"Is everything okay?" I ask with concern.

"Oh yes, fine, fine. Upped my insulin dose is all. I could have told them to do that myself," he grunts.

"I'm glad you're okay. I have to admit, your absence threw me off a little. I've been dying to talk to you." I pause then say, "Are you busy?"

"Lucy, I haven't been busy in decades. Take a seat, young lady."

Instead of heading to the green rocker, I open his closet door and reach into the toe of his loafer. He watches as I pull out two chocolates wrapped up in gold aluminum foil.

"Well, look at that. You're a magician," he says through an astonished expression.

"Art, do these mean anything to you? Go ahead and take a closer look." I pass the candies over to him and watch as he unwraps and sniffs the objects in question.

"Smells like milk chocolate to me. What's the fuss about?"

"These were the gift this year. You know, the gift on my porch. Call me crazy, but I think there's something in them that's causing me to dream some seriously vivid details of my past life events. Things I haven't ever remembered before."

Art's face freezes. He leans forward and slides the glasses down his nose so that we see eyeball to eyeball. "You're telling me that whoever gave these to you infused them with some type of memory targeting substance?"

"I don't know!" I exclaim. "I know it sounds crazy. Is this even possible, from a medical point of view?"

"More like a pharmaceutical point of view," he mutters. "Nothing is impossible."

I go on to tell him about the clues that have been dropped so far, including the locket and the plane ticket. With each word I say, his eyes get wider in awe.

A cafeteria worker drops off a lunch tray, and we both nibble on pieces of a roll.

"You've told me in the past, the gifts are postmarked but the location is blacked out. Is that true for this gift as well?" He asks.

I shake my head. "No. I'm pretty sure this one

was delivered in person."

Art shifts uncomfortably. "I don't like the idea of your taking a mystery drug from a mystery person." He continues, "Have you felt any side effects afterwards?"

"Not at all. Right after I swallow, I get incredibly dizzy right before I pass out. Afterward, everything is very normal."

Art weighs the chocolate in his palm. "Art, you've got to help me," I plead. "I'm willing to do whatever it takes. I want to know the truth about whatever the truth is."

Art studies me for several seconds. "Then there's only one thing to do."

"What's that?" I ask like an overly caffeinated user.

"I will monitor you. Take down your reactions, movements, the amount of time you're out, and I'll be right here when you wake up. I can take a closer look at the consistency of this fourth chocolate while you're out, do some research. When you wake up, we'll have some answers." Art looks excited, a bit like a nerdy kid about to start a science experiment.

"You think I should take number three? Right now?" I say. I glance at the clock, calculating that I have seven hours until my shift starts. The first dream lasted longer than that.

Art spins around in his chair, facing me. "Only if

you're comfortable with it. I would like to see for myself, the effects it has on you. I'd rather you not be alone again while the substance is taking effect."

"Wake me up before my shift starts?" I ask. Art agrees.

I scoot my way into Art's covers and rest my head on his pillow. It is crisp and smells of freshly washed linen. Then I pile some extra pillows up around me to hide my face. I don't want a coworker to walk in and see me snoozing in the client's bed.

"Here's to some answers," I say before resting the chocolate on my tongue. Art scoots back and observes.

When I bite through the thin chocolate coating, I blissfully discover the dark, velvety chocolate of a truffle greeting my taste buds, and I know this is my favorite one yet. I enjoy the glossy, sweet center for an extra few seconds before swallowing.

Art stands over me with his thinking scowl on. I feel his two fingers against my wrist, taking my pulse.

"What is happening now, Lucy?" He asks. But his voice sounds distant and each word echoes before it is lost. It sounds like I'm trapped in a giant enclosed pool, trying to hear him over the rebounding sounds of hundreds of voices.

I try and focus on the saturated red check in his shirt, and soon, red consumes my senses, filling my vision with the color of danger.

*

I feel my nose and eyes pressed against the red polyester, and it starts to move away from me. I hug it tight, trying to stay buried in it, but again it moves left and right with each step. When I look up, I see Mom's face, her chestnut brown hair a lovely compliment to the polyester red dress she wears.

I look up and spot a yellow bird, flush on the wall, and recognize the wallpaper in my kitchen. I look at the guests around and observe a sea of visitors in black. Mom stands out in her striking and bright dress, though her expression is vacant.

I try to hide myself again in the ruffles of red, but she busily moves her way around the kitchen, greeting the guests and ignoring my presence.

I get brave and walk into the front room, where I'm greeted by large prints of my father. Sad glances from guests give away the event. I walk past a heavy, brown casket near the fireplace that is covered by a six-foot bouquet of lilies and roses. I want to hide in the corner and cry, but my young self stands near the casket, tracing the intricate carvings with my finger.

A small gathering of people stands around and watches me, softly weeping. When I finally notice their stares, I run off and lock myself in Mom's bathroom. I sit on the floor for what seems like hours, waiting for my house to become mine again, but the visitors keep coming. I start rummaging through Mom's drawers, trying on her jewelry, testing out her tubes of lipstick. I empty several pill bottles, licking the outside coating to see if any are candy.

Eventually, I reach into the bottom of her garbage and find a small pink cardboard box that has already been opened. The front label says *PT Early Response*. I plunge my hand inside and pull out a white plastic stick with a small window on front. Inside the square window is a bold, black plus sign. Alarms go off in my head, yet my young body doesn't respond. I lose interest and toss the stick back into the garbage.

I'm desperate to take one more glance at the plus sign on the window, but the naïve child in me has moved on. I find an off-white piece of cardstock on the vanity counter. I read my dad's name and stare at the dates depicting his short life. A small, oval shaped picture of him is printed above it. I find scissors in the drawer, and sit down cross-legged on the bathroom floor, cutting out his face and placing it inside my locket. I stand up and leave the mess on the ground.

Now I'm out of the bathroom, wandering around the house. I'm guessing I'm searching for the red dress again. Soon, I'll learn that the woman in that dress isn't around to offer me protection any more, but today, I still hope to receive that comfort from her that I'm so used to.

Finally I find her. She's back in a corner, talking to a small man in a dark suit. I hold on to her leg, burying my face in her fabric. I hear her mumbling words to the man, but their conversation is muffled.

After a minute, Mom shakes me off her leg. I start tapping her wrist incessantly, trying to get her attention. "Mom?" I repeat over and over, with no response from her. She continues conversing with the man. "Mom," I say louder and louder, sounding even to myself like a broken record.

"What? What is it?" she finally cries out, losing her cool.

I'm not used to her using this tone, and my voice comes out timid and sad. "I'm hungry. I haven't eaten anything today."

"Then go eat something!" She demands, turning away from me.

"But Mom, we don't have any food." I pull on her red dress.

"Go ask your dad. I don't feel very well right now." She walks out of the room, leaving me confused and alone, staring up at the small man in the dark suit.

I feel a tear slipping down my cheek. The man crouches down to my eye level. I'm too embarrassed to look up at him through my tears, so I cover my eyes and hide my sadness.

"Lucy. You need to be a brave girl," he says, waiting for me to look up at him.

I don't.

"I know about your mom. I know she is sick." His voice sounds familiar, but his tone is bleak and clashes with any acquaintances I have stored in my collection. He mutters the sentence in a way that makes me believe it's a secret. In a hushed tone he carries on. "There's nothing you can do." The statement is finalized with aggravating silence.

I glance through a crack between my fingers and see the grey tweed of his coat and his arms folded in front of him. My child instincts must be sending out warnings. I take a step back and turn away, but he bends down so that he can whisper directly into my ear.

"I know how it feels."

He took these simple words of comfort and spat them out with a sadistic and bitter twist. It's like hearing the Happy Birthday song transposed into a minor tune.

After a minute, I finally uncover my eyes, finding the courage to look at his face, hoping to find some sort of kindness or misinterpretation, but the man is already out of sight. I look to the front door and spot the tweed jacket. Just as I think he will be gone for good, he turns his head and looks at me from across the room and hisses out more tone-deaf words. "Good luck, Lucy."

This time when he says my name, his familiar diction unlocks all mystery, and the guard of comfort around my heart punctures.

I peer beyond a pair of thick, black glasses and identify cold blue eyes with resentful wrinkles lining underneath. Unruly white hair flops down over his ears. The accustomed sparkle in his eye and brightness of his countenance is void. A feeling of horror shoots into my chest and I gasp for air.

In an instant, my best friend becomes a stranger.

CHAPTER THIRTEEN

My air supply is running low. I thrash left and right trying to catch my breath but I'm tangled in a skein of white sheets. A pocket of light catches my eyes and I swim towards it, freeing myself from the blankets and my dream.

Fresh oxygen fills my lungs but the hazy truth remains intoxicating. I lie in a vulnerable panic on Art's bed, the sheets mangled at my feet, my back moist and rigid. My eyes dart left and right, searching for him, but emptiness surrounds me. The room has morphed to the color of dusk and I can just make out the time on the clock.

Simultaneous alarms go off in my head and down the hall, one a call light, and one alerting me that my shift is starting.

I'm anxious to escape and sit up, finding my bearings. I hear a dull screech from the outside hall that is slowly approaching. Within seconds, the doorknob rattles and turns clockwise.

I can't decide what is worse—my coworkers discovering me in a patient's bed, or coming face to face with a man who has been hiding a lifetime of secrets from me. In a panic, I lie back down and pull the sheet over my head.

The screeching crescendos as the door opens, and Art pushes his walker into the room and closes the door. He is out of breath, trying to keep from panting. The sheet is covering most of my face and my eyes are tightly clenched, but I know it's him. The man behind the walker scoots slowly up to the side of the bed, the metal frame of his walker right next to my face. I can feel his eyes on me, observing my breathing.

My heartbeat is drumming up into my ears but I continue feigning chocolate dreams, doing everything in my power to keep my breathing slow and steady.

After a few seconds, I hear the walker's brakes locked in as it's parked near the foot of the bed. The jingle of keys resonates as they are thrown onto his desk. Then, fast footsteps patter into the bathroom. The sink turns on, and I open my eyes. Without moving the sheet, the only thing I can see through the breach is the nightstand. A half-filled bottle of insulin rests on the surface. Its wrapper seems to be peeling off on one side. I squint harder and spot the words *normal saline* printed on the bottle beneath the loose wrapper.

I feel light headed as I grasp another distortion. He's not diabetic. I wonder if our entire relationship is built on a skillful mask of chicanery. I clench my teeth and find some courage to peek over my sheet.

Indeed, a set of keys is sprawled on his desk, and his walker is parked far from the bathroom. Thoughts drenched in warning flood my intelligence; that I am his prey. I throw the sheet back up over my head and take deep breaths.

The water remains running in the bathroom sink, and the sounds of friction and scrubbing echo against the tile walls. Aghast at my naïveté, I curse myself under the sheets for playing the loner without a fatherly figure. I fell right into his hands, trusting him with my deepest secrets. Part of me pleads for this to be a misunderstanding, wild ideas conjured up by my warped mind. I can't dismiss the idea that Art could be protecting me from something. But the darkness in his voice from my nightmare haunts me still.

I only have one choice, and that's to wake up and get the hell out of here. Art doesn't realize I know he's a suspect, and that gives me the upper hand. I remind myself of this knowledge, and it helps me be braver than I really am.

Loudly, I kick the sheets off and force a stretch. "Art?" I mumble out through a yawn. Art angles his head out of the bathroom.

"Ah, there she is." Hearing his voice is like home, and I want to ignore my premonitions. He steps out of the bathroom without a limp as I sit up. "I've been sitting here for hours waiting for you to wake up." He speaks more quickly than usual through his lie. "Hand me my walker over there, will ya?"

I stand up and push it across the room. "How did you get over there without it?" I try and sound like I'm paying him a compliment.

"Slowly," he says. "Now sit down and tell me everything. I can't wait." I make an obvious glance towards the clock and gulp.

"Shoot, I'm late for my shift. Let's plan on catching up during my break," I say and make my way towards the exit. Art hurdles in front of the door like a veteran of stealth, dragging his useless walker with one hand. His jacket swings open mid air, and I catch the outline of a dark weapon inside his coat pocket, the black metal barrel in naked view.

"Lucy, why don't you sit back down." It's not a request.

"I'd rather not," I say, trying to hide the quiver in my voice.

Art's cool eyes darken and his demeanor mutates in front of me. He straightens his back and now stands fully erect, looking down on me like a disciplinarian. Without a word, he inches closer, like a cat toying with its prey before the end. There is nowhere for me to go and I start backing into the bathroom, staring at the dark, rust colored stains under his fingernails before the light from the windows is completely extinguished.

My heart is racing out of my chest. "Art," I whisper as I back into the darkness, telling myself that he won't hurt me. I hear his breaths following me.

I'm scampering backwards faster now into the blackness. I know the tile wall is coming soon, but before my hands reach for it, I hit my head on the paper towel holder and it knocks me down to my hands and knees, sending me scurrying back as far as I can until I'm nearly flush with the wall.

He doesn't say a word, and the silence is hideous. His heavy boots brush up against the bare skin of my knees. He skims the length of my body with his boot, finally stopping next to my fingers.

My right hand is leaning on a thin cord on the floor. I follow it up a few inches, making sure it is what I think it is. At the same time, Art takes a calculated step and crunches my left fingers with the toe of his boot. I let out a wail and pull the cord in my other hand as hard as I can.

Emergency sirens scream out and a red flashing light pulses throughout the bathroom. I hear a stampede of footsteps racing towards the door, and within seconds, the light flickers on and at least six of my associates are at my side, wide-eyed and looking baffled. I lay panting in a pathetic heap at the foot of the toilet.

"Lucy?" It's Barbara who first recognizes me. There goes my employee of the year plaque. The women circle around me, silently waiting for an explanation. All I want are safe, trusting arms to pull me out of here, but instead, I'm being interrogated. But then again, I'm in my patient's bathroom, in my street clothes, late for work, looking like I've spent some time in Arthur's sack. I'd want some answers too.

I freeze, scraping my brain for a decent lie.

"I need to take a sick day," I finally mutter, pleading the Fifth.

Well that's bound to drown their questions. I help myself up and red-rover through the ladies.

Art and his steel-toed boots must have leisurely made their way back to his desk. I gamble with my grit and decide to steal a last glance in his direction. His slouched body forges the appearance of a feeble old geezer, but his cold eyes hold a look of dangerous victory.

The moment I opened my eyes from dreaming, everything changed. Deceit dripped from his countenance. My main light in the world is now extinguished and replaced with a ghost of my past and all this time I've been leaching onto his lies.

I don't know what he wants, but I don't think he's found it. An irritated flame lights inside me, fully charging my senses. I feel his dark eyes on me, and my anger burns through every vein. I release my crippled fingers, not wanting him to have any sort of satisfaction. My middle finger is twitching, begging to show my resentment. Instead, I leave my trust at the doorstep and exit.

The nurses leave me to my sick day and mostly disperse. My mind has already moved past immediate consequences and is formulating a plan.

I start firing out demands at anyone around me with a badge. "His glucose was off the charts. Quick! Insulin, go." A nurse runs off towards the med cart. An aide passes me. "There are new orders for a Foley catheter. Be firm," I call. A cafeteria worker just walked past with an entire cart full of dinner trays. She takes one, knocks on a door just a few down from me, and disappears through the door. I race over and find the tray to room 301. I skim the paper and find what I'm looking for

Arthur Aldridge

Room 301

Allergies: Beets

I don't know what it is about hospitals and beets. They practically grow out of the med carts and are served at every meal. I take a big fat juicy one off the tray next to Art's, squish it with my hand, and mix it into the sandwich, making Art's Sloppy Joe a little more toxic. I borrow a napkin and try to rub the red stain off my fingers as the lunch lady comes back.

By now, the panicked insulin nurse gives an obligatory knock on Art's door before rushing in with a syringe full of the good stuff. Art will not be compliant, but it will distract him and buy me some time. I watch the cafeteria worker walk over to Art's room with his tray. Just as she's about to enter, I tap her shoulder. "Hey, I left my keys on the desk in there. When you set the tray down, would you mind grabbing them for me?"

Within seconds, I'm sprinting out of the double doors into the parking lot with a commandeered, shiny black fob in hand, breaking more laws in the last two minutes than a seasoned crook. I click the unlock button over and over, desperate to find which car they belong to. I see taillights flickering near the back corner of the lot. As I sprint up to the shiny black car, I read the word *Maserati* on back.

"Art, you piece of crap," I mutter, pushing the unlock button about a thousand more times just to make sure this is the ride I'm taking. I say a silent prayer that it's not a stick shift. I'm not a complete novice when it comes to driving—I've got several hours under my belt from passing my driver's test.

It's been a couple years, but it's probably like riding a bike.

I take the chrome handle and the door glides open. The car is immaculate. Black leather seats, mahogany trim, dark tinted windows, and not a single loose paper or crumb in sight. The screens and buttons look futuristic. I breathe a sigh of relief when I see that it's an automatic.

It takes me way too long to find the correct button to scoot my seat up a few inches. There are two keys on the ring with the fob, and neither of them fits into the keyhole. I'm starting to sweat, looking over my shoulder every few seconds to make sure Art-two-point-O isn't sprinting towards me. Just in case, I lock the doors and roll the windows down a few inches to help with my heat issues. I fiddle with the keys for a few more seconds. Meanwhile, a giant white truck pulls up in the spot next to me. Dr. Beck gets out of his car, and the angle is just right for us to exchange glances through the window crack.

"Lucy? Is that you?" He questions.

I wave sheepishly.

"Whoa, nice car. Looks like you'll be taking me to Eugene next time."

"Oh, hi, Doc. Ha, this old thing? It's…it's my grandma's. Taking it back to her as we speak." The good doctor just raises an eyebrow. "I just can't remember how to start this bad boy up." I am full

155

blown pitting out now and glancing over my shoulder every few seconds like the grand auto thief I am.

"Try the button. That black button there next to the steering wheel." I push it and the engine purrs.

"That's right, silly me." I wipe the sweat from my forehead. "Thanks for your help."

He pauses like he's about to say something, but then turns away, shaking his head, and walks towards the building. I don't think he'll be asking for that ride any time soon. I remember something and jump out of the car.

"Dr. Beck! Hey, Dr. Beck!" He turns around slowly with his hands in his pockets, not wanting to mess with the crazy girl. "Room 301 needs a full length psych eval—ASAP. He could really use some attention tonight." Dr. Beck nods and takes a paper from his shirt pocket, making a note.

I feel powerful and naïve behind the wheel. Turns out that instead of physically shifting gears, I press the touch screen to go in reverse. A screen shows me what's behind, and I no longer have to crane my neck to check on Art's location.

I manage to cruise onto the freeway with no other hiccups. With shaky hands, I push a button that says GPS. A pleasant broad asks where I would like to go. When I request, Eugene, Oregon, she starts chirping out instructions. To my surprise, I'm able to have a complete conversation with an electronic woman. It's a good thing the gas tank is full, because I have a two-hour drive, no wallet, and no time for stops.

Here are the questions I need answered: (1) On a scale of bad guys, how bad is Art and would he hurt me to get what he wants? (2) Why, exactly, am I running from him? (3)What information is he trying to get from me? (4)Who can I trust?

I know where I need to go right now, and I know who can help me get there.

Once I reach Eugene, my new Maserati friend helps me make it to the police station. It's nearly ten o'clock p.m. The door is unlocked, but the lights are dimmed. A cop is seated behind the front desk. He has a dark mustache and pink round cheeks that fizzle his intimidation factor. He removes his feet off the desk and sits up straight when I enter.

"Hi, I'm looking for Mr. Summers. Is he around?" The cop glances through the glass of the front doors, eyeing my ride. Maybe there's a warrant out for my arrest. He snuffs and turns his attentions back to me.

"The chief isn't here at the moment. Anything I can do for you?"

"Could I borrow your phone?"

He slides the black phone set this way without taking his eyes off me. Thanks to the permanent marker, I can still make out the numbers scribbled under my forearm. The cop pretends to sort through some papers. Toph answers on the second ring, and hearing his voice is like heaven.

"Toph, It's Lucy. I need you to.."

"Lucy? Finally! I thought…"

"Toph, listen. I'm at your dad's office—at the station. Can you come here? Now?" My urgency causes the cop to glance up for a half second.

"You're here? In Eugene? For real? Everything okay? I thought you were working tonight."

"Toph, just come here now, okay?" I try to sound as relaxed as possible, and the cop is pretending to buy it.

"I'll be there in five." He hangs up, sensing my tone and I'm left all alone with the officer. I scoot the phone back towards him.

"Thanks. My friend will be here soon."

"Ma'am, sure there's nothing I can do for you?" He leans back and takes a gulp of coffee, wetting the bottom of his mustache. The mug says *World's Greatest Farter, I Mean Father*, across the front. I decide to make use of this time.

"If I wanted access to some records…a deceased family member's records, would that be a possibility?" He raises a bushy eyebrow.

"What kind of records we talking bout? Criminal? Medical? Death certificates? Uh…"

"Yes."

"Well, you'd have to file a request through the state first for permission to release certain information."

"Great," I grumble.

"Not my rules, darlin'. Whose records you needing?"

"My dad's. He passed away about a decade ago."

"Sorry for your loss." The officer twists a pen around in his fingers a few times before quietly asking his next question. "What was your father's name?" He leans up to his keyboard half-heartedly.

"Truman. Truman Lichty." He punches each key slowly with his thick pointer finger. The only view I have is of his face behind the monitor. He moves to the mouse and clicks a few different times. Soon, I see him furrowing those bushy brows. He takes a squinted glance up at me, and then clicks a few more times.

"This file is classified. You're going to have to go through a lot of people before you're able to get in there." He studies me for a minute, trying to figure me out from the three minutes we've shared.

Toph's headlights shine through the windows and seconds later, he bolts through the front doors in his skimpy shorts and a tank. He smells like wild boy, but it doesn't stop him from bear hugging me and burying my head into his armpit. "Are you okay?" He pulls me out and I breathe again.

"I'm fine. Can we talk for a few minutes?"

"As long as you want." He squeezes my hand and walks up to the officer behind the table.

"Larry. What up, dude." Larry answers with a fist bump. "Those maple bars still lying around here somewhere?"

Larry snorts. "Chief's office, if you're lucky." Toph walks past Larry like he owns the place and opens a heavy wood door to his right.

"Come on, we can talk in my dad's office." I follow right behind him like an average Joe holding a VIP pass. Toph yells back out through the door, "Larry, you want one?"

"Nah, only the Chief's son can get away with that crap."

It smells like cold coffee and Pine Sol back here. The blinds covering every window have been twisted shut. Toph leads me past several offices and cubicles before entering the largest one in the back. He turns on the light. Chief Summers's desk is large and tidy with two of everything on top: a couple of monitors, phones, pens, coffee mugs, and radios. On the wall behind the desk is a large map of the city, and several framed certificates and honors surround the map. An American and Oregon state flag are hoisted up by short poles in the corner.

Toph goes straight toward a box of stale donuts resting on top of a filing cabinet before sitting down behind the desk in the Chief's chair. He holds the box out to me, but I wave them away.

"Luce, what's going on? Talk to me." His concern is overshadowed by a mouthful of pastry.

I think through the past ten hours, and after a few minutes of silence, my nails are nearly chewed to the cuticle. Toph sits patiently at first, but I can tell he's getting antsy. He stands up and walks around the desk, taking a seat next to me.

I shake my head, now chewing on two fingers at once. "I don't know who to trust." I look into Toph's eyes and search for safety, refusing to trust my instincts. "You're all I have now. If I lose you too…" I'm unable to finish the sentence, and I slouch down into further mayhem. Toph softly touches my chin and tilts it up, forcing me to look at his face.

"Luce. I did lose you once. I'm not letting that happen again." He's off his chair now, crouching down in front of me. "Trust fate if you can't trust me yet. Even in the crazy short amount of time we've had together, I feel like I know you, I know your heart. And I think you know me too."

I take a deep cleansing breath and sit up straight. Toph takes his seat again and chucks the remainder of his donut into the trash. Because I want to trust him so badly, I spill. "It's Arthur. He's not who he says he is."

"Arthur?"

"Yeah. Art. Art at the nursing home. Art my best friend."

"The old guy? The one who gave you that ring?" He motions towards my hand. I take the shell off my finger and examine it, nodding, before sliding it back on. "Well, who is he then?"

"He's a phony. Doesn't really need to be in a nursing home. He's there to keep an eye on me."

"How? Why?" His words come out quick and impatiently.

"I don't know. He's connected to my dad in some way. I saw him at the funeral."

Toph shifts.

"You told me you didn't remember his funeral." I bite my lip. "You took another one of those chocolates." He shakes his head angrily, and now I know what it is like to feel the wrath of a parent.

"Toph, I'm sorry. I trusted Art…" I feel tears welling up in my eyes and I look away, trying to hide my hurt. Toph looks like he wants to punch something.

"Did he hurt you?"

"I got out of there before he could do anything." I glance down at my swollen fingers. The middle one is turning an offensive shade of purple.

"He did this?" Toph takes my fingers in his hand. I nod.

"I think he's dangerous. I saw a gun inside his jacket. I was just waking up when he came back in the room. I heard him scrubbing his hands under the sink for what seemed like ages. His fingernails…" I stop as chills run up my arms. "Whatever he was scrubbing off was stained under his fingernails."

A horrifying realization suddenly makes me want to throw up. "Renee. I didn't go home to check on her before my shift. " I stand up and pace aimlessly for two seconds. "What if she's not okay? What if he goes over there? What if he already did?" I cover my mouth, gasping for air in a panic stricken sob. Toph is out of his seat heading towards the door.

"I'll call my dad, have the police go check on her."

"She'll never be okay again," I blurt out. "Judy. I need to call Judy first." Toph hands over his phone.

Judy made me memorize her cell number years ago. "Hello, Judy speaking." She answers cheerfully after the third ring.

"Judy, it's Lucy. Did you drop Renee off at home after work? I wasn't there and didn't check on her. I'm worried about her." My fast sentences all run together into a frenzied pile.

"Hi, Lucy. I'm with Renee right now. You want to talk to her?"

"What? You are?" The dread lifts off my chest and I can breathe again. "No, no that's okay. Are you at my house?"

"Yes, I brought her home just after lunch. Poor lady had a rough one today. Couldn't stop talking about Truman. She was in tears, kept saying she saw him. I couldn't get her mind off it. I decided I would stay with her until she fell asleep."

"Judy…" I try to keep my voice from shaking as a tear slides down my cheek. "Judy, thank you." It's going to about kill me to have to ask her this next one. "Judy, I'm in bit of an emergency and can't come home tonight. Is there any way Renee could stay with you, just for tonight?" The line goes silent, and I know I've asked too much.

"Of course, Lucy."

"Judy," I sniffle. "This is a one-time thing. I will repay you somehow."

I hand Toph his cell and collapse back into the chair. My head is swimming. Toph weighs in. "If you think she's in danger, we should call the cops. Isn't staying at Judy's house going to throw her off anyway?"

"Not nearly as much as if some men in uniform come busting through her door. Besides, I don't even know what I would tell them. I can't prove Art is dangerous, and if I tell them about my dreams, they'll discredit anything I say and throw me in the loony bin."

"Well, what now?" Toph is getting more wound up by the second.

"It's time to talk to your dad. That's the reason I hijacked a car and drove out here. And to escape the gun-handling senior citizen."

"I'm sorry, what? Hijacked?"

"Whatever. Just borrowed. Will you call your dad please?"

Toph's jaw is still dropped so I point to his phone. Finally, he shakes the grin off his face.

No answer on both landline and cell. I rub my head in frustration. Toph walks back over and parks behind the desk in the chief's chair. He sits there like a general, mulling over a life-changing matter. At last he speaks. "I might be able to get you what you need. Since you've already committed a misdemeanor, I might as well join you in the slammer. Let's see what my dad's got on Truman." He shakes the mouse and wakes up the computer.

"You know how to access his info?"

"I did an internship here my senior year of high school. That's when I decided I wanted to become an architect."

I laugh and he continues typing.

"Seriously, pops, you should change your passwords," he mutters under his breath. I shut the door and stand behind him, viewing the screen. "This program gives you basic info and records. I'm not sure if Truman will still be in this system, especially since he isn't a resident of Eugene. Let's see." He types in his name and hits enter. While the program processes, he swivels his chair around and looks up at me with a grin.

"Seriously—hijacked?"

"Sorry that I don't have a car," I respond. "I was desperate."

"What about your parents? Don't—didn't they

have a car?"

"They did. I sold it. So we could survive."

Toph nods and squeezes my shoulder, I assume implying that he supports my criminal actions. We turn our attention back to the screen, which is redirecting us to another password screen.

"Restricted, classified files. Government clearance code…" Toph trails off. "Why would Truman's file be classified?"

I shrug and throw my hands up in the air. "We can't get in there, can we?"

"Just a second." Toph swivels his chair around and glides over to the American flag. He pokes his index finger up into the bottom of the hollow pole and pulls out a ripped sliver of paper that's been curled up, hiding in the hole. Written across are three different passcodes, all unlabeled.

"He can't even remember my birthday, let alone all this. He's always got a cheat sheet."

I hold the paper up as Toph tries each code. After the third try, the computer gives us a thinking icon and my heart might beat out of my chest. At last, a file appears, just a single file icon in the center of a white screen. We click on my dad's name and a report pulls up. Toph reads:

Truman R. Lichty
DOB: 1/7/1971
Offense: Domestic abuse secondary to attempted murder.

Toph stops reading and looks up at me. I feel my whole body shaking uncontrollably. He steadies me and pulls me down next to him. He whispers something into my ear but my eyes are locked on the word murder, and I'm drowning in the ugliness. Toph continues reading aloud because I've forgotten how.

VP of lab operations and senior neuroscientist Truman R. Lichty, was ordered to shut down all operations dealing with the government funded Alzheimer's treatment project 'Alzwell' due to adverse affects and inconsistencies in clinical trials. Lichty went rogue on the project and was later accused of injecting spouse Renee Lichty with lethal amounts of the serum. Victim had no previous accounts of dementia on record.

Key Witness

NIA (National Institute of Aging) Director and President Arthur Aldridge stated, "The lethal amount of the serum should have killed her, she is lucky to be alive."

For a more detailed report, see section IV-II

I can't see the screen any more through the flood of tears. "He did this to her," I sob out. I feel a presence in the dark corner of the room and it suffocates my sobs. A gruff voice breaks the silence.

"Don't believe everything you read." I gasp, and

we turn toward the door. A heavy-set man in full uniform nearly fills the entire doorframe. His arms are folded across his chest, and he wears an angry scowl, one that I recognize.

"Dad," Toph sputters. "I tried to call you first. We needed to get information, quick. Lucy is in trou…"

"Exit out. Now." The Chief interrupts.

"Yes, sir." Toph logs out and shuts off the screen. The chief walks towards us, towering over our crime scene.

"There's a reason they keep documents classified," he growls. I hold my breath. "Protection." The chief paces in front of us like a drill sergeant. "If this happens again, there will be consequences." He walks towards the door and stands in front of it abruptly, waiting for us to exit. We jump out of our seats. I follow closely behind Toph. The chief clears his voice as I walk past him. "Lucy, your dad was a good man."

My chills are back for good.

CHAPTER FOURTEEN

We pile into Toph's truck and burn rubber out of there. "I forgot how scary he is," I pant.

"How do you think I learned to run so fast?" Toph huffs, speeding through a yellow light. "I really didn't think we'd get caught."

"I have a feeling that breaking into the system was my only way to ever get info. Your dad was like a brick wall. He still seems to be hiding so much, but when he spoke, he probably gave us more than he could have afforded."

Toph grunts. "He barely said a word. Definitely didn't tell us anything that we didn't already know."

"He didn't say much, but he didn't have to. He couldn't for some reason. But the two clues he gave speak volumes."

"Two clues? Really, Sherlock?"

"Uh, yeah," I say as if talking to a crazy person. "First clue, he said not to believe what we read. Second clue, he said that my dad was a good man." Toph scoffs again.

"Lucy, we already know that your dad is—was a good man."

"But do you know it enough to discredit the federal government?"

"Do you?" He questions. I go mute for a few seconds.

"I trust him. It's just been so long…" I trail off. "It's nice to have an officer of the law reassure me." Toph nods, and pulls into a drive through of a burger joint.

"Why do you women need so much reassurance?"

"You're asking me this right now?"

Toph rolls down the window and turns towards the speaker. "Yeah, I'll take two bacon cheeseburgers and a chocolate shake." He turns towards me. "You want anything babe?"

"Don't babe me."

"Make that three bacon cheeseburgers and two shakes."

The melted cheese and bacon lift my spirits. "The second clue was all about proper tense," I say through a full mouth. Toph is already on to his second burger. Both his wrappers have made their way onto the back floor.

"I really wanted an English lesson today."

"Didn't you catch it?" I ask. "He said 'your dad was a good man.' *Was*," I emphasize. "He was telling me that my dad, Truman Lichty, is not alive."

Toph looks unimpressed by anything but the bottom of his chocolate shake. "Why are you believing the chief? He lied about not knowing about Truman. We pretty much laid out that your dad is the one who gave you the chocolate. He's the only one smart enough to make chocolate that stimulates part of your brain."

"What if it was Art?" I counter. "Obviously he is capable of something like this."

"Why would Art make that mess for himself? We are assuming that he is the villain, correct? From what we know, he is a free bird, while your dad is in hiding. Why would he want you to remember the plane ticket, the locket, me, and himself?"

"I agree. I'm just ruling everything out. There's also the possibility that my dad left these clues before he died and had someone send them." I don't like the direction I'm going. "Where are we heading, by the way?"

"Back to your house to get your last chocolate. I think at this point it's safe to assume it's the quickest way to find what we're looking for." I lean forward and knock my head against the dashboard.

"I don't have it."

"What do you mean, you don't have it?"

"I left it in Art's room." Toph slams his palm onto the steering wheel.

"Great. Now what?"

"Hey, you were the one who told me not to take that 'mystery drug.'"

Toph softens his voice. "I just asked you not to take it without me there." He brushes a stray hair out of my eyes and then focuses back on the road.

"I just need to think. Gather all my information." I close my eyes and let the questions teeter on the edge of my cognition. I mumble aloud. "If Dad is alive, why did he wait ten years to let me know he's alive? Why would he wait this long to reveal the truth? If the chief knows the truth, why can't he uncover it, and how can I?"

Toph sits quietly listening, but eventually can't help but chime in. "Maybe my dad is covering for him. Must have believed he was innocent and was framed by a credible source."

"Art," I accuse. Toph nods.

"Truman must have had a pretty gnarly sentence, after pleading guilty to those charges. There's no way he could have escaped before his trial and faked death without some inside help."

"Enter, Chief Summers," I say. "Or I guess at the time, it would have been Officer Summers. But even if that's actually true, why on earth would Dad have pleaded guilty? Why not fight it?" I'm desperate for answers. Toph's mind is processing and spewing ideas out quicker than an industrial strength copy machine.

"A fast verdict may have sped up the hearing and might have had something to do with the timing of his escape plan." He stares ahead. "Or maybe he was being blackmailed." Toph chews his lip. "Maybe there was overwhelming evidence against him. He couldn't see a way around it and pleading guilty would lessen his sentence." We sit stewing for several more minutes. The maybes build up too high and our confidence tips over.

"Why on earth would my mom be a victim in this? She didn't have Alzheimer's and had no reason to be treated. Did she see something she shouldn't have so he shushed her?" Pretty soon my questions overwhelm our answers and we're left with nothing but shallow ideas.

We drive into Yachats, passing through the familiar air and sounds. I half expect Dad to jump out from behind a tree. I plan out our reuniting ceremony in my head and replay it several times until I wake up and smell the hand sanitizer. I recognize the parking lot Toph is pulling into. He backs into a space near the back, and the glow from the windows is in front of us.

"What are you doing?" I squawk.

"Getting your chocolate back."

"So, what, you're just going to waltz on into his room and politely ask for it?"

"Uh, no, I'm going to bust down his door, steal his gun, and kick him in the crotch."

I laugh in his face. "Do you watch a lot of Ninja Turtles or something? You're in a world of your own. He will annihilate you. You don't know what he's capable of. Neither do I, but I don't want to."

"Let me stop you right there," he says and brings a shushing finger up to my lips. "I'm ninety-nine percent sure he's not going to be in there. In that case, I will search his room for said chocolate, and anything else of interest to us. If that one percent persists against the odds, no need to panic. He doesn't have a clue who I am. I'll ask him if he'd like a complimentary back massage. Then I'll sneak into his pockets and sniff out the chocolate."

"You're off your rocker."

"Tell that to your old boyfriend." He gives me a smirk. "Hide in the back," he orders and locks the doors. After he walks away, I decide to obey him. I crawl into the backseat and shimmy my body into a vertical position on the floor of his car. There is a nice blanket of wrappers, socks, and fries to hide the most of me. My elbow squishes over a ketchup packet and the contents squirt down my arm.

Nice. I turn on just one ceiling light and take a few minutes to clean up the floor. It's like a fast food chain vomited all over in here. When I can finally see the carpet again, I chuck the sack of trash up front, turn off the light, and stuff my appendages into my safety slot. I clutch my locket for comfort and stare through the back window up at the stars. My brain is like a broken record, asking the same questions over. Many things aren't sitting right, and at the top of the list is the fact that Dad would leave me alone to suffer all these years. My heart fights it.

I open my locket, studying each of the engraved words.

Chance favors the prepared mind.

I hate the word chance. Like it's a gamble, finding the truth. If I'm fully prepared, there's still only a chance. I don't want my life to revolve around chance, but right now it's all I've got. So how can I best prepare my mind for the truth? My dreams are showing me some truths, and supposedly Dad planted these dreams. Therefore, Dad is preparing my mind. I stop at this realization. I think I've found the answer to one of my questions, and my heart is beating wildly at the realization. I sit straight up, just as the doors unlock and Toph jumps in.

"Everything okay?" he asks. "Wait, did you clean up in here Luce?" He looks around the truck. "I'm going to have to lock you in my car more often."

"Art. Was he in there?" I ask impatiently and

crawl back into the front seat. I throw the sack of garbage into the back.

"Nope. I've got nothing. Searched every inch of his bedroom too. Thought about stealing some of his plaid. That guy's got some good taste. I see why you had a thing for him."

"You're delusional," I say. "Nothing? We've got nothing? Were the nurses helpful at all?"

"Very helpful. They showed me the fridge with the Jell-o," he answers, turning left out of the lot. "Red berry for the win."

"Toph, listen to me. I just realized something big while you were in there. Like, crazy big."

"Okay, where should I drive while you spill?"

"To my house," I instruct. "Listen, my dad gave me these chocolates, right? These chocolates aren't just a sweet sentiment. There's way more meaning in them. And this necklace isn't just a piece of jewelry he gave me. The saying in it is significant." Toph nods. "There are nine other gifts I was given in between these two gifts, spanning nine years. If dad was the one who gave them to me, I think there must be an alternate meaning to them too."

"You still have them?" Toph asks.

"Every one."

We park two blocks away from my house behind a dumpster. The houses on this street are old and worn out; peeling paint, rusty gates, and weeds past our waists. As we sneak through the overgrown yards and past the dark windows, I remember that it's close to midnight.

"Are you tired?" I whisper. "You have practice in the morning?"

"It's the last thing on my mind. Come on," he motions. "I'll hide out in the yard watching for visitors while you go gather the loot." Toph stops. "Except, what if the old guy is in there waiting for you?" I shiver.

"I've got some mace in my room. I'll grab that first," I say, pretending to be cool.

Toph shakes his head. "I'm coming in."

I'm not about to say no. As we approach the house from the back, I can see that a dim light is on near the kitchen. Toph glances over at me.

"Judy may have left it on." Toph nods.

"Front or back?" He asks.

"Back, it shouldn't be locked."

"Is that supposed to make me feel better?"

He opens the screen door and turns the doorknob. The door creaks open. We peek in and the house appears undisturbed.

"Stay here," Toph orders and marches in alone. When he disappears around the corner, I sneak in and make a straight line to my room. The bedroom door swings nearly closed behind me making the room nearly pitch black. I hurriedly feel around for my dresser drawer. As quietly as possible, I pull the drawer open and paw around for the cylinder can.

From a few yards away, I hear the creak of a floorboard. My heart starts pounding madly.

"Toph?" I whisper into the darkness. No one replies. I frantically feel around for the mace, not thinking anymore about the noise I'm producing, only desperate to find a weapon. The floorboards squeak again and this time it's even closer, I imagine within an arms length. Someone is stepping towards me. I freeze, waiting to be attacked.

Again, silence. No one pounces, and I'm still standing here waiting, quivering, my limbs numb from fright. At last, my hand reaches the can of poison and I grasp the bottle, shakily dismantling the safety valve. I hold it in front of my body like a gun and maneuver away from the drawer as quickly as possible, unwilling to make a target of myself in the dark shadows. I scamper backwards waiting to run into my bed. I take four, then five cautious steps backwards, feeling around for my mattress without success. I've lost my sense of direction now, and without any confidence I continue creeping backwards into the darkness. After two steps, my back rebounds off a stiff, tall, brawny figure. I try to scream but nothing comes out. Instinctively, I crouch, feeling the black shadow towering over me. The body trips over me, collapsing onto all fours. I remember the mace in my hand and blindly spray where I imagine eyelevel is. Rubber soles kick off of me, scuttling away.

"Toph!" I scream, finally able to make use of my vocal chords. I hear the back door screen slam closed and the thud of footsteps running down the hall from the opposite direction. Toph barges in and turns on the light. He's panting, which is saying something for a man who's resting heart rate is forty. When he sees me, he kneels down on the floor next to me, wide eyed, asking for an explanation.

"Someone was in here. He ran out the back door," I gasp. Toph sprints to the door, too late to get any answers. When he comes back in, the blood is drained from his face.

"Hurry. Get your stuff," he says in a throaty voice. I start scrambling around my room, stuffing the gifts into an old suitcase that's big enough for a body to fit in. Toph hovers behind me, not giving me more than a foot or two of space as I flurry throughout different rooms of my house, collecting my treasures.

"That's it, except for my bike—" I curse under my breath. "Which is still at the nursing home." Toph zips up the suitcase and props it up on its legs.

"This will do for now." We leave the lights on and pull the suitcase out of the house. As we travel back through the weeds and bushes, Toph drags the suitcase from one hand, his other holding securely onto my arm. In my free hand, I clench the mace.

Once we're back in the truck, we peel out of

there before any others lurking in the shadows can follow. "Who was it?" Toph asks angrily. I'm surprised by his aggression but I like it.

"No idea, it was too dark. But he felt big."

"You don't think it was Art?"

I shrug. "I guess it could have been. Could have been one of Art's peons. Whoever it was, they left me alone. Didn't try to capture me or hurt me at all, and trust me, he could have. I was pathetic."

"Shoulda watched more Ninja Turtles," Toph says, but his voice still holds concern.

"I almost feel like—like he didn't want to be seen. He was hiding from me," I say.

"Maybe he already found what he was looking for," Toph suggests.

"Yeah, maybe. But what? Thank heavens Mom wasn't there." Toph nods.

"We've got to find somewhere to spread all this stuff out and think."

"The only place open at this hour is the good ol' Yachats bar," I say. "No way they'll let us in."

"No way they'll let *you* in. I'm legal," Toph brags. "I've got an idea."

I'm already uneasy at the thought of another one of Toph's *ideas*. We pull up to the only open convenience store in Yachats; conveniently, it's also the largest. Toph loads our cart up with Red Bull, beef jerky, Oreos, and Skittles. Then he leads me over to the register where there's a small stand with cheap jewelry. He spins the fake bobbles around and stops, eyeing a massive two-karat piece of crap. From a distance, it sparkles like a diamond. Taking my hand, he kneels down on the disgusting tile floor, gifting the cashier with a front row view.

"Lucy Renee Lichty, make me the happiest man in the world…" From the corner of my eye, I see the cashier put her hand over her heart. I roll my eyes. "…and be my wife at the bar?"

I snatch the ring out of his hand and slide it on my finger. "Looks like you robbed the cradle," I say smiling, pulling him off the diseased floor.

The cashier starts ringing us up. "I thought that was you, Lucy," she says. "Congratulations, hon." I glance up and recognize her from the nursing home. That's what happens when you live in a city that has a population smaller than a crowd at a rained out minor league baseball game.

"Ah, you're Thelma's daughter," I concede.

"That's right. Oh, we just love you. Thanks for taking such good care of her. It means the world." My new fiancé stares at me with a look of admiration. "And what a charming young man you've got here. You two are going to have the most handsome children one day."

"Yes. Yes, we will," Toph agrees.

We snicker back to the truck and stash our goods in my backpack.

When we get to our destination, I put the

backpack on but Toph shakes his head. "Let me carry that. You look like a sixteen-year old school girl." I send him daggers. "Hot school girl," he adds.

From the parking lot, the bar looks dead, just like the rest of Yachats. When we walk in, no one is there to appreciate the ring on my finger. The air is smoky and lighting dim. A whiny country tune plays over the radio. One man is at the pool table playing solo, and two others sit in a corner booth, none of which seem to notice us.

Toph motions to a back staircase and we sneak up the steps, shutting ourselves in a large, empty room with thin brown carpet, stacked up folding chairs, and a box TV and VCR set.

"Perfect," Toph announces. "I'll go grab your luggage. You'd better get going on one of those Red Bulls."

"You forget I work nightshift," I call after him, cracking a can open anyway.

Toph lugs the heavy suitcase into the room and unzips it, carefully laying each artifact a foot apart from the next until there are eight items lined up across the room, excluding the bike. Then he stands next to me with his arms folded, staring at the random pieces with an empty gaze. I offer my Red Bull to him, and he takes a giant gulp.

"You really think this junk is going to tell us something?" he asks.

"It's not junk. And yes, the other two gifts--the

chocolate and the locket, weren't just gifts. They both were trying to give me information. I just have to be smart enough to figure it out."

Toph guzzles down the rest of the can and crunches it in his hand. "Let's do this." Like a detective, he strolls past the items, pausing in front of each one. Meanwhile, I take inventory:

-a watch
-an Etch A Sketch
-a game of chess
-a fur blanket
-A book of mind games
-a five-hundred piece puzzle
-a cookbook.
-a stack of VCR tapes.

Toph backs up and stops in front of the puzzle. "You said these items saved you. How did a bazillion-piece puzzle of…" He rifles through the tiny pieces, trying to figure out the big picture.

"The periodic table," I insert.

"How did a life-sized periodic table puzzle come to your rescue? I'm already falling asleep just thinking about it."

"This puzzle was the best thing that happened to me the year I turned ten. I had no friends, no siblings, no cable TV, no extracurricular activities, and obviously no school in the summer. I did that puzzle so much I nearly memorized every element and it's atomic mass." Toph snores loudly, but I carry on. "I got sick of it, of course, and was really frustrated that one of the pieces was missing." My eyes flicker up to Toph's. His eyebrows rise.

"Always missing?" he asks. I nod. "You remember which piece?"

"One somewhere in the middle," I say, unable to hide a smile. "I haven't done it in years." My spirits lift and my energy surges. "I always thought it was a glitch. I'm positive I didn't lose it. It came that way." I bite my bottom lip. "If only I could remember exactly which one was missing." Toph grunts.

"If only it was a corner piece missing. This could take all night." I ignore his pessimism, basking in the realization that this is a sign.

"You start up on that, I'll look over the rest of this stuff," I say.

"Yes, wife."

I shuffle around the objects, laying them in order from youngest to oldest, leaving a gap where the bike belongs. Then I stand back, waiting for a revelation. They look the same as they always have, but I'm hoping perhaps, collectively, something will stand out.

Eventually, I sit down on the floor cross-legged. I peak over at Toph, who is fishing corner and edge pieces out of the sprawling pile. I turn my attention back the assembly line.

A fur blanket, puzzle, recipe book, VCR tape, bike, Etch A Sketch, book of mind exercises, chess game, and a watch. What do all these things have in common? Excluding the blanket and watch, they all require some sort of action. Many of them have taught me. All have different prices, sizes, uses. The eclectic group isn't telling me anything, and I start getting overwhelmed. Time to study one item at a time.

First, I lay the thick, brown, furry blanket flat on the carpet, ignoring the slight urge to curl up in it for a quick bit of shuteye. I take my fingers and carefully press against every square inch, and I realize it's exactly how I teach my old ladies to do a self-breast exam. Whatever. I need a new job.

Nothing is between the pieces of fabric. I'd need to order an ultrasound or come upon a sharp pair of scissors to find anything unobvious. I'm not quite willing to massacre my blankie. I hold the blanket up to the light, searching for any clues or imperfections in the fabric. There's a tag with washing instructions in the bottom right corner. It's faded so I hold it up close to my eyes and barely make out the one and only sentence.

Dry Clean Only

I certainly haven't been compliant with these instructions. I drop the tag and stare into the furry folds. After a second, I snatch the tag back up again. I squint hard, realizing that only certain letters in that sentence are faded, nearly to nothing—four of them to be exact, in an unnatural way. I grab the notebook out of my backpack and sketch down the following missing letters: R, C, L, A.

"Clar…larc…cral…" I mumble. I glance over to Toph who is going gangbusters on one edge of the puzzle. "Toph, do the letters R,C, L, and A mean anything to you?"

Toph looks up, pursing his lips. "An airport code, a university, an acronym of some sort…?"

"Acronym?" I ask.

"Yeah, yeah. Like…Rich Children of Los Angeles. Or Religious Cheerleaders Learning Arabic." Toph laughs at his own joke, turning his attention back to the puzzle.

"So helpful," I groan, already feeling defeated and more stressed by the minute. "I've got to figure this out…like tonight. "I've got a job, and Mom, and…and I don't have time…" My voice is strained. Toph turns back to me.

"Luce, he wouldn't give you something you couldn't figure out. You've got this."

I know he's right.

After borrowing Toph's smartphone and googling the letters, nothing definite pops up except a thought bubble of religious cheerleaders mocking me in Arabic.

I take Toph's advice and try to find things that both Dad and I would have been exposed to or had in common. Problem is, he's been gone for more of my life than he's been present.

I push the negative thoughts away. There's got to be something. What does Dad know that I do too? Where have we both been? Who do we both know?

Suddenly, the answer appears in my head as clear as my first chocolate dream. I start whooping and running around the room like a possessed ape. Toph stands up and stares.

"It's Carl! C-A-R-L. Fish taco-stand Carl. Dad and I used to go there together. I still do! I have to get to Carl!" I explode, making my way towards the door.

"Whoa, easy," Toph says. "Last time I checked, people don't eat fish tacos at two a.m.."

I bite my lip, too anxious to agree. "Can I borrow your truck?" I ask. "The stand isn't far from here. I'll be back in twenty minutes, tops."

Toph thinks about it. "I'll just come with you."

"We don't have time. I need you working your magic on this puzzle. Besides, I ride past this stand on my bike in the middle of the night after every shift. I'll be fine."

Toph grumbles.

"All I'm going to do is scavenge around a bit, see if there's anything out of the ordinary."

I can tell he doesn't like it, but eventually he

tosses me his keys. "Thanks, Toph. Fish tacos on me tomorrow."

"Just be careful. Here, take my phone." He stands up from the floor and pulls his cell out of his pocket, bringing it over to me. I'm not exactly versed in modern technology.

"That's really not necessary. I mean, who would I call since you're not going to be available?"

"911," he says sternly, pushing the phone into my hands.

"Right," I blush. "See you in a few."

I'm much more comfortable driving this old beater truck than the conversing, self-navigating machine of Art's. I look behind my shoulder into the backseat and sweep over the empty seats and floor, reassuring myself that I'm alone.

The previous hour of nighttime has created a thick fog that sits just inches above the streets and lurks out into the ocean waves. I drive cautiously through the eerie, thick air. When I believe I've reached the general area of the taco stand, I angle the truck's lights so that they point directly towards it. Unfortunately, the fog intercepts any visuals.

I park and hop out, locking the doors and clutching Toph's phone. The crashing of waves masks the sounds of my movement, and I am nearly invisible in the fog.

My adrenaline is still racing from my Carl epiphany, and I pray it's not in vain. I walk blindly towards the ocean's symphony, the phone's dim light shining in front of my feet. I look left and right and the fog appears to be getting denser, swallowing me up in its veil. Panic is threatening me to give up, but I push on and march. By now the ocean is so close, soon I'll feel the waves against my toes if I continue. I close my eyes and allow my senses to absorb my whereabouts and direct me.

I take several steps backwards and when I turn around, something solid wallops me right between the eyes, knocking me back a step. I gasp in fear and hold my arms out in front of my head, protecting myself from another blow. I can hear my heart beating out of control. Nothing attacks, so I cautiously hold the phone out and shine the light in front of me.

Looks like the hut found me. I ran smack dab into the taco sign, a solid two by four. I rub between my brows, wondering if *fish tacos* is imprinted on my forehead.

There's no time to waste. Behind the counter I find very little: a bucket of utensils, several metal bowls, cardboard cartons, tiny salsa serving cups, several gallons of oil, some cleaning supplies, and the register. I bite the side of my cheek and push the button that opens the register. Of course it's empty. I examine the perimeter, underneath the plastic table and chairs. I even get so desperate as to dig around in the dirt. Besides some mundane seashells and a dead and rejected fried fish in the sand, I've got nothing.

Toph has me on a short leash and I've got to get back. I close the register and shine the phone's light towards the car, back into the fog.

Just as I'm about to journey back, faint sounds of footsteps stop me dead in my tracks. I put out my light and hold my breath, praying that I'm invisible. The footsteps stop and a flashlight as bright as a strain of the sun suddenly spotlights my entire body. I'm on display, and as vulnerable as ever. I can't see who is on the other side of the light, holding me hostage in this sunbeam. Suddenly, the visitor turns the light around and shines it on himself. A large man with silvery long tresses and deep lines on his face greets me.

"Carl?" I heave out in relief. "Carl, what are you doing here?" I pant.

Carl is as calm as the peaceful lull of ocean waves. "I could ask you the same thing. You set off my alarm." His voice sounds kind, even after being woken up in the nasty hours of nighttime.

"I'm so sorry. Carl, I'm looking for something."

He walks towards me so that we're not yelling anymore.

"What are you looking for, Lucy?" His voice holds a light and lovely Polynesian dialect.

I kick the sand around with my toe. "I don't actually know. I was kind of hoping you would." I sound like a complete moron. Carl studies my eyes for a minute and then takes a step closer so that his whispers can be heard.

"I do know. I've been waiting for you to ask." My eyes go as wide as saucers. Carl shuffles around in his pocket. He pulls out a white, square box about the size of one that might hold an engagement ring. Its corners have been rubbed raw, and cardboard edges are exposed.

"I've carried this with me every day for nine years." His eyes sparkle with relief, like a man who has finally been able to finish his duty. He holds it out to me and drops it into my quaking hands.

The box is light. I touch its surfaces reverently and then hold it tight against my chest. "Thank you," I whisper out, but Carl has already vanished into the fog.

CHAPTER FIFTEEN

Finding the truck through the murk isn't the hard part. Waiting to rip open the box until I get back to civilization, now that's a challenge. I speed through the streets of Yachats, running a few stop signs and yellow lights until the truck is right back where it was in the bar's parking lot. I crack the door open to illuminate the dome light and pull the box out of my pocket. With the corners worn and sides flimsy, the lid nearly falls off on its own. Inside, a noisy, clear wrapper holds pieces of a broken fortune cookie. Carefully, I open the plastic and pull out the hand-written fortune that is still enclosed in a piece of cookie. When I recognize dad's handwriting, I gulp. My speculations were correct. These gifts are from him, and they hold deep meaning. I whisper the fortune, his nine year old clue, aloud:

Believe in the names of those you love

I read it again. Problem is, I don't remember saying those three glorious words to anyone. I love you is reserved for lovers and families. I take a piece of the cookie and crunch on it while contemplating. It's stale, but I chomp down the rest of the pieces and then place the fortune itself in my pocket. Then I run into the bar, skipping two steps at a time up the stairs. I skid to a stop when I see the top of not one but two heads, both busy slaving away on hands and knees over the puzzle. One is Toph's brunette head, the other is a thinning salt and pepper head. Both of them look up at me when I enter.

"You're back!" Toph says with relief, failing to mention anything out of the ordinary. "Tell me you found something."

"Who are you?" I interrupt, sounding accusatory.

Toph stands. "Oh right. Lucy, Giorgio. Giorgio, Lucy," he says informally. "Giorgio here owns the place." Toph slaps him on the back like they are life long chums. "He came up to watch some TV and noticed that we'd taken over his space." Giorgio kindly waves at me and smiles. "He's a puzzle genius. We'll be done before you can say…" He hesitates and crooks his head to the side, staring at me. "Babe…what happened to your forehead?"

He traipses over and stares at the goose egg sprouting between my eyebrows. Giorgio excuses himself, allowing me to tell Toph everything that happened. He nods along, taking in every word.

"So wait, you actually ran into the hut?" He chortles and doesn't even try to hide his amusement.

"Didn't you hear what I said? Look!" I pull the fortune out of my pocket and wave it in front of him. "This is real! This is happening!"

Giorgio comes back with a baggie of ice and hands it to me, bowing his head.

"Yes, thank you, Giorgio," I say. "Take a lesson, Toph."

Toph grabs the ice and holds it to my head, resting his other arm on my shoulder, smiling in that way of his.

"I'm sorry. Luce, I'm totally impressed. But don't think I'm letting you out of my sight again."

I like when he rumbles things out only loud enough for me to hear, especially when he's apologizing for being an idiot. I could sit in his tranquilizing personal bubble all day, but the reality is that I've got work to do. I take the ice and summon him back to the puzzle next to Giorgio.

Those I love. I reread and ponder. It could be an informal love. I love Thomas Edison, Walt Disney, and Bradley Cooper, who doesn't? But these are Dad's clues. Clues that apparently he wrote nine years ago, according to Carl. Nine years ago, I was alone. I still loved the pieces of mom that were left, and the memories of dad.

"Of course I believe in you dad. Why else would I be in a bar at three in the morning trying to find you?" I mumble to myself.

Believe in the names of those you love. It doesn't say, "Believe in those you love." Must be a literal meaning.

"Toph, I need to borrow your phone again." He sends it sailing across the floor without looking up. I pull up a search for the meaning of the name 'Truman' and scroll through the top ten results. Every single site says the same thing. "Faithful, trusty man." Well that's convenient for him. I didn't need a fortune cookie to tell me that.

Mom can't be as lucky. I've loathed the name Renee ever since it replaced 'mom'. When I step back, I realize it is quite lovely sounding.

Renee's results pop up. "French," I mumble. "Rebirth, or born again…" my voice fades and I feel my throat tighten up. There are several meanings to this, but there's only one that pertains to my Renee. I get my bearings and scribble my findings down in my journal. "Toph," I whisper. "Toph, look at this." I kneel down next to him and point in my journal with a shaky hand. Toph reads the name definitions out loud. "What do you think this means?" I ask.

Toph remains in his own thoughts, but Giorgio

clears his throat. "The Bible prophesies that one must be reborn to live with God." For some reason his soft accent gives him credibility. He continues. "Rebirth is a gift. It's a way to see things differently, a second chance at life." Toph and I exchange glances.

"You don't think…" I'm afraid to even say it. "You don't think Renee's condition is reversible? A second chance?"

Toph raises his eyebrows.

"Well, it was induced in the first place," Toph answers. "There's no cure to Alzheimer's, but perhaps there is a cure for drug-induced Alzheimer's."

A violent shudder comes over me.

Toph takes his phone and starts searching and reading. After a minute, he nods his head. "Yep, just what I thought."

"What?" I ask.

"Your name," he says. "It means 'light bringer.'" He looks up from his phone. "Luce, you're going to save your mom."

CHAPTER SIXTEEN

"Why me? Why not dad? Where is dad?" My monologue of questions is endless.

Toph is keeping focused on his task but yells out a few suggestions. "Maybe he can't come out of hiding. Maybe he's being held hostage." I pace faster. Nearly all of the gifts are still here to be explored, perhaps one of those will give his location.

"How much longer have you got?" I fire across the room. The puzzling boys ignore me, but I can see that there's just a small hole in the upper-mid section of the Periodic Table left to be filled in.

I walk to the assembly line of gifts and grab the next one. *The Joy of Cooking*, quite an unusual gift for an eleven year old, yet one that's been used and loved for years. One thousand, one hundred and eleven pages of recipes, and in the seven years I've devoured these pages, I haven't noticed anything out of the ordinary. There are stains on the front white cover; faded red spaghetti sauce splotches and crusty dried up waffle batter. There's a red ribbon bookmarker holding the spot of my beloved buttermilk pancake recipe.

I carefully examine the authors, publishers, and dates. I thumb through the index, glancing over the hundreds of recipes in alphabetical order. Everything is as it seems, and I begin to wonder how a recipe is going to help me find Dad, or help me cure Mom. And why is Dad being so cryptic? Why not just say, 'Hey! Mom was drugged. Here's the pill to fix 'er.'

I hear some whoops and gloats across the room. My new Italian friend is high-fiving Toph. I race over. "Done?" I cry out. The boys stand back and let me eye the prize. Sure enough, just one piece is missing. One element. "Element twenty-six," I breathe out.

Toph pulls out his phone. "I'll look it up," he offers.

"It's iron," I say. "Iron, number twenty-six, transition metal, symbol Fe, atomic mass fifty-five."

"Whoa, seriously?" Toph coughs out.

"Iron...iron...iron," I mutter. "Electronegativity...metal...metalloid..."

"Metal beard, heavy metal, pedal to the metal," Toph jabbers. "Want to include us in your thought process? Or I'm gonna be doing more of that."

"Sorry, of course. Just running through the first things that stand out. It would be nice if we knew what we were looking for, question or answer," I sigh. "How about a group brainstorm? No ideas are bad ideas."

Giorgio has no idea what we're talking about, but he agrees to participate.

"So the symbol is Fe?" Toph asks. I nod. "And the atomic number is twenty-six, atomic mass is fifty-five."

"That's right."

We let our brains stretch as much as they can at four a.m. Toph breaks the silence again. "Is iron something that is used in treatments? Medications? Is he trying to give you the ingredients to the antidote?"

"Gah," I sigh. "Iron is a super important part of our systems. It carries oxygen from our lungs throughout our bodies. Not enough iron means anemia," I explain. "I don't know, seems too complicated," I admit. "Dad can't expect me to build the antidote from some subliminal messages. But I like the way you're thinking."

Giorgio chimes in. "Twenty-six Fe-males. Twenty-six fe-lines. Pump twenty-six pounds of iron."

I stand corrected. There are such things as bad ideas. "Thanks, Giorgio. What are you talking about?" I ask impatiently.

"I don't know much about chemistry. But maybe it doesn't have to do with chemistry. You're looking for another clue, no?"

I nod.

"Giorgio's right," Toph adds. "Maybe Fe is a city code, a stock, a license, an abbreviation."

"Follow that thread," I say. Toph starts searching the world wide web. I take a different route, and I use Giorgio as my muse as I mutter.

"Iron is the missing piece…Iron is missing…Find iron…iron out the wrinkles…iron out the missing pieces…ironic…" I trail off, and Giorgio doesn't follow my thoughts.

"Toph, anything?" I shoot out.

"Nah, not really. Could be referring to an energy corporation, a test taken for physical education, Santa Fe,…"

"Giorgio and I came up with something," I interrupt with excitement.

"We did?" Giorgio asks.

"Yes. So, the last clue, the fortune, was literal. Believe in the names, yadda yadda. Maybe this one is too. Maybe we need to iron, as in the verb. Iron out the wrinkles, iron the pieces…iron this sucker."

Toph points to his masterpiece with a question on his face.

"Yep," I answer.

"Makes sense," he says squinting. "But if it's not meant to be, you ruin your puzzle and start a fire."

I bite my bottom lip. "Giorgio, I'm going to need an iron."

Giorgio walks to a utility closet across the room and pulls out a rusty old iron. "You are my hero," I exclaim. Toph guffaws. Giorgio hands it to me and heads towards the stairs.

"I've got to go clean up downstairs. I'm closing up in an hour. Don't burn my place down," he calls behind his shoulder.

"You've got it, bud!" Toph yells.

I plug in the iron and turn the setting down to *delicate*. The finish on top of the puzzle feels more waxy than papery, which is encouraging. I walk to the closet and find a thin hand towel, which I place on top of the puzzle.

"You want to do the honors?" I ask Toph.

"No way. This is all you," he says, squeezing my shoulder. I take a deep breath and place the iron face down on the towel, holding it for five-second increments across the top left corner. After three sections, I pull the iron off and look to Toph. He removes the towel and we peer at the naked puzzle.

"Nothing," I say, very much disappointed. Toph feels the puzzle with his fingers.

"It's barely even warm to the touch. We need more heat," he orders. I crank up the iron and move the cloth just next to the hole from the missing piece. Again, I bring the iron down on top of the cloth and leave it for five seconds, but this time I feel the iron sinking in deeper to the puzzle. After just one application, I remove the iron and pull up the cloth, but the melted plastic is stuck to the towel.

"Great," I mutter. Toph takes the cloth and pulls slowly, the steaming, sticky plastic stretching and stringing off the top of the puzzle. It's a mess and smells like burning rubber. Giorgio will be up to cuss us out soon.

Toph pulls away at some of the melted wisps, burning his fingers in the meantime. "It looks like there are layers. If we can clear away this top layer, there's this hard shiny board behind it."

"Stop burning yourself," I say. I reach into his pocket and pull out his wallet.

"What's mine is yours, wifey," he says.

"Need this?" I ask, pulling out a library card.

"Not with you around. You're like a book with legs. Long, hot legs." I shake my head and slug him, grinning.

The plastic has hardened again, so I lay down the iron for a few seconds, then pull up the messy cloth and scrape away the rubbish with the edge of the library card.

"Genius," he says, taking over the ironing job and leaving me to the scraping.

"If there's nothing here, I'm never doing a puzzle again," I say.

"That makes two of us."

The warm heat from the iron is enough to send me to sleep while sitting straight up. I continue the scraping motion mechanically, now having cleared at least a quarter of the puzzle. With no evidence in front of me, I hand Toph the library card and mosey over to our sack of goodies. I take a five-minute break and guzzle down another Red Bull and a slew of Skittles, apologizing to my body for the poor treatment.

"Luce!" Toph erupts. My body jolts up to a standing position. "Luce, I see something!" My Red Bull kicks in and I bound over.

Near the bottom left corner are letters written in black permanent marker. I recognize Dad's writing again. Toph furiously scrapes away now with all his energy. I hold the iron over the area, and we work silently with renewed energy.

"It's a number," Toph squints. "Scrape above the number, see if it says anything." I scrape above and reveal two words. I read them aloud.

"*Confirmation number JD7IS9.*" I smile and clap my hands gleefully. The puzzle is still half covered in gooey Periodic Table.

"Confirmation number to what?" Toph asks.

"Think there's more?" I ask dubiously.

"Only one way to find out."

We iron and scrape for the next forty-five minutes, uncovering nothing but white board.

"We'd better get out of here," I say. "Sun will be coming up soon. And we need a computer."

We gather the items back up in my suitcase and load up the truck. Giorgio waves goodbye and sends us with a sack of peanuts.

I pull *The Joy of Cooking* out of the suitcase so I can study it on the way.

"Where should we go?" I ask.

"Probably not my dorm. Practice will be starting soon." He checks the clock.

"Oh man, Toph. I feel so bad. Are they going to kick you off the team?" I ask. "You should go to practice. I'll be fine on my own for a while," I say half-heartedly.

Toph scoffs. "Kick me off? Not if they want to win."

He doesn't even realize the cockiness dripping out of his mouth. To be honest, I can't afford for him not to be. I need him. He carries on, "Coach Sanders's panties are permanently bunched. He's used to it."

I shake my head. "Good thing you're so good. You know you can't act this way in the real world, right?"

"Yes, ma'am."

I'm feeling extra grateful I'm not alone.

"We could go to my parents' house," he suggests.

"My dad will be gone, but my mom will chat your ear off. Ah, we don't have time for that."

I agree with him. I would love to go spend time in a normal family home, especially Toph's. Now's just not the time.

"Unless…", Toph trails off.

"Another one of your ideas?" I mutter.

"My mom won't recognize you. I'll just tell her you're a foreign exchange student and you can duck into the room and say 'Ja, ja' a few times before I shut the door."

"I'm German?"

"You want to go with Chinese? Sure, she might buy that." I roll my eyes.

"She'll recognize me."

"Nah. She's getting old. You can borrow a hat if you really want. I've got something back there you can borrow." He motions to the back seat.

"Fine," I give. But when this is all over, I'm having a heart to heart with Mrs. Summers in English—that is, if she'll still talk to me."

The long drive back to Eugene gives me time to quickly skim each and every page of the cooking bible. Anything out of the ordinary I jot down in my notebook and add the page number to the side. By the time we pull into the parking lot, I have a short list of four, un-telling items, but as Toph turns off the ignition, my attention is diverted to the home standing in front of me.

As I look out my window, the early morning sun shines on a large and stately, two-story red brick home that demands a double take. The driveway circles around the front of the house, and immaculately pruned boxwoods curve around with it. On each side of the double front doors are stone statues: lions, who are in fact sitting on all fours like overgrown mutts. The perfect green grass looks like it's a putting green on a golf course. I look from the house to Toph, and back. He finds a gym-bag perfumed baseball hat and puts it on me.

"What?" He asks when he sees my state of awe.

"Why did you ever move out of here into that smelly cement square of a dorm?"

He shrugs. "I like being on my own."

"The Chief?" I inquire. Toph nods. He carries my suitcase and we saunter in through the front doors like two zombies. I push the baseball hat down over my eyes. The entryway is as impressive as the exterior. Dark cherry wood floors, twenty-foot ceilings, and a heavy chandelier above our heads.

I can see through to the kitchen nook where long windows with rounded tops circle around a table. A plump woman in a pink bathrobe sits drinking her steaming morning coffee. She has a pair of reading glasses on the end of her nose, and a buttered strawberry scone rests next to the newspaper she's perusing. When she sees us, she hops up and tightens her robe.

"Christopher!" She exclaims. "You brought something besides your laundry, so I see?" She speed-walks over.

"Hi, mom," he says. "Yeah we just have a little homework to do. Hope you don't mind if we crash here for a bit."

Mrs. Summers squints her eyes and studies me. I keep my head down, feeling sillier by the minute. "Not at all. First, sit and have some breakfast. Can I get you a scone...Miss?" she asks, waiting for my name. Toph cuts in.

"Helga," he announces. "Yes, Helga Sss...chneider."

"Helga Schneider?" Mrs. Summers repeats.

"Yes," Toph nods. "She's very German." He steps closer to his mom and whispers, "Doesn't speak a lick of English, hairy armpits, you know the type. I'm helping her with some homework."

"Is that so?" Mrs. Summers says before swatting Toph with the dishtowel over her shoulder. "Christopher, you don't study even when you are enrolled in school, and Helga looks a lot like someone I used to know."

Mama Summers's gaze is like a forceful magnet, compelling me to look up. "Hello, Mrs. Summers," I eagerly divulge, taking my hat off and meeting her eyes with apprehension.

"Helga, your English! It's a miracle!" Toph

exclaims. Mrs. Summers shoves him aside before taking my face in her hands and shaking her head back and forth.

"I knew I'd see you again one day." She brings me in for a hug, which is soft and cushy against her pink robe. "Lucy, call me Shari," she says. Eventually she steps back and looks at me from head to toe and inside out. "You look good, dear. Just like your mom."

Toph intercepts. "Mom, we really do have a lot to do, and it's very important," he emphasizes. "Can't explain now. You guys can catch up all you want later, but just leave us alone for the next couple hours?" Shari raises a speculative eyebrow and then eyes the suitcase. Toph is one step ahead of her. "It's not what you think." He unzips half of it and pulls out the chessboard. Shari shakes her head but doesn't ask.

"I'll be in the shower. Help yourself to some breakfast." She starts making her way up the curved staircase. "And maybe when you're done with all of your 'important studying,' you can explain that large rock on Helga's ring finger." Toph and I look at each other.

"Again, not what you think!" Toph calls after her, rolling his eyes as if she's being unreasonable. I put the ring in my pocket and Toph leads me across the house. We make our way down a staircase into the cool, dark basement and into a cozy room, which by the looks of things, used to be Toph's but now doubles as a guest bedroom. There's a queen-sized bed with about seven layers of sheets, down comforters, and quilted blankets. The walls are covered with horizontal wood planks and painted the color of clay. An old TV set sits inside an armoire. On the other side of the room is a wall of built-in shelves, displaying dozens of trophies and medals. Toph gives me more than enough time to admire them as he opens all the curtains and blinds, pretending not to notice his shrine.

Despite the early morning sun peeking through the basement windows, the room has a restful ambiance. I look at the pillowy bed affectionately, but Toph keeps me on track and slides his laptop in front of me. He fetches the piece of tacky puzzle board from the suitcase, which now looks like a dead bird covered in fur blanket fuzz with melted pieces falling off the edges.

"After you," he says, sliding the confirmation number into view.

"*JD7IS9*," I read aloud. "I don't even know what to do with this. I mean, this is as vague as eleven hundred-page cookbook. "What on earth did he confirm? An account? A hotel? Is another package coming?" I ask. "The span of possibilities is nauseating." I look to Toph and notice his eyelids are getting heavy. We've depleted our supply of Red Bull.

Our brains are only allowing simple thoughts and actions, including the desperate act of typing in the confirmation code into every major venue we can think of. Toph was disappointed the code didn't work for Trail Blazers tickets and even more that I wouldn't let him check a Bruno Mars concert.

"Maybe it's not confirming anything at all. Maybe the confirmation code is a code," Toph suggests.

"Shoot me now."

"Let's come back to this," Toph says. "How about the cookbook? I saw you scribbling down some notes."

"Nothing obvious of course," I say dryly. "I feel like I have a billion-page paper to write and it's due in an hour, and I haven't even started."

"And it has to be written in Mandarin," Toph says.

"Click. Has to be written in Click," I mutter.

"That's not even a language."

"The Khoisan in South Africa speak it," I sigh. "It's incomprehensible."

"Aren't you full of a lot of useless facts." Toph says. "It's in your blood, Luce. You'll get it. We just need a lead. How about these videotapes? Have you watched them?" He holds up the stack of five VHS tapes.

"More times than I can count."

"Well what's on them?" Toph asks, opening the doors of the armoire and letting the ancient video player absorb the first tape.

"See for yourself." I kick off my shoes and decide to take a front row seat on top of the mattress. The screen flickers to life. Three opponents stand side by side, staring up at a royal blue board.

"Alex Trebek?" Toph asks.

"That's right, ten glorious hours of him," I say, fluffing a pillow under my head. Toph follows my lead and crawls onto the bed, bringing the remote with him. Instead of taking his half of the bed, he sprawls out in the middle leaving me with the choice of cuddling up next to him or falling off. I stay put and angle my pillow away from his head so he won't be the recipient of my breath. I don't know why I'm worrying, he's still sporting his sweaty tank top.

"So," Toph clarifies, "ten hours, all of Jeopardy?"

"Yep. Two hours on each tape, and if I remember correctly, twenty-one episodes total, commercials included."

"Yikes. Is there a theme? Anything that stands out?"

"A theme? Hmm," I think. "All were shot in the mid-nineties. The contestants have various ages, cultures, and genders. The topics, well, I can't remember clearly enough to deduce a general theme. We'll just have to start from the beginning," I say with a yawn. "I do remember one thing—Alex wears a pink tie somewhere on the fourth tape."

"And?" Toph asks.

"And it's hot," I shrug. Toph grimaces.

"That's not weird. He's older than your dad is, but whatever."

"Older than my dad was," I correct but linger on the thought. "You still think he's alive?" I trail off. My topic change causes Toph to turn and look at me.

"Yeah, I do." His eyes hold the optimism I need. Reassurance is my drug.

"Okay, let's watch," I say, feeling uncomfortable in his gaze. When I reach for the remote, Toph sneaks his arm behind me and scoots closer in one stealthy maneuver. When I sit back, his smooth move is in full effect. Turns out that my body fits so naturally under his wing. I wilt down so that my head is resting against his chest. Our pheromones dance around, masking our expired shower auras. The strong and steady drum of his heart captivates me, and I become lost in the beat. My eyes close and the drum is constant and safe. Toph tightens his arm around me.

I'm a goner.

CHAPTER SEVENTEEN

Somewhere between Double Jeopardy and a final wager, I jerk awake and find myself lying on one side of the bed, neatly tucked under the sheets. I glance over and find the other half of the bed unoccupied and the room empty. I look up to the screen and there he is, Alex Trebek in his pink tie. "No, I'm sorry, the correct answer is *Who is Ernest Hemmingway*," he confidently corrects.

I don't have a clue what time it is, or how long ago I was abandoned by my nap partner, if I can even call him that. If Toph has powered his way through all the episodes up to the pink tie, I could have been snoozing upwards of six hours.

The echo of faint voices is coming from upstairs.

I roll out of bed and find a bathroom down the hall. I splash my face with cold water, scrub my teeth with my pointer finger, and pinch my cheeks. Reset, effective. I'll bet Mama Summers is upstairs trying to squeeze some info out of Toph and I'd better go rescue him.

The staircase opens up into the kitchen, and as I climb the last step, I find Mrs. Summers, alone, vigorously kneading a large ball of dough. She has traded her pink robe for a ruffled apron and her highlighted blond hair is now curled just under her chin.

"Still here? Great. Come on over and take a seat," she says.

"Shari, hi. I thought I might find Toph up here," I stammer.

"Toph? Oh heavens, I thought he was downstairs with you. I'm the last person to ever know where he's run off to."

"So you haven't seen him since this morning?"

"Nope. I obeyed orders and stayed away." She rolls her eyes.

Puzzled, I saunter further into the kitchen and sit down on a stool at the bar per her orders. The kitchen is light and airy in contrast to the basement. "I'm sorry," I say, watching her knead. "I hope we weren't rude this morning. It's been a crazy couple of days. Toph's been nice enough to help me with…" I chose my words carefully, "this project

I've been working on." Mrs. Summers nods. I can tell her head is about to explode with questions, but she takes her frustrations out on the dough. After five more stretches, she pulls two rolling pins out of a drawer and hands me one, then divides the dough in half.

"Roll it into a rectangle, twelve by sixteen or so," she demands with a smile. I obey, taking a palm full of flour and sprinkling it on the counter in front of me. We roll in silence, and I'm becoming curious as to why I've become her sous chef in her kitchen. I'm going to roll a darn perfect rectangle and be on my way.

After a few minutes, I'm pretty proud of my work, and I follow Shari's lead, spreading an unhealthy layer of softened butter across the dough's surface. Finally the silence is broken.

"I'm awfully sorry we turned into strangers," Shari blurts, still spreading the butter. Her voice is full of anxious relief, like she's waited to get this off her chest. A few air bubbles pop inside the layer of dough. "After we moved, I called. Your mother, she just didn't seem to want to see me. I called a couple times, and she became more and more distant, eventually pretending she didn't know me," she says sounding pained. "I just don't know what I did."

I watch her spread another ridiculous layer of butter on top of the previous one, nervously suffocating the dough.

Turns out the chief is tight-lipped. If only I could have stayed down stairs and snuck out the back door. Toph is going to get it.

"Shari, you didn't do anything," I say firmly. We sprinkle cinnamon and sugar on top of the butter until it's a delicious, sparkly brown color. Shari waits for me to say more but I silently roll the dough up length-wise and pinch the edges closed. I cut twelve equal slices and place the rolls in a greased aluminum tin. Shari covers it with a dishtowel. Her eyes are glossy.

"Shari, would it be possible to meet up for lunch next week?" I ask. "I wish so badly we could catch up now, but honestly I can't right now, and next week would be so much better."

Shari places her last roll in a tin and then reaches across the island and pats my doughy hand with her own. "Of course," she answers, placing another dishtowel over her immaculate tin of cinnamon rolls. "These are for you to take home. They'll be ready in an hour or so." She smiles warmly and then turns to the sink, calling over her shoulder, "Stay as long as you like."

It is well into the afternoon and the anxious jitters are coming back over me to finish what I started. I'm going to need to get back to Mom soon, so these next couple hours are crucial for our safety.

Instead of heading straight downstairs, I walk outside through the front doors and confirm that

Toph's truck is gone.

"Classy," I mutter under my breath, making my way back down stairs. If he ran home to shower and change out of his skimpy running clothes, I am supportive.

The fourth Jeopardy tape is now over. I remove it and pop in tape five, this time avoiding the bed. By the looks of things, Toph was a busy boy while I was off visiting the sandman. All of my gifts are scattered throughout the room except the book of crossword puzzles. It is propped up against the wall and a yellow sticky note is poking out from the top, like a bookmark. I race over and open the book, turning to page forty-four where the place is held. Just a few words are scribbled, and when I read it, I think my heart might break.

Luce,
I can't.
I'm so sorry.
Toph

My mouth is hanging open in astonishment. Fury and sadness are fighting for first place, but they're both trumped by confusion.

What exactly can't he do? Solve the riddles? Handle the lack of sleep? Stand to be with me?

I wonder if his choice in the word *can't* implies *not able*, or is it really *not willing*. I just barely used it when I told Mama Summers, "I can't catch up now." In reality, I would love to catch up, but there is something more pressing that must be attended to now. I contemplate giving Toph the benefit of the doubt for half a second. On the other hand, I don't blame him for giving up his role as ringleader in my circus, but to abandon me at his parents' house, vehicle-less, while I'm sleeping, without any forewarning or explanation?

"Ooh!" I bellow, crumpling his note in my angry palm. I truly don't have time to come up with any excuses for his sudden departure. I tell myself I'm strong enough to focus on the task at hand. Picking up the wrinkled note, I turn back to page forty-four of the crosswords where he left this barbaric bookmark.

This book of crosswords has around two hundred pages, all of which have been completed by my fifteen-year old self over summer break three years ago. I paced myself, only allowing two to three puzzles per day. This is what I had to look forward to, and oh boy, did I.

I examine page forty-four carefully, wondering how I skipped the bubbly, cutesy handwriting phase. My manuscript has stayed boyish and scribbly since the beginning.

Page forty-four has some unobvious variations, the first being the paper: same size, indistinguishable shades of white, but different textures. The black ink outlining the puzzle is more saturated than all the other pages in the book. The number font inside the squares is millimeters larger. I gloat over my cleverness but then remember the credit belongs to someone else. Though he is a pig, he proved his usefulness.

Each puzzle in this book has a theme, a label at the top of the page. This one is titled "Key." There are eleven questions down and eight across. I don't recollect completing this particular puzzle, but my work is all over it.

I begin skimming, trying not to be critical of Dad's skills as a puzzler, and focus purely on its meaning. I begin with one down and read: *Known for his principles of vaccination, pasteurization, and microbial fermentation.* I glance up to the puzzle to verify the answer I already know. Answer: *Louis Pasteur.* Moving on to one across: *Lois Lowry writes of Jonas, the receiver of memory.* Answer: *The Giver.*

Seems as though the name Louis is a common thread, one I'm not in the mood to pull at. I keep reading. Two down: *Chance or luck as an external, arbitrary force.* Again, I glance to the puzzle. Answer: *Fortune.*

Unlike the name Louis, the word fortune piques my interest, and I reach for the fortune in my pocket, confirming its validity before continuing. Three down: *The difference or change in a certain quantity.* I glance up to the puzzle for the answer. *Delta.*

I'm in a rush to find more pertinent words and hastily, I cheat the questions and skim the puzzle itself for any more intriguing terms. I read aloud the answers in no particular order.

Three hundred and seven, beeline, freeze, punctual, Louis Pasteur, blackmail, chocolate, daily double…

I double check my vision and reread the words that strike a major chord with my recent life. *Chocolate, fortune, daily double, blackmail.* These familiar phrases are like Waldo amidst the sea of words around them that hold no significance, but it doesn't matter. I stare at five down like it's a rodent caught in a trap. "Daily Double," I read, glancing up to Alex Trebek. "Five down, is daily double. Whatever Dad is trying to tell me must be in a Daily Double." I do some quick math and figure that there are approximately sixty-three Daily Doubles in these tapes. There must be something else to help narrow it down. These other answers must correlate in some way. I study two down, the other obvious tip-off. "Fortune," I mumble. And then in one glorious realization, I get it.

The title says it all. This puzzle is the key, the key to figuring out exactly what each gift means. The numbers correlate to the gift's numbers. My second gift was the blanket, which led to Carl, who gave me the fortune. My fifth present was the video tapes, and now I may need dig through sixty-three Daily Doubles in hopes of discovering a revelation.

One thing remains a mystery. The "across" words hold no parallel with the gifts. I'll deal with that later. Right now, I take out my notebook and make a quick chart, the first column being the gifts in chronological receiving order, the second column being the crossword *down* answers, one through eleven.

Gift	Crossword answers
1- necklace	1-Louis Pasteur
2- blanket	2-fortune
3-puzzle	3-Delta
4-cookbook	4-three hundred and seven
5-jeopardy	5-Daily Double
6-bike	6-third and sixth
7-crossword	7-key
8-watch	8-battery
9-Etch A Sketch	9-freeze
10-chess	10-office
11-chocolates	11-watch

I'm going to decipher these gifs one by one until there isn't a single question left. I take my necklace and open the locket, staring at the quote inside. Toph's computer is still across the room, plugged into the wall.

I feel a pang of sadness when I see it. Why isn't he here? There's the possibility that he may come back, but his note certainly didn't suggest that. I'm just realizing that it's a bit awkward being in his home without him, but that's too bad. I need his wi-fi and a safe place. Plus, the idiot left me stranded here.

The laptop is charged up and waiting for me. I type in the quote and confirm that it came straight out of Louis Pasteur's mouth. Unless this locket holds any more secrets I haven't yet discovered, I'm guessing one down is a template, enlightening me to the correlation between gift and puzzle.

I've already earned the bragging rights to two down, revealing the fortune without the crossword's help, but gift three has had me stumped. I look over at the confirmation code that once hid under pieces of the periodic table.

A delta could be referring to a mathematical symbol, a flood plain, or a Greek symbol, but I push this information aside and turn back to the computer. My nerves come alive as I type in the keys that will take me to the website for Delta Airlines. I have a feeling that very soon, I will know exactly where to find my dad.

I type in the confirmation code exactly as written and hold my breath as the computer searches.

Within seconds, a bright white screen glows in front of my face, and a ticket stub appears. As I search the words on the screen, I gasp and take in the details as fast as my eyes will process.

I was wrong. This isn't Dad's old ticket stub.

This is a plane ticket, but it is for me, with my full name in all caps across the top. Departing from Eugene, Oregon, arriving in Sydney, Australia. No return flight. I scroll down and view a second ticket with the same information, except instead of my name; it's Renee's.

My head is swimming in unanswered questions, the main being Dad's location. Is he already in Australia, waiting for us? I get a sick feeling in my stomach when a realization hits me. I may have misinterpreted the fortune cookie. Perhaps Renee's rebirth doesn't refer to a cure; perhaps it's a rebirth of our family, starting over in Australia, away from lies and the American government.

On second hand, if Dad isn't alive, why would he have booked Renee and me a ticket out of here?

Overwhelmed, I look at the list of the gifts and crosswords, relying heavily on them to answer more of my questions.

I turn back to the computer when I realize that I haven't even checked the date that I'm fleeing the country.

"This isn't possible," I mutter, double-checking my watch's calendar against the listed date.

Looks like I won't be getting much sleep tonight either.

I've always wanted to fly.

CHAPTER EIGHTEEN

The redeye leaves eight hours from now. Figuring out the rest of these clues is crucial if I'm even considering making an informed decision, which, right now I'm not. Being spontaneous, traveling, and having the chance to escape my situation have never been in the realm of possibilities. My attachments here are shallow, and I keep eyeing the handwritten note lying on the floor in front of me as evidence.

As I prioritize the things to get done within this eight-hour window, packing our life belongings comes second to only one thing. I don't have a passport. Right now, I'm banking on the hope that one of these clues will lead me to a processed pair of passports, or this op is over. A sedative for Renee would also be nice, if not necessary. It's time to get back to the crossword.

My brain needs to be fired up and shooting out answers faster than it ever has. Unfortunately for me, it's thwarted, staring at the pathetic piece of paper on the floor, and I can't help but wonder if Toph discovered these plane tickets first while I was sleeping. My gaze sits heavily on the word "can't." To him this means the end of our friendship, and anything else it could have led to. I'm no relationship expert, but Mr. Darcy didn't give up without a fight.

"Wuss," I mutter and throw the note into the garbage for good.

My next clue is the one thousand one hundred and twenty-two page cookbook. Lucky for me, the crossword clue is *three hundred and seven*. I flip through the pages until I see 307. Three partial recipes are on this page, the first is lemon meringue pie and only the final steps are listed. The third, dark chocolate mousse pie has about half the ingredients listed, but it ends on page three hundred and eight. Only the second one is complete, top to bottom: banana cream pie. It deserves to be the winner, considering it's the tastiest. Unfortunately, it holds no significance or sentimental value to me.

I scavenge the remains of my chocolate dreams, trying to place banana cream pie somewhere. I beg for memories, for a spark, but I'm left with nothing but a tasteless cookbook in front of me. I get specific, looking for clues in the ingredients: the butter, bananas, heavy cream, sugar.

I hold the cookbook under a table lamp, looking for a hidden clue in the title. I start to feel stressed, hot, even nauseated, fighting minute to minute against the clock. I find myself wishing again that he were here. Right now I'm so desperate, I'd even take Giorgio, but Toph's words from somewhere in the middle of the crazy night resurface, and I know that my dad wouldn't give me anything I couldn't handle.

Shari is still upstairs, bustling around in the kitchen. I have half a mind to head back up there and ask if we can whip up a banana cream pie and wait for the answer to fall into my wooden-spoon wielding hands. That luxury immediately expires when I glance at the clock and see that my timer is down to seven and a half hours.

Thinking back to the previous clues, the meanings have been literal, even a little witty. I follow that lead.

The recipes on this page have one thing in common: silky, sweet, rich pie. Pie is a classic dessert, comprised of crust and a filling. It isn't always necessarily a dessert; there's shepherd's pie and chicken pot pie, but those are hardly worth mentioning, considering my sweet tooth.

I think a few months back to Mr. Reynold's class

when we celebrated pie day, stuffing our teenaged faces with every kind of cheap store-bought pie you could think of. Math class had never been so sweet.

"Math," I stammer, hearing Mr. Reynold's lecturing voice in the background. "It's not pie day, it's pi day," I whoop, talking to my reflection in the mirror. I grab my notebook and jot down the number 3.14. Pi has 'Dad' written all over it. When I try and imagine Dad in the kitchen with an apron, I know I'm right. Always stick with the math and science.

Now I'm left dealing with another clue, possibly a date. After ten minutes, I officially hate March fourteenth. I can't think of any significance for this date pertaining to my family. I mull over dates, times, and more of the pi numerals before running up the stairs in search of some brain fuel. My tin of cinnamon rolls is unguarded, cooling on the counter. Mama Summers has vacated the kitchen so I confiscate my tasty treat and bring it down into the cave.

It irks me, moving on to five down before figuring out four, but that's the name of the crossword game. Often you have to work backwards to figure out the obscure ones, which is pretty much like my relationship with Toph. Haven't talked to the guy in a decade. I spill everything, he disappears.

"You suck, Toph," I mutter to make myself feel

better. But I don't.

The fast forward button on the remote is going to get some heavy action, as I've got sixty-three Daily Doubles to work my way through. Starting at the beginning, I place tape number one back in and fast forward until the first Daily Double square dances and flips across the screen with the accompanying laser like tune. A man named Charles with a smashing comb-over and large, pearly white teeth wagers a meager eight hundred dollars once he hears that the topic is "Plants." Alex reads:

"This kidney-shaped nut comes from the evergreen tree, anacardium occidentale, that may grow to forty feet in height." Charles doesn't skip a beat and answers.

"What is cashew."

Charles is right, of course.

My mind conjures up all sorts of nonsensical meanings for this answer:

(1)Dad plans to meet me under a cashew tree.

(2)I need to feed mom cashews.

(3)My next clue is hidden under a cashew tree.

Yeah, powering my way through five-dozen Daily Doubles isn't going to cut it. I stuff in half of a gooey cinnamon roll, chomping carnivorously as I think. There's got to be something more specific. I bite my lip in frustration and realize I'm right back where I started with four down. That's when I decide to try and put the pi and the daily double together.

"Three point one four," I murmur. "Third Daily Double, fourteenth episode," I brain storm. "Third contestant, fourteenth daily double…" Logistically, neither of those makes sense. I try again. "Three minutes and fourteen seconds in…"

Unfortunately, there's not a daily double at the 3.14 minute mark, nor is there one three hours and fourteen minutes later.

I scratch my head, unwilling to believe the two clues don't correspond. I decide to try tape three, minute fourteen, but first I devour the other half of the cinnamon roll, licking the frosting off my fingers before switching the tapes.

At minute fourteen on tape three, the glorious blue square dances before a savvy thirty-something year old brunette man. I push pause and throw my arms up in the air, mouthing hallelujah to the heavens. Then I rewind a few seconds to see the topic. "Physiology," I read, agreeing that this fits within my "dad" criteria of purely pertaining to math and science.

I ignore the wager and wait breathlessly for Alex to give me what I've been looking for. At last he reads.

"Y-shaped proteins which identify and help remove foreign antigens, also called immunoglobulins."

"Antibodies," the contestant and I say together.

I click the off button and rub my head, recalling the basics of antibodies.

(1)They are the superheroes of the immune system.

(2)Our bodies make these to get rid of the harmful germs and viruses that try to set up camp.

Enthusiasm flares inside me as I prance around the possibility that Dad's plan is still based on curing mom—curing mom in Australia, apparently.

Out of the eleven 'down' crosswords, I've got five figured out. I'm nearly half way to finishing this, but I can't stay here any longer. Despite the fact that Art is a traitor and an enemy, my real enemy here is time. It's time to make my way back to Yachats, and by now, I could make that drive in my sleep, I've been back and forth so much.

If I speed, it will take an hour and forty-five minutes to get there, and unfortunately an hour and forty-five minutes to get back to the Eugene airport. There goes fifty percent of my time. When I factor in packing up our belongings, getting to the airport an hour early, and the small task of finding the means to get to and from these locations, my brainstorming time is shot. I'll need to use every precious second driving in the car to figure out the rest of the clues.

My list of desperate ideas to beam me back to Yachats include:

    (1) Waiting for the bus. No time.

    (2) Begging a ride off Shari Summers. Last resort.

(3) Going back to the Police station and seeing if my borrowed Maserati is still available. The fob is still in my pocket, and not on purpose. I meant to ditch it into a shrubbery but forgot about it. Must be a sign.

Everything is thrown back into the suitcase, and it's time to go beg a ride off Shari, but only to the police station. The round tin of cinnamon rolls is half eaten, and I bury the evidence in my backpack and wipe the dried flakes of frosting off my face.

The TV in the family room is on. I leave my suitcase in the kitchen and peek my head around the corner. "Shari? You in there?" I walk towards the couch. Shari doesn't answer. Instead, a teenaged girl stands up and looks me up and down. Her face is caked in heavy, dark make-up, so much that I can't make out her eye color. Her long stringy blonde hair is nearly bleached white, and the short leather skirt she has on could double as a scarf.

"Hey, I'm a friend of Toph's, " I say. "Are you one of his special friends as well?" I don't mean for it to come out like an awkward ex-girlfriend, but it does.

"Ew. Never," she shutters. "I'm Jenny. Little sister." I try not to let my eyes bug out of my head. Looks like the chief has his hands full. "My mom isn't here. I don't know where she went," she says and pushes play again. It's obvious I'm interrupting her reality smut.

"Jenny, I'm so sorry to ask this of you, but your awesome older brother left me stranded here and my car is at your dad's office. Is there any possible way you could give me a lift?"

I'm getting ignored and desperate. "I'll uh…make Toph do your laundry for a week." She doesn't budge except to roll her eyes. "Okay," I say, pulling out the big guns. "I know some hot college guys I can line you up with."

I don't. She pushes pause and turns towards me.

"How hot?" she spews.

"College football, hot." I'm on fire.

"Fine," she huffs. I unzip my bag and hand over the crumpled paper containing the phone number of the beefy fella from the campus bus ride, days ago.

I throw my luggage in the trunk of her shiny red sedan and we don't exchange a single word to the station. She's out of the lot before I even have time to say thank you or find out what color her eyes are.

It takes me one turn around the parking lot to realize that Art reclaimed his car. Defeated, I sit myself down on the pavement in front of the police station and contemplate my next act of desperation.

Just down the street, a white truck hauls around the corner and speeds into the parking lot, screeching to an abrupt stop in front of me. Toph hops out. I leave my bag unattended and dive into a lilac bush.

He doesn't notice the luggage or my maneuver. He's got a crazy look in his eye. I watch as he storms through the front doors like I've never seen him. I follow my curiosity and lurk behind him, passing through the doors he throws open like his shadow. He butt's his way into the chief's office and I stand outside the door, all ears, ignoring the stares of staff.

"I can't!" I hear him yell with a great amount of emotion. A deep, darker voice answers.

"You must."

"It's not fair," Toph whimpers.

The voices dampen. The dark one whispers, "Unless you want to destroy your family, you will stay as far away from this as possible."

I hold my breath and dare to steal a hidden glimpse of the dark voice from behind the desk, though I already know who it belongs to. The chief rubs his eyes. When he brings his hand down, I cover my mouth to silence the gasp.

His eyes are swollen nearly shut but the slits that show are blood-red. I back away slowly with a lump in my throat too big to swallow.

The large-framed figure matches up.

I maced the chief.

CHAPTER NINETEEN

The Summers men continue to grumble and bark at each other in six-inch whispers but I don't stick around to witness any more of it. I fly through the heavy front doors, hoist my suitcase into the bed of the truck, and say a prayer of gratitude that Toph has a habit of leaving his keys in the ignition.

Whatever it was Toph had to choose between, he didn't choose me. I'm not angry or resentful, but I'm stealing his truck.

No one comes chasing after me as I peel out and exit the lot. I refuse to blink so that the mists welled up in my eyes can't become tears. It's not about the chief. I don't know what business he had in my house, but from what he said, he wants to stay away from the poisonous situation I'm in.

I blink and a tear escapes down ɪ one.

That was the last time I would see Toph.

On my way to the freeway, I stop at a red light and glance over at the crossword that is lying in the seat next to me. The words turn to letters and the letters become a blurry haze through my unfocused vision. I demand myself to focus and at last the letters reappear and form words. I read them thoughtlessly, jumping down from word to meaningless word. After about the fifth one, *mummy*, I pause. My senses sharpen. A car behind me honks, and then another. I drive through the green light and pull over, staring at the eight words that seem to read like a sentence, one on top of the other. I haven't given much thought to the 'across' words but now the answer is so obvious; it's shocking I didn't see it before. I read each answer to the across words, one through eight in order.

"Giver-fourth-bonbon-two-mummy-beeline-punctual-watch," I read. Then I read it again. I look to the questions, checking their significance.

1-Lowry's Newberry medal winner in which the main character is the "receiver of memory."

2-Shakespeare wrote a play about this particular Henry.

I read on, becoming more confident that Lois Lowry and Henry IV are just formalities in devising what was meant for my eyes.

Most of the message makes sense. I read aloud how I choose to interpret Dad's message. "Give fourth chocolate to Mom. Be punctual, watch."

The glory of the epiphany settles and I'm sick to my stomach. If that fourth chocolate is meant to cure Mom, nothing else matters. Right this instant, I shift my priorities, pushing aside packing and the plane tickets.

I am on a manhunt for Arthur D. Aldridge. The ticking clock is looming over my head, not just because of the flight, but because of the order to be punctual. The word punctual is specific, meaning on time, at a proper meeting time, or at a particular point in time.

His request is too specific and his clue is too broad.

The sun is shining through the car window onto my face. I'm flustered, hot, bothered, but more determined than I've ever been in my life.

The last word of the sentence is a sentence all on its own, as well as a separate demand. "Watch," I whisper and brainstorm. Watch the clock. Watch a person. Watch the effects on Mom. Watch for Dad to clue me.

I've been sitting here, pulled over on the side of the road just blocks from the station for ten minutes. I should already have been arrested for joyriding. Lousy cops.

A gas station is just down the street. I pull into the lot and park the truck behind the building, out of view. A graffitied payphone is on the side of the building. I find a stack of coins in Toph's ashtray and slink over to last century's means of communication.

A middle-aged man with long straggly hair and filthy hands is at the end of his joint and is eyeing my every move, not even trying to be discreet. It throws my already high levels of stress into a new tier of crazy. I throw coins down the phone's slot. My hands are damp and shaking and I'm not paying any attention to how much change has gone in, I'm just praying for that dial tone. The change slides back down into the return slot. I leave it and run around the side of the building, through the front doors. Out of breath, I face the cashier who is more inked than Dennis Rodman. The gauges in his earlobes allow me to see through to the other side of the store.

"Do you have a phone I can borrow?" He doesn't say a word and pushes the store phone over and sends me a wink. I dial 911.

"Yes, I would like to file a report for a stolen Maserati."

The calm woman on the other end asks my location. I envy her composure.

"Yachats, no, I mean Eugene, Oregon."

"What's your name?" She asks. I glance through

the earlobes and eye the Camel cigarettes.

"Uh, Camille. Camille Aldridge. But this is my grandfather's car I'm calling about. His name is Arthur Aldridge."

"Yes, Miss Aldridge, I see that there has already been a report filed—yesterday, on behalf of Mr. Aldridge. His car has already been located."

"Oh, what a relief," I falsify impressively. "Look, do you have his information updated? His phone number and such?"

"Yes, ma'am. Everything should be current."

"Do you have the address on file for the nursing home he just moved in to?" The woman on the other end pauses and I hear her typing in the background.

"From what I can tell, he lives at home in Eugene."

"No, his current residence is at Amber Waves Nursing Home in Yachats, Oregon," I say, making her take down the new address. "What about his work address? Is that out of date as well?" I try to sound huffy in order to retrieve the info I'm after.

"I have 2580 Winding Knight Oaks," she divulges. I grab a leaky Bic pen next to the cash register and write it on the underside of my arm. "Yep," I say. "You got it. All right, well, I'll tell Gramps that his car has been found and, well, thank you, I appreciate it."

The store's front doors automatically glide open,

and I sprint through towards the truck. The old ogler is gone but as I'm about to get in, I do a double-take of the truck bed. The sight is enough to make me vomit.

My suitcase has been ripped open, and the remaining contents are strewn about. Through my hyperventilating, I take inventory. The chess-board and pieces are dumped all over the floor. I immediately notice my furry blanket is gone. The cookbook remains and the Etch A Sketch is there. What else could he have taken?

My watch. I dig through the suitcase and scavenge the truck bed to be sure. That old, broken watch has been stolen. Though the blanket is sentimental, I've already figured its significance. I have to get my watch back.

I sprint to the front of the store near the street and survey the area. Across four lanes of traffic and a block south, a see the old greasy thief hobbling down the sidewalk with the fur blanket around his shoulders.

I won't be calling the cops, and even though I might be able to take him down myself, I run back into the store and face the tattooed winker.

"That man!" I shout, pointing across the street. "That man stole my watch and blanket!"

His earlobes swing as he gallops out from behind the desk and tears out of the store without a word. I watch through the glass doors as he cuts through the traffic and tracks down the only lunatic carrying a fur blanket in the sweaty summer. A group of us is now watching as my hero ransacks the swindler and proceeds to do a rough and thorough pat-down, forcing my watch out from the depths of his pants pocket.

We all cheer as the clerk comes trotting back with my stolen treasure, like prince charming from the hood.

The clerk's name is Damien, and he hands me back my effects with a final wink, and I find myself wishing there was some way to repay him. I hope karma finds its way back to him.

I hold the blanket away from my body like a stinky garment and discard it and the other items back into my suitcase, but I place the aged, dead watch around my wrist, just up from the newer one that replaced it. This watch is trying to tell me something, and I'm going to keep it close. I could have kept the old one and replaced the battery, but to be honest, it was and still is a piece of crap. The band is frayed and the image inside is Minnie Mouse, her gloved pink hands pointing to the numbers. It was always a tad juvenile for me, but I needed it for work.

I glance to the crossword table to read the clue that corresponds to the watch. I need something to occupy my mind as I drive to 2580 Winding Knight Oaks.

The watch was gift number eight, and I read the affiliated clue.

Bill Clinton's 1992 campaign slogan.

The answer in the box is seven letters, and my imagination runs away once I see it.

"It's time."

Minnie Mouse holds the answer, well actually, she's pointing to the answer. I thank the heavens above I didn't change the clock battery.

Thanks to the crossword *across* epiphany, I can conclude that the last word, "watch," was meant as a noun instead of a verb. Be punctual; watch. In order to be punctual in giving mom the fourth chocolate, I need to give it to her at the time it says when my watch battery went caput. I adore how specific his instructions are.

Dad must have given me a juvenile trashy watch so I'd replace it and not bother changing the batteries. Genius.

I look to where Minnie Mouse's gloves are pointing. Small arm is on the nine, large arm between the twelve and one. I'm calling it nine o' three. This watch has a date listed as well, and before I look, I pray I haven't already missed it. It stopped ticking on 6-29, exactly two years ago, to the day. I shiver.

I shouldn't be surprised. Dad worked this out to every last detail, and I just hope I'm doing his plan justice. Every single thing he planned had an exact purpose, and I have chills at the thought and time he put into this to make it perfect. I've got to get this right.

I look to my good watch. I have three hours to reclaim my chocolate and get Mom.

After driving a couple blocks I find a working payphone and call Amber Waves. A wave of nostalgia hits me as I realize I've worked my last shift and can't say goodbye to the patients. I have six hours until I leave this country, possibly for good. It will all be worth it.

The nurse gives me the information I need; that Art has gone AWOL. I don't know why he would be hanging out there with the geezers, but I had to cross it off as a possibility.

I don't bother giving my two weeks' notice before hanging up. I think of my employee of the year plaque. One day I can tell Dad about it. He'll be proud of me.

This leaves Art's home and Art's work as the most likely places to track him down. I don't think he'd be at home. I assume he's either on a manhunt for Dad or he's in his lab dissecting Mom's chocolate. I'm banking on the latter.

Turns out that Winding Knight Oaks isn't in Eugene. I rip the map out of the phone book next to the pay phone. It shows a lonely road north and west of Eugene, about forty-five minutes or so outside of Yachats. If he isn't here, at least I'm well on my way back home to get my stuff.

I have a pretty accurate built-in compass and it'd better be pointing due north today. I don't have any time to waste trying to find this place.

As I drive through the windy roads navigating through blankets of tall pine trees, I have the remaining clues on my mind. There are only two left to be deciphered: the Etch A Sketch and the game of chess. The crossword clues are "freeze," in reference to the Etch A Sketch, and "office," corresponding with the game.

The first thing I'm going to do when I get to Art's office is find the break room and toss the Etch A Sketch in the freezer. As far as the chess goes, I haven't checkmated in years. As far as ransacking Art's place, I'm nuts. He seems willing to hurt me, and I need to be willing to do the same. He's ruined my family's life, it's the least I can do. The movie *Miss Congeniality* has taught me all I need to know to strike a man in the most lethal, vulnerable areas.

My false confidence is a joke. I'm just going to have to outfox him. The chances of his being at his office are slim, and if all the stars are aligned, he left the precious in his lab, all in one glorious piece, ready for me to reclaim.

My stomach rumbles. I look to the empty food wrappers on the floor and miss Toph. The cowardly pig.

The name-calling is starting to help.

There is a turnoff a few yards ahead. I pull off and check the map before following onto a dirt road even more saturated with trees.

I follow Winding Knight Oaks for a mile or so before I start to suspect I've gone too far. The trees start to intertwine. The road narrows and a creek follows me on the right. I drive about ten more seconds and then slam on my brakes—Toph's brakes. To my right, completely shaded and nestled amidst the trees stands a surprisingly large, rectangular building. It almost could be mistaken for a power plant or water engineering building, but the windows are barred shut. There is no sign or label anywhere. There is only one thing on the front, next to the frosted glass door on front: the numbers 2580.

I'm here.

The building looks environmental but corporate, and very private. There's a front parking lot and it's completely empty. My hopes drop. If this is a government building, there's not a chance of me MacGyvering my way in if it's deserted and locked.

I drive around the side toward the back where there's a separate entrance, a dark brown metal door. Parked directly in front of it is a shiny, silver Maserati.

I nearly scream in horror. I fly past the car, through the lot's exit and park back behind the creek, hidden by a row of thick redwoods. The truck is hidden, but through a small opening I can see the dark brown door. I pray the noisy creek muted the sound of Toph's truck.

I didn't think this through. I'm out in the woods, approaching night-time, with my stalker, the liar, the most dangerous man I know, just feet away, and probably waiting for me.

I need courage and I need a weapon. I'm going in. This is it, my family's chance. Dad didn't sacrifice the last ten years of his life for nothing.

Quickly, I scavenge through the glove box. Surely a cop's son carries something useful for protection.

The heaviest thing I find is a tire pressure gauge and a smelly shoe. Toph is the last person to hold a concealed weapons permit, the good for nothing pansy.

Sneaking in is impossible. The back door is likely the only one unlocked and for all I know, it could lead me directly to the devil.

I have a plan and I pray like crazy it's not a suicide mission.

I take Toph's duffle bag and stuff in the chess game and Etch A Sketch. I put on an air of fake confidence, slam the truck's door shut, and march to the dreaded, heavy, metal door. Vigorously, I knock and yell.

"Art! Art! Are you in there? Art, help!" I hear a scuffle from inside, and it takes everything I have to steady my shaky hands and slow my breathing. Slow footsteps from inside unnerve me even more. Then there's a pause. I gather my courage and start all over.

"Art! Please, if you're in there, I need you." The desperation in my voice is genuine. At last, the door swings open and I take a final breath. Art stands erect in front of me. His eyes are angry and red and terrifying, but I don't let him make the first move.

"Art!" I grab his arm softly, feigning comfort. "Art, I've been looking everywhere for you. I need your help." He sneers at me, ready to pounce. I hurry on. "I, I think my dad is alive, and I think you do too." I pause and dare to look into those murderous eyes. He doesn't say a word, but his pause encourages me to carry on. "I think he's trying to kill Renee. I'm so confused. I need help," I cry out. Out of the corner of my eye, I look past him into the building, and a vague sense of déjà vu washes over me. I see beakers, scales, microscopes, and computers. When I see the lab table, I gasp. I've been here before, many times.

This was Dad's lab. I fold my arms, trying to hide the goose bumps.

Art's white hair is standing out from his head and his sharp eyes don't hold a hint of the warmth they used to. "Why would you think that?" he growls.

"My last dream. Chocolate three, in your room," I pause dramatically. "I wasn't ready to say anything.

But I am now." I accidentally catch a glimpse of the heavy silver weapon inside his inner coat pocket but do everything in my power to ignore it.

Art glares skeptically. "You ran away. Stole my car. Why would you trust me now?"

"Art, I know you were following me, watching me at the nursing home. I know you work for the government. I know you are trying to protect me and Renee, and I know that I know too much," I spill. "I'm not supposed to know that Dad's still alive. But I do."

He buys it. With a snuff he relaxes his tense body and takes a few steps back. I slowly step over the threshold and enter his office. He shuts the heavy door behind me.

The room is dimly lit. There are four computers, several monitors and desks spread throughout the room. Along the back wall is the lab table, and I spy something that resembles chocolate dust on a scale.

"What did you dream?" he asks. I wish he would at least try and talk in the sweet, kind voice that he used to. He should be on Broadway with those acting skills.

I sit in a lab chair, directly across from my former best friend. "It was awful." I sniffle and pause for effect. "Dad was alive. We were like a normal family again, but then he drugged Renee and she was seizing." I fake a soft sob. "The look on his face. It haunts me," I cry out. "Art, I think he's going to kill

Renee. He's already tried once, I read the report. This time he'll succeed. I'm scared," I cry. "These dreams have been telling the truth the whole time, and I think the third one is predicting his plans. He wants me to know. It's so twisted. He wants me to be freed of Renee. Like he is."

I bury my head in my hands. I've gone too far. There's no way he's going to believe this nonsense. I look up and he's staring across the room past me with a very bewildered look on his face. I run with it.

"The only thing I can think to do now, is to take that last chocolate. It is my only way of knowing if all this is real."

"Let me get this straight," he snarls. "You believe Truman is alive, and that he crafted and delivered these chocolates." I nod. "Why on this hellish earth would he expose his true intentions and tell you?" My lies are getting deeper and more unbelievable. I have only one purpose, and that's to get that chocolate and make it out of here alive.

"I think he wants me to come with him." I wipe a fabricated tear from my eye. "That's why you have to find him before he finds me! Tell me you still have that fourth chocolate. I could take it, get more details of his plans, and while I'm sleeping, you could begin tracking him down?"

I'm heavily banking on the hope that Dad already knows Art is after him and is waiting in Australia, safe and sound. He left me a freaking long to do list and I have to get Art off my back some way.

Art's expression is in a deep thought. At last, he walks back to the lab and scrapes the obliterated crumbles of remaining chocolate and dust onto a plain white piece of paper. He walks back to me and places it on a desk next to us. We both stare at the pile.

"Do you think it will still work?" I ask out of my own curiosity. "And what did you find after dissecting it?" I blurt before he has a chance to answer my first question. He ignores me and lines up three small desks in a row so there aren't any gaps between them.

"The properties all remain. It will still work," he says coldly.

My plan is working. I stare at the desks he lined up against the wall and realize he's expecting this to be my resting place. I hop up onto the desks and pick up the paper with the remains of mom's cure.

"Excuse me one minute," I say, walking towards the back lab tables. "I'm going to add some water to this in hopes of congealing it back into one piece."

His eyes follow me to the back. I turn on the sink and it splashes noisily against the stainless steel. There is a lip on the edge of the table that will hide some of my actions if I'm shifty. I feel his pointed eyes on me but I carry on, rolling a small beaker down off the table. I shimmy it down between my body and the front of the table. When it gets down to my knees, I squeeze it tightly between my legs. I splash around in the sink with one hand as a distraction and funnel the contents in the white paper, sliding it ever so carefully to the edge and ultimately, tipping it and spilling the contents down in front of me. Most of the chocolate gold spills into the beaker. I continue to squeeze it tightly between my quavering legs. I take the mostly empty white paper and siphon it up to my mouth, loudly chewing the dust remnants, purposefully smearing some of the chocolate dust on my lip. I drop the paper, and it glides onto the floor by my feet. I bend down to pick it up, and take the beaker full of chocolate between my legs and push it into the corner under the desk.

Art continues to stare coldly into my soul as I walk back to him and lie down on his altar. I might as well be lying in a casket. Nightfall is quickly approaching, and an eerie, dark premonition swallows me whole. Panic ensues. My pupils dilate, my breathing is shallow and rapid, and my palms are damp, pressing against the hard wooden table. I want to abort. It's too late.

Art stands over my horizontal body. I look up and notice the deep downward wrinkles on either side of his mouth. They're molded from what can only be explained by a permanent, heinous scowl he wears, and I wonder how I overlooked it back at

Amber Waves.

I cover my panic attack with chocolate symptoms, thinking back to the metallic after taste and the spinning.

"I'm dizzy, really dizzy," I slur, forcing my respirations to slow. I let my eyelids droop down, not yet willing to completely close out the villain from my view. I look up to his face and his long wiry eyebrows, now easily finding fault in his wicked features.

His eyes are studying my movements, moving from my eyes, down the length of my body, and slowly back up. Finally they stop, just above my mouth. He leans down gently, breathing heavily, and drags his callused finger across my lip, erasing the remnant of chocolate I'd planted. A piercing shiver convulses through the deepest parts of me. I feel the violent urge to vomit but I hold my breath and shut my eyes, closing out any chance to escape. I'm in the dark now, feigning chocolate dreams.

CHAPTER TWENTY

I've been lying as a lifeless corpse for several minutes, relying on my ears alone to follow Art. He should be out the door by now on his way to ambush Dad, but I feel his dark, silent presence watching me dream, and I smell his acrid, stale breath wafting from each exhale.

My enemy stands over me in complete control of whether I live or die. But this is the only way. He won't kill me, he needs me. He needs me to tell him what that last dream is about. He needs me alive if he wants to find Dad. I rest assured that the heavy weapon will stay put in his coat pocket.

It's been around ten minutes that I've been in the dark. The backs of my eyelids no longer show pink.

Black is the only color engulfing my senses and I feel the sun's absence. Despite my best efforts to believe in my positive thinking, my body is rigid, waiting any second to be attacked, and dreading his coarse and evil fingers touching any part of me again.

At last, Art stands up and takes several steps towards the back lab desk. I hear him gathering things and placing them inside a bag of sorts with a heavy-duty zipper. I panic thinking of the beaker holding mom's salvation, but in this darkness it would be nearly impossible to stumble across.

I lay completely frozen and exposed on the hard wooden table, begging to hear the slam of the door and the hum of his Maserati, leaving me alone to complete my tasks. But the plod of his heavy boots gets closer and louder until finally, he stops mere inches away. I'm sweating, ill, and desperate to open my eyes and locate him.

Two more steps. He's up near my head. I wonder how dark it really is, if he can see my tense and rigid limbs, the goose bumps up and down my arms, and hear galloping beat of my heart. I hold my breath.

He touches my chin. His large feelers slide slowly down and stop on my neck. I feel two fingers against my carotid artery. They stay there.

As he checks my pulse I quiet my nerves, but not enough to slow my violent pulse. Tachycardia is a believable side effect of the chocolate. I need to breathe again.

He is thorough, taking at least a sixty-second pulse read. The silence in the room is intoxicating.

At last his fingers retract, but it's a short hiatus. Now two hands glide past my chin, one on each side, patiently falling lower, eventually circling around my neck, warm and constricting. They get heavier. Then they get tighter.

My body jerks upward, only to be suppressed by his force. I gasp involuntarily, taking in a last large gulp of air. But it's too late. My eyes explode open and adjust to the bleakness, focusing on the dark outline of his eyes, six inches from mine. He breaks the silence. His voice is strained and merciless.

"The thing is, I know Truman better than anyone."

His hands are synched around my neck like a cobra. I squirm and kick with every drop of my energy, but I'm powerless, trapped under his weight. I swing my arms wildly, thrashing around for contact, but his face is out of reach. I sink my fingernails deep into the skin of his hands, but it only spurs him on.

"He would do anything for her," he spews inches from my face. "But the reality is, he can't save your mom, and I couldn't save mine."

I hear him but his words are starting to echo, floating far from me and my cognition.

"This is the extinction of all Lichtys. Renee will

be the easiest," he chides. "With you and your mother out of the picture, Truman won't have anything left to live for, especially once he's convicted for killing the two of you." He gasps out.

I feel the intensity of my physical being wilting. Complete blackness surrounds now, with heaviness in my chest and burning in my lungs. I beg myself to fight on. But everything slows. The only thing I hear is the anxious thudding of my heart, obtrusively beating up into my ears, drowning out any other noises. I feel hot and then cold, and I'm drifting away from my body. I think of heaven, realizing Dad won't be there waiting for me. It gives me one last motivation to fight. I don't want to die.

I use every ounce of my energy and swing my arms up, praying for one fatal blow. I expect to feel flesh but my arms swing around, engulfing only the air.

From a few feet above me, a noisy but dull clang vibrates throughout the air and the pressure is released. At once, my lungs are filled with oxygen. Two hands gently embrace my face. His voice is panicked. The damp light seeps back as I crack open my eyes.

Toph cradles me in his arms, caressing my cheek and the marks across my neck.

I see Art lying in a heap on the floor. A large metal shovel is next to him.

CHAPTER TWENTY-ONE

I only want to savor the moment, but I can't.

"Get his gun." My voice is raspy. "Inside pocket of his jacket." Toph places me down gingerly, then kicks unconscious Art over so he's lying on his back.

"Always knew this guy was a moron," he says, pulling open the tweed jacket and confiscating his weapon. He hands it to me and then grandly winds up, seconds away from kicking the elderly assassin in the crotch.

"Don't wake him up!" I screech. "Do something with him. Get him out of here!" Toph pauses, clearly disappointed.

"Guess what, princess. I just saved your life."

And with that, he roundhouses Art squarely in the groin. Art curls his body up in the fetal position and starts coughing pathetically.

"On your feet," Toph barks. "Arms in the air." Toph reclaims the weapon from me, pointing it at Art's head, looking much too comfortable with it. Apparently he's learned a thing or two from daddy.

Gradually, Art comes to. Toph walks over so he's standing between the two of us. Art is bent over like a true geriatric, gingerly making his way onto his feet.

"What do you suggest I do with him?" Toph asks maliciously, still pointing the gun at the wounded.

"Are you freaking kidding me Toph? You don't have a plan?" I'm livid. "Couldn't you have waited a few minutes to kick him in the crotch?" I yell. Before I can even take half a breath to begin yelling again, Art suddenly darts towards Toph, leaping in the air, stripping every ounce of his senior citizen façade. The gun is knocked out of Toph's unsuspecting hands. Toph curses. The gun slides on the floor across the room and to my horror, both men dive towards the loaded weapon. Art's shifty little body makes its way onto the bottom of the pile. I can see him cradling the gun between both hands, trying to get a proper grip.

Once I realize that the shrieking is coming from my own mouth, I shut up and make myself useful, going after the shovel.

"Get out of here!" Toph yells at me, surely knowing I won't obey. I grab the heavy garden tool he ingeniously saved my life with earlier and wait for my opportunity. But Art is buried under Toph's long lanky body and I am helpless. With every ounce of my being, I pray that I won't hear a gunshot.

On a desk just feet away, I spy a cell phone and don't recognize it as Toph's. I sprint over to it and dial 911 with trembling fingers. I am mortified when the recorded voice tells me I'm out of cell range. I watch in terror, just feet away from the scuffle.

Toph's top lip is puffing up and oozing blood but his face holds only a look of determination. He waits for the right angle and from behind, sucker punches the old man in the liver, simultaneously kicking the gun out of his hands. It launches across the room and slides out of sight under the lab table.

Toph dives for it, but Art runs the opposite direction. I get my gumption back and chase after Art with the shovel, ready to javelin it towards his core. But Art tears across the room and dives out the same door I came in.

"Lucy, stop!" Toph roars at me. And for once, I obey, slowing my stride. Toph holds the gun in his hand and races towards the door. Just before he launches his body into it, a loud, mechanical locking noise echoes throughout the building. Toph's body ricochets against the door, sending him tumbling back towards me. He leaps back up on his feet and tries again, pounding against the metal door in frustration.

"He's locked us in," I pant. Toph darts to the front of the building, and I hear him denied again. He kicks the door with all his might but the metal is impenetrable.

I slink towards the back window next to where Art exited and slowly pull down one of the plastic blinds, peering past the metal bars. Though it's nearly dark, I see him, directly in front of me, six feet away. His face is bloody and bruised with blues and purples consuming the entire left side. He takes the key out of his pocket and climbs into the driver's seat of his sports car. To my horror, he catches my eye and leans back out. He doesn't come any closer. Just smiles a horrible, heinous grin of victory before driving away.

I crumple into a ball on the floor.

CHAPTER TWENTY-TWO

I survived my suicide mission, and now I hold her freedom in my hands. But as long as I'm trapped, so is she.

I peer through the clear glass beaker at the chocolate fragments and dust sprinkled across the bottom. Then I glance at the two watches, still side-by-side and clasped to my left wrist. Minnie Mouse sternly points to the numbers, urging me to do something.

Nine-o-three is less than two hours away and I'm expertly locked in a government building hidden by a forest while Art freely lurks throughout the streets. The thought of his vile expression is enough to incapacitate me again. But every second matters now.

Toph rummages through every drawer and crevice convinced there is a way out. He's torn and distracted, pacing through the rooms, but checking in on me every few minutes. His injuries look much worse than mine, though he won't let me address them.

The last traces of sunlight are extinguished and I'm down one sense. Until Toph figures a way to get us out of here, I'll need to use every second to unravel my last two clues. Keeping my brain occupied will numb the panic of Renee's safety and Dad's travel plans.

I need to find a freezer. I tuck the Etch A Sketch under my arm and follow Toph who is guided by his phone's light, at least for a few more minutes until his battery will die. When he sees me following, he takes my hand without hesitation. I shadow him closely, feeling the protection of his presence and the warmth of his touch. He unlocks more emotion than I would like.

"He's going to find her. Art's going to find my mom." He hears the panic in my voice and turns around, facing me. The look on his face is a combination of relief and guilt.

"Luce, don't be mad," he says. "Your mom is protected. I sent the police to go pick her up hours ago. Actually, to pick both of you up. I knew you didn't want to involve the cops, but I couldn't stand the thought of you being in danger." He squeezes my hand and avoids my eyes. "I hope you understand."

I close my eyes and rub my forehead, squirming at what I have to ask him. "Toph, please tell me you didn't send your dad. Please," I plead with some fire behind my question. He sends me a look of suspicion.

"Do you know?" he asks.

"That he was the one I maced? Yep," I fire out. "That he was the one sneaking around my house like a creep in the dark? Yeah. What I don't understand is why you called the cops and took off without an explanation. Or why you're here, when you thought I was safe and sound being babysat by your hired help."

"Obviously, I was right!" Toph fires back. "He almost killed you. What are you thinking, meeting him here on your own? It's suicide."

"If I had anyone else to help, anyone else who cared, I wouldn't have had to come on my own." My voice is weak, angry, and shaking. Toph grabs my hands again and won't let me pull away.

"I'm here." He pulls me in tight. My lungs are burning with each labored and emotional breath.

"I care so much," he says.

The room is filled up with unanswered questions but he holds me in silence, wrapping his arms even tighter around me and resting his chin on my ponytail. I daydream back to our first date, reminiscing in the laughter and remembering the way he hugged me. I want to be back there.

Toph talks without letting go. "I didn't send my dad to get Renee," he says. I breathe a sigh of relief. "The squad from Yachats is keeping her company. My dad…" he trails off. "My dad is deeper in this than we thought. He's the reason I had to leave you."

I furrow my eyebrows. "What do you mean? I thought it was because you wanted the cops to handle it. Or maybe even because you didn't want me on that plane."

Toph leans back, getting a good look at me. "What plane?"

"I thought you knew about the plane ticket," I reply, shaking my head and overwhelmed by the confusion. "Clearly we have a lot of catching up to do. But I am losing time. Toph, I have an hour and half to find Renee and get her to swallow everything that's in that beaker."

Toph sighs and turns the light off his phone. "Let's sit, quickly catch up so we're on the same page, and make a plan. I found an emergency kit with matches in it near the kitchenette. There are a couple of scented candles. Let's light those and preserve what's left of my phone battery in case I can get a signal."

"Done. Is there a freezer in the break room?" I

blindly feel the desks around me until I find the Etch A Sketch.

"Yeah, I think so." He leads me by the shoulders back to a break room of sorts. We light two conflicting scents; pine and pomegranate. I have a future sense that these smells will always remind me of this night. I need there to be a happy ending.

The flickering candlelight is just enough that I can see his outline. As I throw my game in the freezer, he spreads a thin gauze blanket from the emergency pack on the floor. We sit cross-legged across from each other. It seems too far away.

"Ladies first," he says. I like the way his low voice rumbles when he speaks softly. "No way," I argue. "Why don't you start out by answering why you left me alone with your mother."

Toph shakes his head.

"What you should be asking is how I got here. You stole my truck, thief.

"Oh, please," I sigh. "Fair punishment for abandonment." Toph grins but soon it disappears as he decides how to start.

"Well, you fell asleep. Like immediately, all snuggled up in my bed. Trust me, I didn't want to leave," he grins again. "But I heard the chief upstairs. I'd been worried about your safety for a while and I thought it would be a good time to let him in on how bad the situation really was." Toph rubs his whiskery chin. "In hindsight, he's the last person I should have gone to."

"Toph, tell me why he was in my house," I say sternly. Toph bites his bottom lip.

"I think he was looking for Truman."

"So he knows he's alive?"

"Now he does," he replies.

"Well, is he trying to help him or what?"

"Actually," he pauses uncomfortably, "his job depends on Truman being dead. And he would do anything for his job, trust me."

"Why? I don't understand," I say. "What does my dad have to do with him—all these years later?"

"The chief didn't spell everything out for me, just enough to let me know that if I act on anything, or do anything, it will be the end of him and our family. He breathed down my throat and made me promise not to get involved with your plans." He pauses. "I knew I couldn't betray him, but I also knew I couldn't leave you in danger on your own. So I left and decided to do what I could for both of you."

"Which was?"

"Let the Yachats cops deal with Arthur so my dad stays out of it, and in the meantime, keep you and Renee safe."

"But what about my dad? Apparently your dad wants him dead and Art wants him destroyed."

Toph drops his head. "My dad wants him to remain fake-dead. Stay in the closet."

"That's not fair!" I shout. "He's spent years putting this plan together to save my family, and you're trying to shut it down and leave him to the vultures."

"It's not true," Toph says softly. "I'm here. I saw the across words on the crossword puzzle and swore that I would do what it takes to get that chocolate back from Art. You just beat me to it."

"What could my dad have done that made your dad, the chief, his best friend, want him dead?" I ask.

"It's more what he didn't do," Toph replies. "Our earlier assumptions were correct. Your dad faked his death. It would have been nearly impossible for him to pull that off on his own, unless he had some high-ranking help."

"The chief," I whisper. Toph nods.

"My dad must have known Truman was innocent but couldn't prove it due to the overwhelming evidence ingeniously planted by Arthur Aldridge, who happens to hold a decent amount of sway in his government job," Toph explains. "So, my dad helped Truman fake his death."

"But why would Dad do that?" I urge. "Why not fight it? Why not take the sentence? It couldn't have been worse than having to live in the shadows, pretending to be dead?"

"I think that's where your mom's cure comes in. If he went to jail, he wouldn't have had the chance to work on a cure for Renee. And apparently, it's time sensitive." He glances to my watches.

"Whoa," I stop him there. "So he didn't have time to plead innocent or guilty. He had to fake his death to buy him the time to work. But that still doesn't answer why your dad isn't supportive."

"At the time my dad helped your dad, he wasn't the chief. He's climbed the ladder these last few years. If the division ever found out he was the primary accomplice of an attempted murderer, he'd be out of a job and behind bars," Toph says. "When I was in his office, my dad was yelling things like, "I tried! Told him to forget his old life, start over. There's nothing more to be done."

"So your dad saved him from decades in prison and sent him on his way, hoping that he would start a new life, and forget the one he had in Yachats."

"But he couldn't do that," Toph says with a smile. "He couldn't ever abandon you and Renee. He made a plan, sent gifts, ultimately waiting until the time was right and you could assist him in curing Renee. And, apparently, flee the country?" Toph asks.

"Yeah, remember the confirmation code behind the puzzle?"

"How could I forget?"

"Turns out it's not a ticket stub to a Bon Jovi concert," I say. "It's an airline ticket confirmation. Two one-way tickets to Australia for Renee and me." I decide to leave out the detail that it leaves in four hours.

"Wow." Toph is silent but still nodding. Finally he asks.

"Are you going to go?" So much emotion comes out with the question but he tries to mask it with a shrug.

I nod. "Yeah." It comes out soft but decidedly. Silence fills the room for several confusing seconds. Finally Toph speaks.

"But if we're locked in this building forever, I guess you can't go." He manages to smile.

I scoot forward on my knees so that we are eye to eye. "If my mom's sanity wasn't ticking away, all I'd want to do is be with you. Anywhere." It's hard to breathe again. "But every second matters. And I need you."

Toph's eyes flicker in the candlelight as he ponders over my statement. "I guess I can't be selfish then. Renee deserves it," he says in a throaty, low voice. "You deserve it, Luce."

We hug and electricity passes between the two of us like a loose and dangerous raw wire. More precious seconds pass and I don't regret even one of them. It's a hug of comfort, encouragement, friendship, and heat. He releases first and slowly brushes his lips across my cheek. I have to forcibly restrain myself not to jump on him, and he knows it, playing it cool.

I remove myself from his magnetic zone and take a candle with me over to the freezer. "I'm going to figure out these last two gifts and clues, you work on getting us out of here," I say, just a tad annoyed over his self-control. I glance over at him and he looks to be in a melancholy trance, but when he hears my orders, he hops up and gets to work.

The tiny freezer has lost its energy source for longer than I would like but is still frosty. When I pull the red toy out and hold the candle up to the glass drawing window, magic has transpired. Excitement dances in the pit of my stomach. There are three short lines of writing sketched across the previously blank board.

The dim heat from the candle is warming up the glass just enough to send thawed clumps of aluminum powder towards the glass face. Letter by letter, the writing fades until there is an empty screen.

The lines weren't easily legible in the few seconds I had. I run back to the freezer, tripping over some cords in the darkness. I feel around in the freezer, noting its contents and the fact that I'm releasing precious frozen air that I might not be able to get back.

My hand skims across a frozen TV dinner. I place the frozen turkey and mashed potatoes flat against my Etch A Sketch, hoping it will bring its temperature down enough. Then I grab my notebook and paper, ready to translate.

I impatiently wait thirty seconds, hearing Toph hammering away at something a few rooms down.

"Toph!" I yell out. "Toph can you come here for a minute?" He comes jogging in wearing a tool belt and holding a sledgehammer. Art's gun is tucked in one of the pockets. I try my hardest not to get distracted at this lovely sight.

"I need to use the light from your phone. Will you shine it on this?" I hold up the frozen dinner clapped onto the Etch A Sketch. He pulls his phone out of another one of those handy pockets.

"Sure, but I'm not sure how much time it'll give us before it dies."

"Okay," I say. "There are three different lines of writing across here." I point to the surface of the board under the frozen din. "When I say go, you're going to shine your light on the board and read each letter, one by one clearly and quickly while I write them down, got it?"

"I'm ready when you are."

I take a deep breath. "Now!" I remove the frozen dinner and grab my pen. Toph starts shouting out letters and numbers like a drill sergeant.

"T-L-I-C-H-T-Y-6-6-4-2, next line"

"Go!" I assert.

"F-exclamation mark-N-D-T-H-3-C-U-R-3."

"Next line now!" I bark.

"C-colon-slash-slash-uhh…T or an L?" He

wavers. "It's disappearing, gone now. Only a few letters left."

I sigh and hold the rapidly thawing frozen dinner back on the Etch A Sketch and place the pair back in the freezer.

"What's going on here?" He peers over my shoulder at the two and a half lines I wrote on my notebook.

"T Lichty," I mutter under my breath. "It's some sort of username and password to something of Dad's."

"What's the next line say?" Toph asks, looking at my hastily jotted down symbols.

F!ndth3cur3

"The password is 'find the cure.'" I bite my lip. "Our ancient computer at home doesn't require a username and password. It's got to be something here, where he used to work."

Toph is just staring at me with a confused expression. "One more quick round of catch up?" He asks. "You have all the clues or gifts figured out except the Etch A Sketch and the chess game, right?"

"Yeah, that's right."

"And what made you figure out that you should freeze the Etch A Sketch?"

"Have you ever played with aluminum powder?"

I ask.

"Uh, I don't know?" Toph answers defensively.

"Well, it sticks to everything. It's what coats the glass surface of the Etch A Sketch. When you turn the knobs, a stylus scrapes off the aluminum powder leaving you with a line or a design, or in my case, writing. However, when the aluminum powder freezes, it doesn't stick anymore and it drops to the bottom, leaving Dad's message in naked view."

"Thanks for the lesson," Toph chides. "But how on earth did you know to freeze it?"

"Oh, the crossword puzzle," I reply. "You figured out that the across words were a message. But the down words all correspond to the gifts. My ninth gift was the Etch A Sketch, and the answer to nine down was *freeze*." I pat my notebook. "Very handy."

"So what is the clue that goes with the chess game?" He asks. I imagine the sledgehammer did him no good and now he's hoping to help out in a different way.

"Office," I reply. "Office is the clue word."

"Which is why you came here?" He asks.

"No, actually. I came here to find Art and get my chocolate back, same as you." I answer. "But when I entered, I felt all sorts of nostalgia. Right up until Art started to strangle me."

"Did this place used to be your dad's office?"

"I'm nearly possitive."

"Well here's what I think," Toph says. "There is something in here on one of these computers that's for your eyes only." He points to the notebook with the username and password. "The clues we figured out together correspond in some way, these must as well."

"Yeah, the cookbook and the jeopardy tape went hand in hand also." I look up to Toph. "If this is the office dad was referring to, the only way we could have gotten in is if we had a key." We both stare at the game of chess. I glance up at Toph.

"You think this game is going to lead us to a key?"

He nods. "And if that key can get us in, it can get us out."

I finally have a glimmer of hope again. "Help me translate this last frozen line," I say with new energy.

"C-colon-slash-slash-T-R-L."

"That's it?" I ask.

"Yep," Toph answers, peeling back the lid on the TV dinner. He throws the entire serving of turkey into his mouth. His phone light goes off.

"That's the end of that," he says.

I hold my notebook over the candle, careful not to singe the paper. I stare at the third line written in my notebook.

C://trl

"We have a username, password, and a file. Now all we need is some power or I'll never know what's in that file."

"Acutally," Toph chomps, "there's one computer over there that's plugged into a UPS."

"What's that?" I ask, knowing all too well he's enjoying my naïveté.

"Uninterrupted power supply. It's for emergency backup. If we're lucky it will give us twenty minutes or so of battery.

"That's enough time to check inside the folder and also find some way to contact help." I follow Toph across the room to the computer he was referring to. It has a large monitor and purrs to life at the touch of a button.

"Let's just hope IT was lazy enough not to deactivate his account," Toph says.

"I got this Etch A Sketch two years ago. If Dad made this clue then, the account must have still been active." Toph scratches his whiskery chin.

"How are you sure he didn't make all these clues within the first year and then have them sent out every year on your birthday?"

I scowl. "You don't think he's alive any more, do you?"

"I hope he is."

"That last gift, the chocolate," I stammer with emotion, "was hand delivered. Who else would have delivered that?"

Toph closes his eyes painfully. "I did." When he finally opens them he searches desperately to meet my eyes. "Luce, I meant to tell you earlier. I found it in my dad's office. It was ready to be sent in the mail. It had a stamp and a sticker with your name and address. I was curious. I wanted to see you again after all these years. So I took off the sticker and stamp and decided to deliver it to you in person." He tries to take my hand but I won't let him. "I drove out to your house on the afternoon of the twenty-fifth, but no one was home. So I wrote your name on the front and left it in your back door." He rubs his forehead. "I don't know why I did it, and I don't know why I didn't tell you earlier."

My brain frog clears enough to get angry. "So you lied to me, this whole time."

"I never meant to lie, I never meant any harm, Luce. Please trust me, I'll explain everything. But right now, you need to type in that username and password because we're wasting battery."

I send him a look meant to kill and then turn all my attention to the blinking cursor in front of me. The light shining out from the screen is bright to my unadjusted eyes. I pray with all my being that this account still exists and that Dad still exists. I type each key precisely as written and wait.

Before I can say another prayer, the black screen parts outward unlocking a new blue screen. It still works. And whether dad set it up recently to work or he made sure it would work a decade ago, I count my blessings and search through the files until I find a folder labeled *C*.

"This is it," I say, not forgetting Toph's betrayal but still grateful I'm not alone. He leans in. I click on the folder and find more than a dozen files in here. None of them say *trl*. I start clicking on each one starting at the top and find they redirect me to a page of jibberish code. Finally, I reach the last one.

"Truman R Lichty," I read aloud. "T-r-l." Toph puts a supportive hand on my shoulder. I want to shake it off, but instead I focus on the screen in front of me. When I double click, the screen goes black and an arrow pointing right shows up in the middle.

"It's a video," Toph says. I grab my pen and push play.

The screen flickers, and an image of a timer shows up. "It's loading," Toph says.

"How much time does the battery have left?"

"Maybe ten minutes. Shouldn't take that long." He scrolls over the video. "Looks like it's only a couple minutes long."

I nearly lose the air inside of me as I wonder if I'm going to see Dad in this video. My hands start shaking, and I have to physically tell myself to breath. "Here." I hand Toph my pen. "You take notes—I'm too shaky."

We wait in silence, watching the white bars tick around in a circle, round and round. The room around us is completely silent and black except the spotlight of white air bursting out of the screen.

At last the video starts playing. It is fuzzy and the shot is distant, but I recognize the location. It's Dad's office—before it had been renovated. Nearly the same place I'm standing now, but years ago. It looks like this is a surveillance tape, as it's looking down on the room. The room is a creamy yellow color with a stainless steel lab table.

Three people enter the room: a man, a woman, and a child. The video pauses, trying to load again. "Who is that?" Toph asks.

"I don't know." Toph takes the cursor and zooms in on the frozen image.

I gasp.

I recognize Art first. He is younger, similar to how he looked at Dad's funeral. He has on a white lab coat and thick black circular spectacles. In his right hand, he holds two syringes. A long roll of butcher paper sits across the lab table, not unlike at a doctor's office. At last, the video starts playing again. Toph turns the volume up as loud as it will go.

The woman and child sit on top of the paper-covered table. I recognize her voice immediately. It's Mom. She speaks to Art. "Hopefully Truman will understand. With my family history, I can't risk it.

My grandma got Alzheimer's at seventy-five, and my mother at sixty. For all I know, I could only have a few years left."

Art nods. "This is completely precautionary and made for people exactly with your family history. There is no reason the government should have shut it down so abruptly. Your husband spent his life on this, and you trust him, now don't you?"

Renee rolls up her sleeve. I notice she's wearing a loose white blouse with crocheting around the neckline and sleeves. I wear that shirt all the time. It looks amazing on her with her loose brown curls.

"Of course I trust him, but he told me it wasn't time."

Art takes the cap off the syringe and taps the air bubbles out. Then he takes an alcohol swab and cleans off her deltoid. "It's now or never." Without another word, he plunges the syringe deep into her arm, slowly pushing the serum into her blood stream.

The child is blond and thin, deeply distracted by her Rubik's Cube and oblivious to the world around her.

Art tosses the syringe into a red sharps container on the wall and then speaks again. "Go ahead and wash the area with soap and water. The bathroom is just down the hall."

Renee turns towards the girl. "Lucy, I'll be right back. Stay put." Renee exits, and there I am, alone with Arthur Aldridge for the first of many times. He looks toward Renee who is nowhere in the shot, then pulls the second syringe out of his pocket and takes the cap off. Silently, he slowly moves the needle towards my arm and pierces through my skin without warning. I watch as the little girl jumps, reacting. And then in a blurry blaze, Renee sprints across the screen, shoving the little girl out of the way. The needle exits my arm, and in the confusion, enters the back of Renee's arm. Art's thumb is on the plunger, having extinguished all the serum into both of us.

"What have you done?" Art stares at the empty syringe, mortified.

"You injected my baby?" She screams. "You had no right! I trusted you."

"I was doing what is best for both of you," he says. "She carries your genes—your fate—as well. But because of your actions, you've received a dose and half of the serum. These amounts can be toxic."

"I will press charges," Renee says. "This is criminal."

"You are as much at fault as I am," Art hisses. "You agreed to taking a drug the government prohibited. You say one word and we're both in trouble."

Renee's expression is livid. "Come on, Lucy." Renee grabs her purse and my hand and the screen goes black.

Back up power is out.

CHAPTER TWENTY-THREE

The still, dark room swallows me as I sit frozen in time, forgetting anything else around me. After several minutes, I realize I'm stroking my left arm where the serum was injected ten years ago. I have no recollection of this, but it happened, and the evidence is waiting in a folder in Dad's secret file for the world to see.

"Why?" I finally speak into the silence. "If he had this video, why didn't he turn him in?"

Toph finds a chair and rolls over to me. "Maybe it was a more recent acquisition," Toph suggests. "We already know your dad is innocent. I don't think that's the main thing he wanted you to see in that video."

A phantom pain pricks my skin and I rub my arm again. "He wanted me to see that I have some of the medicine in me. More like—toxin."

Toph clears his throat. "So, in your system there's a small dose of a long acting, precautionary anti-Alzheimer's vaccine. Do you think that's the reason Truman was able to give you chocolate and target those dreams and memories?"

My head is swimming in thick confusion and I'm tired, hungry, and overwhelmed. "I have no idea. I don't know what's true, what's not true, who I can trust, how to get out of here, why you lied to me, or if I should hop on a one-way plane in three hours and flee this country of dishonest fleabags."

"Three hours?" Toph exclaims. "Tell me you're not leaving tonight."

"Yeah. I need to get Mom the chocolate in one hour from now, and hop on the red eye in two." I throw my head back in defeat.

Toph stands up and walks away. I hear him rummaging through the fridge again. He comes back with the candle, half a bag of frozen peas, two string cheeses, and a mostly full bag of lunchmeat.

"Luce, you've come so far. We're not giving up." He drops the food onto the blanket. "Here, munch on this hors d'oeuvre while we make sense of everything."

I nibble on the end of a string cheese. "Can't wait for the main course."

"I didn't lie to you. I did withhold some shameful information but only because it was embarrassing."

"Omission is a sin."

"I may have acted surprised when you told me about the present on your door step, but I didn't know it was drugged up chocolate, and I didn't know who they were from. Nor did I know why they were in my dad's office! He never told me, and I never asked."

I take a deep breath. "Remember that night on the beach, that conversation we had? You told me you thought my dad was still alive. But a few minutes ago, you said you thought my dad had made all these gifts within a year and then had your dad send them out each year. It doesn't make sense. Which is it?"

"I really did believe your dad was alive when we had that conversation. I still think he did all the work as quickly as he could, gave it all to my dad, and asked him to give you one each year. He probably did this just in case he wasn't alive to do it himself. And because he had to be in hiding."

"Okay," I process. "Then tell me what's changed. Why do you think he may not be alive anymore?"

"There are two high-ranking men out there who want Truman dead, both to cover their own dirty tracks. Art, for obvious reasons," he points to the darkened computer screen, "and my dad to save his job." Toph closes his eyes and I can tell this is hard for him.

"Art thought Truman was dead, until you went and told him otherwise, right?"

"That's right," I agree.

"And now that he believes he's alive, he's out on a manhunt." Toph exhales. "But my dad isn't hunting at all. He's hiding in the corner of his office, ordering me to stay as far away from it as possible. Why isn't he out looking for him as well?"

I can't believe what I'm hearing. "You think your dad already finished him."

Toph shrugs, hiding his face from me. He has gone silent, but I venture on.

"That's why he was hiding out at my house that night. My dad was there. He had to have been. Judy took my mom home early because Mom couldn't stop talking about how she had seen him," I sniffle, "Dad." I'm filled with regret. "I wish for once I would have listened to her. She could have been telling the truth."

The air is dead around us and our energy wilted. I only see the shadow of Toph's long figure, hunched over, pitiful on the chair.

In this moment of aching and sadness, all I see is my truest friend in pain.

Blindly, I walk over to where he sits. I find his face with my hands. His cheeks are wet with sorrow and it breaks me. I curl myself up onto his lap and gently hug around his shoulders, resting my head against his strong chest. He wraps his own arms around me, hugging me fiercely. Time seems to stand still for a few precious minutes as we accept hard truths.

My head is buried in the soft fabric of his shirt when at once, all the lights burst on across the entire building. I jump to my feet and look around us for intruders. Toph takes my hand and walks in front of me like a bodyguard, checking each room.

"Gotta be the backup generator," he says. "Just kicked on."

I run to the back door and shove my body into the handle. Still locked.

"At least we have light," I say. I glance down at my watch. It's eight fifteen. Mom's chocolate will expire in forty-five minutes.

"How long will it take to get from here to mom in Yachats?"

Toph crunches some numbers in his head. "We're somewhere outside of Florence in the Bush," he says. "I'd say forty minutes or so, plus or minus ten."

"If the officer who is holding mom gets a message to meet us half way, that saves us twenty minutes, best case scenario. That leaves us with about twenty minutes to find a way out of here," I figure. My brain gets ahead of me. "We have power now and could send out a message for help!" I exclaim.

"Email?" Toph asks.

"But wait, even if they did see the message and make it here in record time, the building is locked down, inside out."

"We've got to find the key," Toph replies solemnly.

We make our way over to the chessboard, both wired and frantic, now aware of our time restriction. I pick up each game piece, feeling if any is weighted more heavily. Toph examines the board and the instructions, looking for something, anything out of the ordinary. I'm in such a frenzy, my brain is moving from one question to another without allowing myself time to think deeply about any of them. Luckily, Toph is taking charge.

"I'll take white, you take black, start setting up the pieces."

I find my eight black pawns and line them up on the second row. Then I find the king and queen and they take their spots on the back row. The two rooks are next and then the knights. My hands are shaking and clammy.

"Do you have my other knight over there?" I ask. Toph's pieces are all accounted for and set up properly. He stands up, searching the area.

"No, but there's this checker piece," he answers.

I look up and freeze. "That's it," I whisper. "That's the clue. There never were two black nights.

Last time I played, I substituted this checker for the missing knight."

"A missing black knight," Toph repeats. "How does a black knight get us into a government building…"

"The address," I exclaim. "Twenty-five-eighty Winding *Knight* Oaks. The clue 'office' was pretty obscure. The missing knight is a clue that this is the office he was referring to."

Toph furrows his brows. "So, that's the clue? Do you think there's a key after all?" He asks. "I mean, maybe he assumed you'd come during business hours."

"This place doesn't have business hours." I smirk, looking around.

"I'll bet the locking system is magnetic," Toph says. "Maybe these game pieces have magnets of some type in them."

I'm desperate enough to try anything. As we drag the pieces near the locks, there isn't any sort of pull or charge. Our time is evaporating into thin air. I can actually hear the ticking second hand pass after each second.

When there are mere seconds left, Toph resorts back to the sledgehammer, pounding with all his might at the walls, barred windows, and metal doors. We are in denial that our twenty minutes is up, as we pound through sheet rock, only to be stopped by metal walls.

Sweat is streaming down Toph's temples and over his scabbed cheek as he fights with all his might for our freedom. I have to physically restrain him to finally get it across that our time is up. Renee will not get what was intended for her.

"I'm so sorry, Luce," he cries out through sweat and blood. He still holds the sledgehammer, but falls against the wall to the floor.

For the first time in a while, I finally regain my composure. "We did everything we could," I stammer. Toph takes my hand and pulls me down next to him. "It was a lot to ask," I say feeling subdued. Toph turns towards my face and cradles my cheek. His eyes try and console me.

"So what now? Your plane leaves in what, a little over two hours?"

I want to free myself from this failure, from the weight of this day of impossibles. I put my hand on Toph's knee and then slide my body so it's snug up against his. Like a gift, the lights all die at that moment and we are left in complete darkness.

"Lights are probably on a timer. Generator is still on," Toph mentions, a little out of breath. We sit in still silence for several seconds, both of us breathing a little heavier, waiting for what is going to come next. I'm not one to make the move, but with time ticking away and my international flight quickly approaching, I know Toph isn't about to try and swoop in and monopolize any of my precious time.

So I do.

Slowly, I slide my body into his lap so he's cradling me and rest my head on his shoulder. He welcomes me in, running his warm hand up and down my arm. I reach up feeling the whiskers along his jaw, wishing there was enough light to see his face. He pulls me in tighter, his warm breath tickling my neck and sending tingles down my arms. With his free hand, he gently runs his hand through my long hair, softly combing his fingers through the wavy locks. I feel like I have entered a different world, one that's impossible to leave. I cling tighter around his shoulders and he turns to me, our faces are pressed together, our lips just centimeters apart. He rests his forehead against mine and keeps his lips agonizing millimeters away before he turns and quietly rumbles a line into my ear.

"Play chess with me?" By the tone of his voice, he is still lingering in the 'whooped zone' but that line was enough to snap me back into reality.

"Is chess code for something else?"

Toph laughs.

"What? Right Now?" I ask.

"If I only get to spend a few more minutes with you, let's make it interesting."

I know exactly how I want to spend my last few minutes with him, and it doesn't involve chess. I slide off of his lap feeling punished and wait while he lights what remains of our candles. We set up the board, and his eyes study me, seeming to read more than just my outward reactions.

"You can go first," I scowl. "And just so you know, I'm really good."

Toph musters a grin. "Would you be willing to bet on it?"

I tilt my head back and smooth my hair into a long ponytail. Toph watches my every move and I'm getting him right where I want him. "What did you have in mind?"

"If you win, I promise I'll get you and your mom to Australia."

I nod approvingly.

"But if I win, I get to kiss you," he says, taking my face into his palm and eying the outline of my lips. "Before I get you onto that plane."

The flush and heat are creeping back into my cheeks. "Those are your terms?" I whisper.

Toph nods, leaning back, eyeing his pieces. I feel bad for the poor guy. He could have gotten what he wanted for free, but now he's going to have to come find me across seas to collect his kiss.

I've never lost.

He moves his first pawn out methodically. I immediately follow, already sure of the strategy I will use. We play in silence, and Toph is starting to sweat. I have my pawns barricading in the center of the board.

"Interesting strategy," he remarks.

"As is yours. You could have had exactly what you wanted, yet you decided to sit back, move your bishop, bet on your odds. I even let you go first," I say. "You could have had me. And now your moves don't stand a chance."

Toph grins. "Those lips are mine, Lichty."

I make my next move shaking my head. "Your bishop is mine, Summers."

He looks down at the board with his mouth gaping open. He makes a point to close it quickly, and concocts a brisk, confident move. "So I'm guessing I'm not your first?" he asks.

"Of course not. My first time was years ago, in the library of my middle school. I took advantage of Sheldon Reeves. Poor nerd." I sigh remembering my first checkmate.

I make another move, getting Toph's king right where I want him. He appears oblivious.

"Took advantage huh? Lucky guy. I thought I might have to teach you a thing or two." He leans back studying me more than the game.

"I'm quite experienced," I gloat.

"Well then maybe you should teach me a thing or two," he grins, moving his pawns and making them utterly useless.

"I will, Christopher, I will." I yawn and stretch, laying myself out in front of the board. I undo my ponytail and shake my hair out left and right.

"You play dirty."

I ignore him. "It's not your first time, is it?" I ask.

"Jane Winters. Seventh grade. Behind the dumpsters," he answers. "It was all right."

"So she won?" I assume.

Toph raises an eyebrow. "Won what, my heart?" he asks. "No way. Woof. Her shiny bubble gum flavored lip smacker lured me in like a moth to a flame."

I gulp. I misread our conversation real hard. First chess match and first kiss don't belong in the same sentence, let alone same conversation. At least my lie was innocent, and my lip virginity remains my own secret.

"First times are supposed to be unlike anything else, you know? Full of anticipation, electricity, bragging rights." I surround his knight while he continues. "If I could take it back, I would. Save it for the girl of my dreams." I confiscate his knight, but he rambles on. "Perhaps a leggy blonde who happens to be an auto thief, and also a professional butt wiper. Maybe even a chess master," he leans in towards me, talking real smooth and sexy. "An Australian goddess," he whispers, so close now I can feel his heat.

"You had me at butt wiper," I answer in a sultry voice, just before pushing his face away. "Focus, Summers, or you ain't gettin' nothin'."

One more move and I'll win the quickest and

easiest game of my life. I'm furious at the idiotic bet he made. I mean, he can't possibly think he's doing well.

I consider pretending to lose, but it's too late. At this point, I can't lose unless I forfeit. Seconds tick by and I'm getting flustered over the passing time and his incompetence. Without warning, I lose it.

"You are the worst chess player. Ever. You are absolutely terrible!" I cry. I move my queen and take his king. "Checkmate!" I yell and throw the piece at him.

He seems a bit taken back by my sudden huffing and puffing, but not at all surprised by his total annihilation.

"You don't really want to kiss me, do you?" I yell, picking up a handful of pawns and chucking them at him one by one. He shields his face from the metal pieces, but I grab a handful more. "You were the one who made this bet. You could have just saved me the time and politely declined. I'm sort of in a hurry here."

Toph shields his face from the chess bullets and finally moves towards me, reaching down to the board where I'm scrambling for more ammo. He forcefully pins my hands down under his. Our heads hover over the playing board.

"You think I don't want to?" He yells though my face is inches away. "Well, you're right. I don't," he growls, looking pained. "Kissing those lips would be like torture. Day and night, they haunt me. You are like a drug that I can't get enough of. How can I recover after this?" His body is rigid and his eyes glossy but fiery. "I thought I could do it, but every second I'm not with you makes me realize I'm not strong enough. It's like you are the one thing keeping me going in this world. If I kiss you, it will wreak havoc on me even more. Because I can't have you. And I've never wanted anything so bad." He exhales, finally unpinning my hands. He looks away. "And yeah, I suck at chess." He kicks a chair and it goes sailing across the room.

I study him in the silence, shocked at his revelation. Even his shadow looks rigid and explosive. His words leave me speechless and my heart torn.

"You don't need me," I finally mutter. "I'm just a part of your journey. I'm dispensable. You're just comfortable with me," I shrug. "I'm…I'm like a fish taco," I say, finally getting his attention and an eyebrow raise. "You think you like me, but it's just because you haven't had…sushi," I suggest.

"I hate sushi."

"Lobster. You haven't had lobster. You are so used to your dang fish taco. It's convenient and cheap. But one day, you'll want something more."

Toph stands with his hands on his hips, scowling at me. "That is the absolute worst analogy I've ever heard." He is nearly grinning now at my stupidity.

"Comfortable with you? Wrong. I've had a pack of Tums in my back pocket since the day we met. Convenient? Yeah, please let me drive to Yachats one more time," he begs. "Please let me get my A kicked again by a senior citizen. Please," he grumbles. I can't help but giggle.

"The only thing that's dispensable about you," he says, "is me." He takes a deep breath and turns away, walking back towards the tools.

"Hey! What about me?" I shout, pushing another chair so it sails across the room and blocks his route. He trips over a wheel and turns around.

"What about you?"

"What about what I want?"

Toph sighs. "What do you want, Lucy?"

I slowly walk over to where he stands, finding his shadow in the dark.

"I want my best friend to give me my first kiss before I can't ever get it back."

"Your first kiss?" His voice is low and thick.

I nod, letting go of my insecurities and placing myself right in front of him, begging for his arms to take me. "I know it's a lot to ask, but for once in my life, I'm going to be selfish. Please." I whisper with my head tilted up just inches from his lips.

He takes both of my hands, interlocking my fingers with his own, our arms still down at our sides, our bodies finally close enough to touch. I close my eyes waiting for the moment, feeling his face, his whiskers, his nose skimming against my cheek. He unclasps one of our hands, brushing locks of hair away from my face, and caressing my cheek, then my chin. Tingles of pleasure spring up from my neck and down my back. I open my eyes to see his own, closed, and his lips hovering just above mine. And then on cue, I close my eyes. His warm, soft lips brush against mine and teach me what to do. I don't know where I am, or what time it is, nor do I care.

He pulls me in tighter, and my hands are in his hair, on his neck. We kiss hard, his fingers pressed into the skin on my lower back. Nothing can stop this because it feels so right. But then, he does. Gently, he kisses me one last time before stepping back and grazing my sanded lips with his finger. I open my eyes and feel dizzy and short of breath. Toph swoops a rolling chair under me.

"Thank you," I laugh, squeezing his hand. "I will never forget that."

"Me either." We let the moment linger a few extra sacred seconds. "Now I've got to keep my end of the bargain and find you a way out of here."

I bite my lip. "I think I know how."

"What?"

"Just thought of it."

"While we were…?" He points back and forth between the two of us.

"No," I laugh. "While you were taking ages to

make your chess moves. So, in that video footage my dad sent, Art was standing over here." I point to the area back by the lab table. Toph follows me with the candles. "In the video, this is where he was standing. Once my mom left, he went back into a room to get something, out of the video shot." I motion behind me and point to the solid back wall.

"This wasn't here before?" Toph asks.

"Exactly. There was a door right here. And for some reason, it's been covered up by the remodel."

"So what you're saying is…" Toph lingers, "this building isn't impenetrable after all?"

"I'm thinking you're going to need that sledgehammer."

Toph prances off to get it before I even finish my sentence. He comes back, swinging it around like it's batting practice.

"I'm guessing they just covered it up with sheet rock. And even if they replaced the exterior with that thick aluminum, it will be a smaller replaced piece instead of a solid slab, easier to pound through."

"Excellent. Show me where."

I sit on the lab table, just like in the video and close my eyes, remembering Art's movements. Then I point to the spot and open my eyes. Toph motions for me to stand back, and he pounds his way through the sheet rock, meeting the aluminum with a clang. He takes the flat end of the hammer and breaks through about six feet high and three feet wide of sheet rock, then clears it away. We are left with shiny metal facing us.

"Here goes nothing" Toph hands me the sledgehammer, takes several large steps backwards then sprints towards the wall, hurling his shoulder into the metal with great speed and force. I close my eyes and tense up every muscle in my body.

A heavy, powerful thud sounds and then vibrations echo and are freed. I hear the trickle of a stream and breathe in fresh air from the outside world, peeking through the Toph sized hole in the wall.

"You've got to be kidding me—you did it!" I slip through the hole and find Toph. But my voice is muffled by the sound of a car. Two blinding headlights accelerate towards us. I gasp and pull Toph up from the ground. He stands in front of me protectively. Slowly we back up until we are flush with the building.

"Is it Art?" I whisper in dread. "Should we go back in and hide?" Toph is making up his mind and as he does, he pulls Art's weapon out of his pocket and holds it down to his side, still pancaking me against the wall protectively.

The headlights turn ninety degrees and the car parks abruptly. A man jumps out of the driver's seat and runs towards the metal door. We jump, just as a loud metal clang echoes through all corner of the building.

"Whoever he is, he has a key," Toph says.

"He didn't see us?" I ask. Toph shakes his head.

"I'm going to get your chocolate."

"No, wait. Toph, stop." Right then, a switch sounds and bright light streams through the hole in the wall. The light shines on the parked car in front of us, highlighting the writing on the side.

"Yachats City Police," I read, giddy with relief. Toph scrunches his brow. "Wait, what are these guys doing here? Something's not right about this."

At that moment, we notice movement in the back seat of the vehicle.

"Stay here," Toph demands. He holds his gun in front of him and slinks to the side of the car, crouching beneath the passenger window. My body is frozen as I watch in horror. Slowly, he reaches his hand up towards the door handle. In one fluid motion, he cranks the door open and points his weapon at the suspect.

Gasping, he drops the gun to the ground. It hits the gravel with a thud. I take several steps forward and join him at his side, anxious to see what he sees.

"Renee," I gasp.

CHAPTER
TWENTY-FOUR

"Hurry and get the chocolate in the beaker," I plead. "Maybe it's not too late."

Toph crouches back through the hole in the wall and disappears. I enter the cop car, sitting in the back seat opposite Renee who is cowering in the corner. Guilt and worry flood over me as I see the state she is in. A bag of fluid is hanging on a hook above her head, and leading down from it is a line, attached into her forearm. Her arm has been heavily bandaged, almost like a noncompliant kid who needed some reinforcement. The bag is steadily dripping, about one drop every second.

"Renee, why are you hooked up to an IV?" I stammer, reaching for the bag of fluid. "Midazolam in LR," I read. "Who did this to you?" I cry. But Renee is slouched into the corner and turned as far away from me as possible, her body in a tense ball, her expression devoid of emotion.

A tear slips down my cheek, and I reach for Renee's hand. She flinches and turns farther away, hiding her hands from me. I hear the rush of Toph's footsteps on the gravel. He swings the door and crouches his head inside the car.

"How is she?" He hands me the beaker. I shake my head.

"Not good. She's been hospitalized," I whimper. "They have her on IV versed."

"What's that?"

"A sedative." I sniffle. "We use it in the nursing home on some aggressive and psychotic patients." I think of Mr. Schroeder. "I can't even imagine what she's been through."

"It won't be all for nothing." Toph wipes my tear with his thumb.

I find an empty coffee mug in the front seat of the cop car and poor the contents from the beaker into the cup.

"Renee, I have some chocolate in this cup. Here, I want you to try some." I offer the cup out to her, but she recoils even more, pressed against the door. Deep down, I knew this was going to be ludicrous. Without physically forcing her, I don't know what to do. She has completely shut down. I hold back more tears and decide to beg.

"Renee, this is the only thing I will ever ask of you. And it's the most important thing you could ever do for me. I want to be a family again," I plead. "Please, as your daughter, I beg you to swallow this chocolate."

I let silence swallow up two minutes while I wait for her to give me anything. Renee is in her own dark place well beyond interaction. I hit my head back against the headrest desperate not to admit defeat. I won't ever give up trying.

"Did you find the cop?" I ask, suddenly angry for what he's put Renee through. Toph shakes his head, still leaning in through the back seat window. "No, but I heard him rummaging around in the supplies closet."

At once, the unmistakable sound of a gun cocking fills the air. I gasp, eyeing a black muzzle pointed at Toph's head. The officer holds the weapon with two trembling hands. I can't see his face, but I don't have to. I know his voice.

"Step away from her," he says. "Please. I don't want to hurt you. Just step- away."

Mom sits up, suddenly alive in this world. Tears stream down my cheeks.

Toph backs away slowly, his arms up in the air. The officer's weapon follows him. There is silence. I break it.

"Dad?" I beg, waiting for someone to fill the

void.

The door opens. The officer drops to his knees on the gravel. Dad's calming, gentle, familiar voice cracks. "Lucy. Darling. Is it really you?" He drops the gun.

I gasp. The world around me freezes in time. I try to find air as I look down at the officer. He removes his hat. His eyes are welling with tears, new lines creased below them. His hair is gray. His face is bearded. His voice is home.

"Dad." I shake my head in disbelief. My body is shaking uncontrollably. Dad takes my hands and holds them tightly, bringing them up to his face and kissing them over and over. Tears roll down his cheeks and onto my fingers. He sits on the seat next to me. I cry on his shoulder, taking in his smell, his mannerisms, his emotions. He holds me tight, waiting as long as it takes for me to come back up. I do, against my better judgment. Delicately, he wraps one arm around Renee and keeps the other around me. She doesn't fight. We are a family again. My heart might burst.

At last he looks at me, searching, trying to take in my adult self. His eyes twinkle, and I have a feeling this is the first time he has smiled in a long, long time. "You are amazing. Beautiful. Just so, so beautiful," he stammers through his emotions.

All at once I'm weighted down with hundreds of questions. I'm so overwhelmed with mystery, I don't even know where to start but Dad reads my mind.

"I will answer everything—all of your questions. But first, I need to know, are you coming with me?" He asks. He looks me squarely in the eye, but his question doesn't evoke pressure.

"Do you have my passport?"

He closes his eyes and smiles, sighing relief. "Yes."

I study his features. He looks like he hasn't slept in years. He's too thin, his skin is pale, and it seems he has a tremor in both hands.

Toph steps out from behind the car. "Guys, we have company. Truman, you expecting someone?"

Dad's eyes turn from relief to panic. We squint at the distant headlights. "Everyone, in the car now. I'll explain everything on the way." We pile into the police car, our hearts pounding. Dad is at the wheel, Toph is in the passenger seat, and I'm in the back next to Mom. I buckle her in. She doesn't budge.

Dad leaves the headlights off and swings around the parking lot, exiting through a way that I didn't enter, maneuvering over a curb. Slowly, we glide through the thick bushes scraping the sides of the car. We travel only five miles per hour, and no one says a word for three excruciating minutes. Everyone I love is sitting in this car, and I feel the weight of that.

At last, we reach a paved road. Dad turns his

headlights on dim and we settle into a normal speed. Behind us, the burst from an explosion erupts. I glance out the back window and see a massive blaze of fire, right where we came from.

"What was that?" I ask, alarmed.

"Arthur covering his tracks," Toph says. Dad nods.

"He blew up his entire building?" I ask. But Dad is focused on the task at hand.

"Time?" he asks, like a surgeon to his nurse.

"Ten-twenty-one," I report. Toph looks back to me and smiles but his eyes can't hide the worry.

Dad nods. "Forty minutes until take off." He pauses. "It's time. Christopher, lights please." Toph clicks on the passenger lights. Every few seconds, Dad glances in the rear view mirror at Renee, his sweetheart. I can see the pain and color draining from his face with every glance.

"I assume you watched the Daily Double, the secret footage on my C drive, and are prepared for this moment," Dad says.

"Prepared for this moment? Dad, I couldn't get the chocolate to mom on time, and I hate myself for it."

"Lucy, that chocolate was a precursor to this moment. Yes, it would have been a nice cushion, but it isn't a deal breaker."

"I don't understand. That chocolate isn't the antidote? Aren't we trying to reverse her condition?"

I ask in a panic. "Seriously, what's going on?" I'm so frustrated I could scream.

"Darling, we have one shot at saving your mother. A window. That window starts in nine minutes, and ends in ten. The Daily Double, what did it say?"

I scramble, firing my brain into life or death mode. "Something about antibodies- and their purpose," I answer.

"Very good. Now in the video footage you watched, Arthur gave your mom nearly twice the dose recommended, poisoning her. She didn't know it at the time, but she was pregnant." He pauses, his voice softening. "There's no way she could have known before she agreed to Arthur's plan. We had been trying to conceive for years without success. She took a test the day I left." Dad takes a deep, slow breath.

I gasp, holding my chest. The visions of the pregnancy test resurface from my latest dream. I hadn't thought about that until this second. Dad goes on, clearly trying to stay focused, but I can't even fathom the pain he feels.

"Pregnancy alters the metabolism of drugs. This particular dose caused her to abort the fetus, increasing the toxicity of the overdose. Her brain has been covered with thick amyloid plaque, similar to typical Alzheimer's patients, day-by-day tangling more and suffocating her memories."

I search for understanding but Dad doesn't have time to further explain.

"In eight minutes, the high dose she received will reach its peak. That's the beauty, and the danger of this drug. Normally, a drug reaches its half-life much, much sooner. Alzwell has the potential to be a miracle drug, but in our situation, it's a ticking time bomb. After this point, if untreated, her brain will start shrinking and decaying, resulting in irreversible damage."

I shudder in horror. He continues. "The beauty of the half-life is that the concentration will be officially reduced to one half its initial potency; in seven and a half minutes, that is. We have a sixty second window where the drug's potency is halved and the antibodies are potentially able to reach through that plaque, clearing the fog away, bringing her back to us before she's gone for good."

"I don't understand. Where are these antibodies coming from? Surely her own antibodies would have fought it off by now if they could." And then without another word from Dad, I get it. I replay the video in my head, watching Art poke my arm and inject a small amount of the medicine into my blood stream.

"My body created its own antibodies when I was poked," I say aloud. Dad nods.

"You are her freedom." I cover my mouth in astonishment. "Your dose reaches its half-life in," he glances to his watch, "six and a half minutes. For some glorious reason, your body responded beautifully to the antidote. You've been building these antibodies for ten years, and it's time, before the half-life reaches, to use what you've been building."

A shiver runs through my whole body. "Are you suggesting…" I pause. "Dad, what was the fourth chocolate for?" I ask.

"It was to prepare her body for a rapid blood transfusion, to prevent adverse reactions, and prevent clotting." I shake my head and try to focus.

"This seems insane. I mean, is our blood even compatible?"

"You're O negative," he answers.

"The universal donor," we say in unison.

"Christopher, you have four minutes to draw Lucy's blood."

"Whoa, what?" he exclaims.

"Wait, Dad. Quick question," I interrupt. "What if I had shared that chocolate birthday present with somebody?"

Dad makes eye contact with me through the rear view mirror. "Lucy, you don't share chocolate." We share a quick smile. Man, I've missed him. Dad carries on. "Lucy, at ten thirty to the second, you will take that precious blood and directly connect it to her IV catheter. Do you understand?" Toph squirms in his seat.

"Yes," I answer.

"Sir, I…" Toph stammers.

"Open the briefcase," Dad orders. Toph looks to me with a pale face. "First take the alcohol packet and clean Lucy's anticubital fossa."

I take the alcohol swab from him and clean the inside crook of my elbow.

"Take the tourniquet and tie it tightly above her elbow."

Toph obeys, getting out of his seatbelt. He turns around, facing me, following orders.

"Now, there is a butterfly needle…" He trails off, eyeing his rear view mirror. The freeway is crowded, but he suddenly pushes on the gas and weaves in and out of cars. I hear the revving of a car on our tail.

"Who is after us?" I ask. "Art or the chief?"

"Chief Summers?" Dad questions. "He isn't involved in this mess anymore. And he doesn't need to be—all right, Christopher? I need this operation to stay clean. Right now you need to focus. Take that butterfly needle, take the cap off, and insert it right up through that vein, bevel of the needle up please."

Toph looks white as ghost. I think he may pass out.

"Here, put this under your nose so you don't pass out," I whisper. Toph places the alcohol swab just under his nostrils, but I see his eyes rolling back.

"Give that to me," I order. I swipe the needle out of his hand, biting the cap off with my teeth and spiting it to the ground. I've seen enough phlebotomists drawing blood on my patients to know the basics. I flick my vein and it bounces, ready to give me what I need. Carefully, I thread it through the center of my vein. Sharp tingles shoot outwards just before the thick, dark blood seeps through the tubing and up into the container, filling it slowly and steadily. I release the tourniquet and it flows more freely. Up in the front, Toph is sniffing hard on that alcohol swab, fighting hard for his manhood.

I am ecstatic with my first attempt success when suddenly, our car veers left and right whipping us sideways. My needle threatens to dislodge. I hold tight to my arm, pressing against the needle securely. I ignore my lightheadedness.

Dad mumbles curses under his breath. In the excitement, Toph snaps out of his blood delirium and focuses on the predicament.

"Art?" Toph mumbles under his breath. I see Dad nod. "Why doesn't he just let you go?"

"I have something that he wants."

"Why don't you show the world that footage? Free yourselves."

"If I do that, many people I care about will get hurt. Including your father and my wife."

Toph is quiet. I hear the car behind us again. Dad

glances from his side mirror and back to the road several times. "I can't let him follow us to the airport."

Toph throws his body into the back, sliding me into the middle seat. He rolls down the window and leans his body out, simultaneously pulling his confiscated weapon out.

"Toph! Get in here!" I scream.

"Veer right," he orders, and we surge sideways. He aims at the car and takes two shots, then ducks back into his seat.

"Got one of his tires."

Dad nods in approval. I'm getting woozier by the second. "I hate this," I announce. "Dad, are you a cop?"

"No, honey. I borrowed a nice officer's car. And clothes," he adds.

Without warning, he slams on the brakes, sending us weightless in the air, only suspended by our seatbelts. He pulls off into the median and flips around into the screaming traffic on the opposite freeway. Toph, who still isn't buckled in, plummets into the console. I gasp, covering my eyes.

"Where will the next exit take me?" Dad asks, clenching his teeth and oblivious to Toph's blow. He grips the steering wheel, his knuckles white, trying to control the shaking in his hands. I realize why he put Toph in charge of poking me instead of himself.

"Not this one. Take 272 going west. It'll get us back on track," Toph says, pulling himself back into his seat.

For once, I'm jealous of oblivious Renee. I check my own pulse, positive my heart isn't going to make it through this.

"Get your seatbelt on!" I hiss at Toph. He ignores me. Dad glances back at me through his mirror.

"Lucy, that's enough blood. Save some for yourself. You're going to need your energy."

Toph looks at me and through the haze, I see the concern on his face. He grabs a cotton ball and holds his breath, removing the needle from my arm. Blood bubbles up, pooling in the crook of my arm. Toph swallows hard and holds the cotton ball down.

"Sixty seconds," Truman states, glancing at me in the mirror. I nod, as delirious as the beginnings of my chocolate dreams. I fight it, taking an alcohol swab to clean off the port of Mom's tubing, but I have to sit back.

"She's not going to make it," Toph yells towards Dad.

I lean forward with my head between my knees, trying to remember to breathe, but the unconscious world wants me, tempting me with an escape. I bite my lip as hard as I can, tasting blood and reminding me of what matters. Toph lifts the saturated cotton ball from my arm. More blood spurts out. He grabs a two-by-four piece of gauze and presses down harder. "It won't clot," he yells up front, holding my face with his other hand, trying to keep my gaze.

Dad is ripping through the traffic. The trees and surrounding vehicles blur into a colorful mirage against the black backdrop. At once, I see the blinding flash of red and blue lights. I'm not sure if they are real. The ringing of sirens is deafening.

"Fifteen seconds." His voice tempts me to stay present. I know I have a job to do, and I'm stuck in a different realm.

The sharp sting of alcohol under my nostrils revives me. My dilated pupils narrow, focusing on Toph, who is cleaning off Mom's port with a fresh swab of alcohol and firmly putting pressure on my arm with his other hand.

The lights surround us left, right, forward, backward. Dad's strained countenance takes on more stress. "Art framed me again. To all of them, I hijacked a police car and am running off with hostages."

We're forced to slow and eventually come to a complete stop under a freeway bridge. But with the precious seconds ticking, the armies that face us aren't our priority.

Sweat drips down Dad's forehead. "Christopher—buy me some time. I need sixty seconds to infuse the minimum amount, or this is all for nothing." He takes my blood and the tubing, not waiting for an answer.

Amplified voices demand we step out with our hands up.

"Go," Dad pleads. A whimper escapes my lips as Toph nods and heads onto the front lines, unarmed. We lock eyes before he shuts the door.

I see the shadow of his face between the blinking flares of red and blue lights, his arms up in the air. It's as if the air is knocked out of me. I have to look away.

I glance down at my arm and lift the cotton. It's clotted.

The air is charged in the car, keeping me where I need to be. It's time. Dad is leaning over the console facing us, ducking his head and holding the two lines up in front of his eyes. The dim passenger lights flicker. His breaths are quick and heavy as he brings the tubes together, but the shaking in his hands is too fierce.

Feeling the weight of each second tick away is sickening. With my steady hands, I take Dad's in my own and together, we connect the lines. I twist the valve onto Mom's securely. Dad finds the clamp and frees it. We hold our breath, watching the blood drip by drip as it colors the clear tubing red.

Dread consumes me as I wait for a bad reaction. How I wish I could have gotten that last chocolate to her. I feel sick in my stomach about Toph, wondering if he's safe, how many more seconds he can buy us, and if it will be enough. My nerves are on fire, and that hazy world that offered me an escape has closed its doors.

Dad looks to me for just a second, reading my emotions. "Fear is the opposite of faith, Lucy." His voice is warm, comforting. He takes my hand in his and turns his attention back to Mom.

Mom's eyes are closed, but her breathing is even and unlabored. I'm grateful Dad was wise enough to give her a sedative. I take her cold hand in my free hand.

"You've given up everything, and given her everything," Dad says to me, his gaze turning towards me. His voice is tender. "And now, you're giving her this." We stare at the blood, halfway infused. "I couldn't ask for anything more. You're a selfless, smart, gracious daughter. Thank you forever, Lucy."

A hot tear slips down my cheek. His few words are payoff for a decade of hardship, gifting me with a life free of regret.

"How long will it take?" I ask. "If it works, I mean. How long until she'll remember?"

"Realistically, years. And we shouldn't plan on a full recovery. But day by day, things will come back to her as the antibodies fight. Eventually, she will recognize us. It might take— " Dad stops speaking. I look up and see that Mom's eyes are open, fixed on Dad, just inches from her face. She reaches her hand up and caresses Dad's cheek. In a heartbeat, her voice is filled with life. "Truman. You're back."

Dad's eyes are glassy, bewildered, unbelieving. He places his trembling hand over hers, still on his cheek, his eyes searching for understanding. He nods. "I'm back," he stammers. "Are you?"

Mom squeezes my hand and looks over to me. Tears overflow from her eyes as she takes me in. "I'm here." She smiles with certainty. "And I'm so glad I am."

Dad lets out a sob and leans in, kissing her tenderly. Mom wipes the tears from his cheek and brings me into their huddle. We're a complete unit. My world is full again, ten years of emptiness filled in a heartbeat. We hold each other as the infusion completes, vaguely aware of the sacrifices each of us has made to enable this moment. I can't imagine ever needing more. But then I think of Toph.

"It doesn't make sense," Dad says. "Lucy, your antibodies. Physically, it's not possible…"

It seems I'm the only one aware that the minute of time we begged off Toph is well up. As Dad ponders the impossible, the outside reality forces me to look. When I do, the sight makes my stomach flip.

Toph stands in front of our car, one arm around a man's neck, his other pointing a gun at the man's head. Spotlights are blaring into their faces.

"Oh no. No," I plead.

Dad looks out. "Is that Art?"

I nod. "Toph's holding him hostage." I see Toph's eyes dart back towards us for half a second. His weary expression informs me that our time is up.

I reach over Mom and open the door. Fresh air pours into the car. The lights are blinding. Still holding each other, we step out one at a time, standing behind Toph and his victim.

Dad holds us protectively. "I'm sorry. It wasn't supposed to end like this," he whispers.

Mom pulls us in closer. "This is only the beginning."

Art flinches at Mom's lucid words.

When Toph can see that we're out, he drops his gun, holding his hands up in the air. The second the gun hits the ground, the SWAT team swarms.

Dad and Toph are forced to the ground face down and handcuffed. Mom holds my hand tight, not letting anybody separate us. I'm not sure if it's due to my weakness and pallor or the bag of empty blood still connected to Mom's arm, but we are ushered back to an ambulance. In the commotion and masses of professionals, I lose sight of Dad and Toph.

I assume they're treating us as victims instead of suspects, clear up until they handcuff one of my wrists to a metal rod attached to the interior of the ambulance. They do the same to Mom, who sits on a stretcher parallel to the bench I sit on. Three professionals in medic scrubs examine us, only asking medical questions. I'm sure the interrogation will come later. If only I'd had time to ask Dad what he planned on telling the cops so we could be on the same page. But I already know—I will tell the truth. The absolute truth.

They restart our IVs, pouring saline into our systems and treating us kindly. The cold fluid seeps through my veins and makes me shiver. A kind nurse puts a white blanket over me.

The outside world is closed out behind the safe doors of the ambulance. I wish I could see Dad and Toph. The ambulance crew steps out to talk with an official who is looking for a medical update.

"Are you okay, Lucy?" Mom's words bring me back. I glance over at her, concern all over her face. Concern for me. I can't help but smile.

"Yeah. We'll be all right."

"We," she closes her eyes, shaking her head. "I don't know where I've been, but I do know that you never left my side. Might be the only thing I'm sure of." She smiles, and the confidence and peace I see in her are overwhelming. I watch her clear, focused eyes as she continues. "Luce, it makes me sick trying to imagine the last—what—eight? Nine? Ten years of your life?"

I nod and she brings her hand to her chest, indicating that her heart is broken.

"I hate that I missed out, that I wasn't there for you when you needed me. But above all, I'm grateful. I'm proud. And I don't know how I can ever thank you." Her chin is quivering.

I smile, reaching my arm across for a hug. She stretches too, but our hands only stretch far enough to rest on each other's shoulders. We both laugh.

"One hour ago, I didn't have either of you. Now I have two amazing parents. I have a family again. I couldn't ask for anything more."

Mom is glowing. A tear falls down her cheek. "How about you tell me about that boy out there you're worried sick about. He's a looker."

I throw my head back and laugh. "You know that's Christopher Summers, right, Mom?" Her eyes get wide.

"No!" she whispers. I nod my head, still laughing.

Through our giggles we hear the hum of a low voice next to the ambulance doors. "This is a former patient of mine. I'll just need two minutes of her time," he says, the back doors opening and quickly shutting behind him. The ID he flashed to the medic crew disappears into his pocket.

When I glance up, I'm so mortified, I've completely lost the capability to scream. Art's sadistic face glares under the damp ambulance lights.

"If you scream, I will shoot you." His placid tone

sends a piercing shiver through my entire body.

Mom is white as a ghost, closing her eyes, undoubtedly praying. I make a life or death decision, betting against him. I take a deep breath and scream. But Art's hand plummets over my face, smothering my volume. With one hand still firmly over my mouth, he pins me down onto the metal bench and seals my mouth shut with medical tape. Renee is quietly shaking in the corner, and I watch as he does the same to her.

With only one arm handcuffed, I tear the tape off my mouth and glance around wildly, trying to find anything to use as a weapon, but I am an arm's length away from anything useful.

Art stands in front of us, his dark wrinkles even more prominent than just hours earlier. The cold look in his eyes is horrifying. "This time, there's nothing you can do," he says, pulling a syringe out of the inside of his jacket pocket.

"This must look familiar." He holds the syringe in front of Renee, teasing her with it. "Every last drop of Alzwell, a toxic dose. I've been saving it for a special occasion." He exhales with forged displeasure. "Your daughter is going to inject you herself. I wouldn't want to soil my clean record. I have to admit, I'm curious to know the effect a dose this size will have on you. My guess is complete, irreversible brain damage." The corners of his lips curl up in a perverted smile. He turns his attention to me. "I framed Truman, and now I'm framing you. How does it feel?"

Without a second thought, I hurl my body towards him fist first. My hand knocks into his shoulder and sends him skidding into the opposite wall of the ambulance. His head hits an emergency kit, sending syringes and glass bottles falling to the floor. I fight with all my might, but I'm still stuck to the opposite wall, just feet from him.

Someone must have heard the noise. Someone will come in. His two minutes will be up soon.

Art drops to his knees and picks up two glass ampules that fell out of the metal kit he ran into. I glance over his shoulder, discerning the labels.

Epinephrine.

Holding the full syringe of *Alzwell* in his mouth, he breaks the tops off the ampules and opens the packaging to a new syringe. With speed and precision, he draws up the fluid from both into one single syringe, identical to the one he's clenching between his teeth.

"You're a fool," he says under his breath. "It's time that you're silenced. How about we change our story? Truman drugged both of you. One of you, with *Alzwell*. The other, epinephrine. Enough epinephrine to make your heart stop, immediately." He takes both syringes and shuffles them in his hands so they become indistinguishable. "Who wants to go first? Pick a hand," he says to Mom like a lethal spider, toying with its prey. "Funny thing is, you'll never know which of you chose brain damage and which one chose immediate death."

"Help!" I screech with everything I have in me. Art turns around and backhands me, his hand slapping my face hard enough that I fall back into the wall where my handcuffs are locked.

Without another word, he takes the lid off one syringe and darts towards Renee.

I jerk the IV needle out of my arm that's still dripping with fluid and fling the IV tubing around his neck, wrenching both ends of the cord. Art stumbles back and falls onto the hard floor, his elbows taking the brunt of his weight. The syringe that was millimeters away from Mom's arm falls to the floor next to my feet. My hand seizes it without a second thought and I missile it down into Art's unsuspecting neck, pushing the plunger down and extricating every ounce of fluid.

Before I have time to fully withdraw the needle from his skin, Art turns and seizes my arm, yanking me down towards him. With my arm still cuffed to the wall, I'm bent awkwardly, halfway on the stretcher and partially on the floor. His eyes are wild and erratic, blind and awaiting his own fate. I'm pinned under his weight and have lost the air to scream.

Blood drips out of the hole in my arm where the IV needle was, and weakness ensues. As he bites the cap off the last syringe, I give one last attempt to wriggle free but I'm utterly trapped. My body is rigid. I close my eyes as he plunges the syringe down towards me.

I feel nothing.

I open my eyes and see Mom's arm draped across me, Art's syringe emptied into her blood stream in a split second. Art collapses into the corner, attempting to hold his head steady. I pull the empty, dangling syringe out of her arm.

"No!" I cry, witnessing the immediate effects take action. I fall down to the ground with her. Her face turns pale and her body starts shaking. I reach across and touch her neck, anxious to feel her pulse. "Mom, don't go." My own blood and tears are running rampant.

Her breaths become short and labored and I recognize the symptoms of cardiac arrest. She pulls my hand away from her neck, away from her weakening pulse. She clutches my hand with both of hers, holding it tight like she did when we exited the car, braving her destiny. I lay my spiraling head down on her chest, feeling it rise and fall a few final times until she is still.

As she enters a new world, I beg to go with her, drowning in my own tears and sorrow. Faintness is all consuming and offers me respite. I take it, holding tight to her hand.

CHAPTER TWENTY-FIVE

Though I'm certain there's a deafening commotion here inside the ambulance, all I hear is a faint ringing as I watch the chaos from above. My emotions are left back with my body. I'm nothing more than an outsider watching from an unseen observation window.

I view an elderly man, crouched in the corner, holding his head.

A young woman, pale, but life's enchantment is still flowing through her body.

A middle-aged woman, her spirit withdrawn from her soul. I look around, wondering if she's watching from above also, but she's nowhere to be seen.

The severe mark of blood is splattered across the floor and stained down the young girl. Empty syringes lay on the floor, their bevels sharp and unprotected.

A medic walks in and releases a panic signal. Within seconds the double doors are flung wide open and the ambulance is saturated with personnel, the cramped space immediately infiltrated. Blinding lights illuminate the scene. Three crowd around the woman, vigorously performing emergency CPR. Two take the girl's arm, clotting off the dribbling IV site while restarting another. The man in the corner is interrogated, but his blank expression leaves them frantic for answers.

A gradual crescendo of sound brings me closer to the scene. I hear the constant beep of a machine, breathless, desperate counts during chest compressions, and finally a man's voice. "Fire up the AED. Is everybody clear?"

Two paddles full of electricity are placed on the woman's chest, then another voice. "Separate their hands or Lucy will get shocked too."

Lucy. I recognize my name. The second my hand is ripped away from hers, my spirit and body connect and I gasp in a breath of the present.

Mom's chest convulses with the powerful shock and I can't watch nor can I look away.

"Ventricular fibrillation stabilized," a medic reports.

"Pulse?" another medic demands.

"One hundred ten."

"Pulse?" I say. "She has a pulse?"

The medics ignore my cry. I sob unbelieving tears of joy and sit back on the bench, watching them force life back into her.

Someone removes my IV before all the fluid has had a chance to finish hydrating my system.

A heavily armed officer approaches me.

"Lucy Lichty?"

"Yeah, that's me."

"You're under arrest. Please stand." I wipe away my tears of relief just before the officer locks both hands behind my back. He leads me out of the ambulance doors and into the dark night, where the ominous flashing lights surround us. I follow directions, knowing all this will be sorted out soon. Nothing can dampen the fact that Mom is alive. I glance around for Toph and Dad, but they are missing.

"Do you know where my dad is?" I ask. "Or when I'll be able to speak with him?"

"Miss Lichty, you are being charged with two accounts of first degree attempted murder. You can speak with an attorney tomorrow."

I feel the color drain from my face, imagining the scene they stepped into when entering the ambulance—

-My IV tubing around Art's neck

-Art's glassed over expression

-The depleted syringe I pulled out from Mom's arm, lying right next to me.

Both syringes contain my fingerprints.

I was the only one who didn't get injected.

This is unreal.

Art was right. I've been framed.

CHAPTER TWENTY-SIX

The smell of the pee-crusted metal toilet an inch away from my thin cot is revolting.

I can't eat. I can't sleep. It's four a.m. I miss my family.

I'm supposed to be in Australia, not prison.

They tell me to go to sleep, that I'll get used to it. I refuse to—I'm innocent.

Five days ago, my father was dead and my mom was a vegetable. Five days ago, I didn't know that the guy I've fallen for still existed. And ironically, five days ago, I would have been charged as a minor.

My emotions are fried. I keep telling myself, hour after hour, that things will work themselves out. That truth will be heard. Justice will be found.

But being quarantined for five hours and counting and treated as a convicted felon is playing unhealthy tricks on my morale.

I've scrutinized the situation for proof to buy my freedom and bring my family back to a whole. So far, everything leads back to the fact that we were fleeing the country and my fingerprints are on both syringes. Mom's miraculous recovery was credited to Art, National Institute of Aging president, with officials believing I tried to finish her off once her mind was back.

I eye the toilet again, ignoring Mother Nature's call. With the slotted prison bars, privacy is a joke. I will wait. But for what? My trial? Some obvious evidence to appear? Dad to fake his death again and break me out?

The truth is evident—I could be here for a while. But I still refuse to use that abominable can. I won't give in that easily. I deserve a proper bathroom with soap.

A pile of starched, white sheets lie in a pile on the corner of the cot. I run my hand over them. They feel more like sandpaper, but that beats whatever scum is growing on this mattress. I think of the line of women who've lain here before me. What their crimes were, how long they served, why they couldn't hit the bowl of the toilet. What a legacy to follow. Hardly a bedtime story.

I lay my head down, thinking of Dad and Toph,

if they share the same fate as me, or worse. Again, I try and convince myself that everything will get worked out.

A carving on the cement wall parallel to my line of vision sidetracks my bleak thoughts. I welcome the distraction, trying to decipher the letters through the little light that's coming into my cell through the bars.

There are three words, all in caps. When I finally put them together, I wish I hadn't.

KILL ME NOW

CHAPTER TWENTY-SEVEN

Happy clouds of cotton dot the sky with streams of sunshine breaking through. I feel the heat from the sun's rays resting on my limbs, warming my soul with the promise of summer. Brightly colored wild flowers are sprung up from every surface, sharing their nectar with fuzzy bubble bees.

A sweet and warm aroma of maple and sugar fills my nostrils. I hear the crunch and swallow of horses grazing on hay nearby. Their munching gets louder and all too soon, becomes obnoxious. Soon, these impolite horses are ruining my perfect summer afternoon.

I open my eyes.

My florescent orange jumpsuit beams me back to

this cruel reality. I glance through the bars. Sitting on a metal folding chair right in front of my cell, is a cop—same one who brought me here yesterday. He's noisily grazing on a pastry and watching the harsh facts seep back into my groggy head.

"Mornin', Sunshine," he says in between noisy swallows. "Glad you got some sleep. I'm here to discuss…"

"How's Renee?" I interrupt in a groggy morning voice. "How's my mom?"

"Oh, she'll be fine."

His casual tone is infuriating.

"In fact, if they can get all their testing done, I'll bet the hospital will release her today."

"Then soon she'll tell you all that I'm innocent," I say. "As are my dad and Toph Summers."

The cop grins. "You know, a mother would do anything for her child, even after betrayal."

I shake my head in disgust. "If you're not here to listen to me, then why are you here?" I'm fuming, wishing I could stuff that doughnut into his fat face.

"Great question. I'm meeting someone. Ah, here he is now."

A weaselly man in an oversized suit enters from the right, stopping in front of my cell. He shakes hands with the cop.

"Miss Lichty, as you know, you have the right to an attorney. This is yours, Mr. L.W. Walsh, Oregon State Defense Attorney."

I nod my head politely in place of a handshake.

"Maple bar, Lyle?" The cop grabs the cardboard box next to his chair and holds it out to my attorney.

"Don't mind if I do." He pulls up a second metal chair next to the cop's and sits down in front of me.

"Nice to meet you, Miss Lichty." His voice is deep. He doesn't have the look of someone who's won a lot of cases, but he has kind eyes.

A kitchen worker slumps by and slides in my breakfast tray. Half a boiled egg—the yolk is smelly green and matches the shade of Mr. Walsh's baggy suit. A burnt piece of dry wheat toast sits cold and unwelcoming next to the egg.

I stay on my cot.

"Better eat, young lady. Don't want to hurt the cook's feelings," the cop snickers and elbows the attorney playfully. I stare at them blankly while the cop takes a giant bite of his pastry. To my delight, the red jelly squishes out and plops down the front of his uniform.

For the first time since admission, I grin.

L.W. Walsh doesn't try and hide his smile as he takes his maple bar that's centered on a napkin and slides it under my cell.

"Now what do you think you're doing?" the cop yells.

"These metal bars seperating us don't cause humanity to disappear."

I like this guy.

I'm not hungry, but I take a bite of the maple bar to show my gratitude. After one bite, I remember that I'm actually starving. I gobble the rest of it down, licking my fingers and realizing that might be the last time something edible crosses through these bars.

"Miss Lichty, I'm here to discuss your rights, your specific charges, your hearing schedule and so forth. But first, I want to answer any questions you may have for me."

"Thanks," I say. "I appreciate you being here, and yeah, I have a question."

"Just one?"

"That depends on your answer."

"Go ahead then," he says.

I look him straight in his kind eyes. "Do you believe me?"

Mr. Walsh's eyes don't falter as he answers firmly. "I will believe every word you tell me."

The cop produces a nasal guffaw, still scrubbing the jelly stain off his shirt.

I smile and exhale. "Well, then, I have a lot more, but first, some backstory."

"Ten years ago, Arthur Aldridge injected both my mother and me in his work lab. My father came across surveillance footage of this exact scene, probably a year or so after he had already been falsely convicted. At this point, he was in hiding."

The attorney nods, scribbling down in his notebook.

"I have seen this footage with my own eyes, as has Christopher Summers."

The fat cop interrupts me. "If he had proof of his innocence years ago, why didn't he bring it forward? This is ludicrous."

"For several reasons," I say pointedly. "First of all, this was the first time that he saw what had really happened. Arthur Aldridge injected my Mother and then, while she was out of the room, he tried to inoculate me as well. But he didn't get very far. My mom intercepted him and inadvertently got stabbed by the syringe intended for me. She received way more than was intended for her, thus causing her early on-set dementia."

"You're saying that you received some of the Alzwell, correct?" asks Mr. Walsh.

"That's right. When my dad saw this, he knew he had to come up with a plan to try and reverse the effects—mess with the half-life, come up with some type of antidote. He had to play his cards wisely, considering he had a mad man closely watching his wife and daughter. If he had just turned that footage in, Arthur Aldridge would have killed him or us, or, the government would have locked him up, not giving him the time he needed to come up with a reversal. My dad has spent the last ten years of his life waiting for the moment when my mom could be cured. He didn't kill her, he saved her, in the most selfless way possible. My dad was worried he would get caught or killed before it was time for the cure, so he came up with a series of clues to lead me to our salvation."

"So, Miss Lichty, where is this surveillance footage you are talking about? Seems like this could buy you and your loved ones your freedom."

"Blown up in his lab building on 2580 Winding Knight Oaks."

The cop is rubbing his head, getting impatient. "It's a great story. With zero evidence. You got two more minutes, then you need to start up on your prison duties. It'll be like the first day of school."

I feel panicked and flustered. I think about bringing up Chief Summers and how he helped Dad fake his death. But even if he does come forward, it won't prove my father was innocent. It will only get the chief in trouble.

Something comes to me. "I know. How about the fact that Art was a fake resident in the nursing home I worked at?"

"We pulled those records," the cop says apathetically, his arms resting on his belly. "All of his tests come back positive for diabetes. He was a real resident."

"Well then he rigged those tests!" I yell. "He's a fraud! He's a monster! He's been stalking me for years to make sure I don't remember his transgression. He didn't cure my mom, I don't care what you say about him being the NIA director. I saved my mom with my own blood! Check it!" I yell, out of breath.

The cop just shakes his head calmly and sighs. "Thirty seconds left." He starts gathering the donuts and garbage under his chair. Mr. Walsh is still scribbling things down in his notebook.

"Miss Lichty," Mr. Walsh says.

"It's Lucy."

"Lucy, your preliminary hearing will be in two weeks, during which, the court will determine if sufficient evident exists for you to stand trial."

"Two weeks?" I say, mortified by my lack of options. "I have to sit here for two weeks and just wait?" I feel tears well up in my eyes and I see the genuine sympathy in my attorney's. He twists a ring around his finger habitually, looking for some words to uplift.

"Search your mind for details, trails, any possible evidence. I will gather as much as I can in the mean time."

He stands up and collects his things. I saunter to the back of my cell, burying my head in my arms, wishing I could disappear.

"Keep your chin up," he says before turning and walking out of view.

My world as I've known it, already a shade of grey, is now black. I feel cold, with no way to get warm. Stiff, with no way to get comfortable. Alone, with no one to wrap their arms around me. While I'm grateful for the concern the attorney showed, his bleak expression clued me in to my future verdict. I think of his slouched posture, the ring he twisted round and around.

That ring…my thoughts trail off somewhere. And then, an epic epiphany hits me straight in the face. In a millisecond, my brain exports the idea into evidence. I can hardly catch my breath, like the wind has been knocked out of me. When I finally do, I yell at the top of my lungs.

"Mr. Walsh! Wait! Mr. Walsh!"

After ten seconds, my attorney saunters back into view, a curious expression on his face.

"I've got it. Possible evidence to prove my innocence," I say.

My new nemesis walks around the corner. "Your time is up, princess. Time to go put some of those CNA skills to work. They got cleaning, and bed makin' and all sorts of fun. You might even meet your new cell mates if—"

Mr. Walsh holds his hand up so sternly that the cop goes silent mid ridicule. All of his attention is on me.

"Go on, Lucy."

I gulp and nod. "When they arrested me, they took all of my personal items. It mostly consisted of the things I was wearing. They said they would store them here, sealed in an envelope. I need you to go get them."

"You can't have them," the cop starts.

"You'll go get that envelope immediately, Officer." A dark shadow emerges from the corner. His familiar voice is dripping with authority.

"Yes, Chief Summers. Right away."

The chief comes into view as the officer scrambles away. Mr. Walsh follows behind. The chief nods at the men before turning and addressing me.

"Lucy, it is finally time that we spoke."

Still surprised by his appearance, I stare ahead at the large, commanding man. "My dad already told me you aren't involved in this anymore," I say, a hint of anger in my voice.

"As long as I know the truth, I am involved. You see, the plan was for your father to cure Renee, and disappear with the two of you to Australia and live a full and happy life. Unfortunately for both of us, that didn't work. Due to the recent, unexpected turn of events, I will come forward and fight for your freedom, no matter what the cost. I don't want you to sit there alone, thinking you don't have anyone standing behind you. Believe it or not, I always have been."

"You—you are going to fight for us? Even if it means losing your job?"

"Whatever it takes," he answers.

"Wow." I pause to absorb this new knowledge. "Does Toph know?" I ask. "Does he know that you're—a good guy?"

The chief smiles. "I've spoken with my son."

Another question comes to mind. "But why were you in my house that night? The night I sprayed you with mace? Apparently you weren't hunting my Dad."

The chief nods and I swear I see his eye twitch. "As you know, Christopher took that final gift out of my office without telling me. I was panicked. I made a promise to Truman, years ago, that I would get every single one of those gifts to you. I broke into your house that night out of desperation, to see if someone had dropped it in the mail, to see if you had, by some chance, received it."

My previous anger is lifted and I feel nothing but respect and gratitude for this man. "We owe you, Chief," I say. "Thank you for everything you've done." I pause. "But I'm worried. Even if you come forward and stand for my dad's innocence, do you hold any new proof? Or are you just his best friend who happens to be the chief of police?"

The chief shuts his eyes as if already accepting the new consequences his actions will create. "I don't know. But we have to try."

We hear footsteps down the hall. We both lean in. "Before you tell the world that you covered for a convicted criminal," I whisper, "wait."

The cop strolls in and holds the envelope out to the chief.

"Poor it out," the chief demands, pointing to the floor. The cop obeys.

"That, right there," I point.

Walsh picks up a ring with a large, mesmerizing stone in the center.

"Abalone," I say. "Art gave it to me as a gift. He told me it was once used to communicate with heaven. But—" I rub my head, wondering if my hypothesis could be correct.

"But it was a selfish gift. He was using it as his own means of one-sided communication, to keep tabs on me."

"You think there's a tracker in there?" Walsh asks.

"I'll bet it does, but more importantly, I think there's a microphone. Yesterday, I came unannounced to his lab while he was dissecting a chocolate from my dad. I'm guessing he wasn't tracking me at the time because his efforts were focused on hunting my dad. However, when I got close to him, I heard a weird sound come from his phone. The sound of feedback. Every time he got closer to me, that static-like noise would screech. I don't know how I didn't think of it before," I admit. "I need you to get Art's phone. The two have got to be connected in some way."

Walsh and Chief Summers are out of there

before I even have time to say thank you.

*

Two hours later, I'm digging trash out of a gutter that's running along the prison perimeter. To be honest, it's cleaner work than what I'm used to at the nursing home. I hear chatter amongst my jail mates. I turn around to see what the fuss is about. A prison guard blows her whistle to get us back on task, but I can't look away.

Inside the prison grounds, walking towards us, are four suited men, all wearing sunglasses and looking like a scene straight from Men In Black.

I drop my shovel when I recognize Walsh and the chief, resulting in a loud clang against the cement. I bypass the prison guard and run up to them, begging for good news, knowing I only have seconds until the nasty guard piles on extra duties. The chief doesn't say a word while he pulls a familiar cell phone out of a sealed plastic bag. I recognize it from the lab. He pushes an icon that says *Voice Tracker* and then types in yesterday's date.

"Why don't you go ahead and listen in at 2316," he says, handing the phone to me.

I push play, turning the volume up. Equal amounts of static increase as well.

I hear heavy, panicked breathing, most likely my own. When I hear his voice for the first time, chills crawl up and down my arms and I feel sick, right back in that ambulance, desperate to fight for our lives. His voice will forever haunt me. But I listen.

"I framed Truman, and now I'm framing you. How does it feel?"

My mouth drops. It's the most glorious thing I've ever heard exit someone's mouth. So much cynicism and hate and perfection all wrapped up in one exonerating phrase.

The chief pushes pause and reclaims the evidence. I'm relieved I don't have to relive any more of that scene. "The judge listened to the entire ambulance happenings—twice. Your actions were brave and impressive, Lucy. There's more than enough hard evidence to set you and your daddy free. On account of the State of Oregon Department of Justice, you are officially released of all charges."

"Immediately?" I ask, wide eyed. "My father as well?" He nods.

"And Toph Summers?" I ask.

"And Christopher Summers," the chief smiles with a sparkle in his eye.

I close my eyes, thinking of the weight of the last five days, the last ten years. For the first time in a decade, I feel the bonds and doubt and fear released. I am liberated in every way.

I throw my arms around my new best friends. "Thank you," I say, fresh tears running down my cheeks.

"Lets get you home."

"One thing first," I say, sniffling.

"What's that?"

"Please take me to a public restroom."

CHAPTER TWENTY-EIGHT

One year later

Six plump steaks sizzle on the grill. Dad tightens his apron and flips each sirloin, ensuring perfect grill marks. Chief Summers stands to Dad's side and together they chuckle and exchange stories behind the smoking grill. Their animated actions are entertaining enough to ignore my book and enjoy the show from my chaise lounge.

The yard looks immaculate. The trees have been pruned and the grass is a rich green. Most of the patches have filled in, their root fibers weaving together to fill the vacancies—not unlike the efforts my parents made to heal our family, so eager to fill the gaps from the ten years they can't get back.

Shari Summers opens the door and walks out onto the patio holding glasses of icy lemonade on a silver tray. Mom follows behind carrying a triple layer coconut cream cake. It is bigger and more decadent than a wedding cake.

"Mom! Are you serious?" I yell across the yard.

"Shh," she silences me. "Get used to it, birthday girl."

I close my eyes and giggle, soaking in every second of this. Howie saunters over and jumps onto my lap, his moist dog breath a smelly cloud in my face. When I scratch his head, his entire body collapses on top of me in pure doggie ecstasy. I can barely breathe but I love this overgrown mutt too much to kick him off.

"You stole my seat, Howie. Move it, fatty."

I open my eyes to find Toph, smiling down on us. He's holding some flowers and a wrapped rectangular box, always and forever in his cross-country garb.

"Put some pants on, Summers," I smirk.

"Happy birthday, Luce." He kneels down and hands me a gorgeous bouquet of peonies, giving me a look that might actually cause me to stop breathing. I sit up and Howie rolls off, onto the grass.

"Open it," he says, handing me the box.

"Is it present time?" Mom calls. "Wait for us!"

They pull some chairs over so that we're in a circle of sorts. I tear open the wrapping paper, grinning at Toph suspiciously. I open the box and find a green University of Oregon tee shirt and matching sweat pants.

"I love them!" I exclaim. "Perfect. Just what I need."

"Not that I don't love seeing you in that lab coat every day," Toph says.

I snicker. "Thanks so much, Toph. I love them."

"Can I steal you for one second?" he asks, suddenly serious.

"Yeah, sure. Is everything okay?"

He nods, taking me by the hand and leading me around the corner of the house, away from the suspicious eyes of our parents.

"What's up?" I ask.

"I didn't think you'd want your parents to see the other part of your gift." And before I have time to ask what he's talking about, he grabs my arm and pulls me in, planting his lips on mine, kissing me like it's the only thing that matters. He wraps his arms around me, lifting me up to his same level, literally sweeping me off my feet. I'm dizzy, swimming in bliss, when a voice around the corner brings me back to reality.

"Get a room, you two!"

Shari is onto us. I giggle and peck Toph one more time on his soft lips.

"Don't even think about it!" my dad shouts after her. This time, Toph laughs.

I walk back sheepishly, my rosy cheeks giving us away. Meanwhile, Toph scolds our parents. "What do you think we are, animals? I was just showing Lucy my latest breakdance move. It's not ready yet for your eyes."

"All right, Lucy. My turn," Dad says, handing me a small package. I rip the paper off and find a box of gourmet, hand-dipped chocolates.

"Very funny, Dad," I say grinning, standing up to give him a hug.

"This has been the perfect birthday. Thank you all so much for making it special. But I can't deny that I'll miss those mystery presents that showed up on the doorstep, year after year. I guess I have both of you to thank for that," I say, speaking both to Dad and the chief.

"Well, it's not over yet," Dad replies.

"What's not over?" I ask.

"Your yearly delivery. I should specify, not the delivery itself, but the clue attached to it."

I raise an eyebrow. "I'm listening."

"While I was in hiding, I gave you ten gifts, one per year. Nine of them, you deciphered and used on your journey to cure Mom. The tenth clue has yet to be identified."

I turn to Toph. "We didn't figure all of them out?"

Toph sends me a one-sided grin. "Your bike—it was at the nursing home, so we didn't take it with us to the bar with the rest of the gifts."

"And we were able to figure out Dad's message without it." I turn to Dad. "So, you want me to go hunt it down? I gotta admit, some of those clues, no, all of those clues, were next to impossible to figure out. This could take me the rest of the year to solve, especially considering no one's life is on the line. That feeling of impending doom was very useful."

"Trust me," Dad says with a grin. "It will be worth it."

I stand up and jog to the side of the house and eye my aged, well-used bike. Just looking at it brings on warm feelings and I'm reminded of the first time I laid eyes on it—the shiny baby blue paint, the perfectly woven basket that would eventually hold groceries and schoolbooks. Even the ugly zip-tied surf rack holds so much sentimental value.

I wheel it back to my birthday party posse, nudging the kickstand so it's on display in the center of the circle.

"It's here?" Toph asks, motioning for Dad to drop a steak down on his plate. "I thought you had it on campus."

"I brought it on the bus today and rode it home from the bus stop. I've been wanting to ride it through Yachats like old times."

Toph nods, taking a carnivorous bite of his steak.

"You should be glad. Now you all get to watch me suffer through this last clue."

"Have some dinner first, Luce," Dad says with a large steak hanging down from his fork.

"Nope. I'll eat after."

"Oh, here we go," Toph says.

I run inside the house and make my way to the back of my closet. I pull a large, sealed box out of the corner and open it. Immediately I find the book of crossword puzzles and flip to the page titled *Key*. I find six across and read the answer:

Third and sixth

I run back out to the bike with a victorious grin spread across my face.

"So what's the clue, Luce?" Toph asks.

"Third and sixth," I answer. "Not to be confused with three and six. Third and sixth. This type of language could represent the third and sixth day of the year, or third and sixth place in ranking, the third and sixth volume of something," I trail off. "But I don't think it's any of those."

Mom and Dad are thoroughly entertained by my monologue, like it's dinner and a show. All remain quietly munching while I continue.

"This bike has twenty-one gears, with numbers one through three on my left hand here, and numbers one through seven on my right. If I'm correct, Dad's reference to third and sixth pertains to the gears. Third gear on the left, sixth gear on the right." I don't even look up from my charade to see if Dad's face gives away any clues to my accuracy.

I hop on my bike and switch to the golden gears, pedaling around on my grass until the bike has finished shifting. Then I hop off and take a gander at the chains, expecting a revelation. After several minutes of looking for patterns or clues, I walk the bike back to the dinner party.

"Luce, how about a birthday steak now?" Dad asks. I ignore his question.

"Do you have a blacklight?"

"No, not here," Dad replies.

"I do." The chief reaches into his pocket and pulls out a keychain with all sorts of random things connected to it including a Leatherman and mace. I clap my hands as he removes it from the chain.

"Don't ask to borrow the mace," he says with a smirk.

"Don't worry, I have my own."

Mom and Shari laugh nervously, but between the chief and I, we know we're good.

I wheel the bike back into the dark shed, shutting the door behind me. I shine the light on every square inch of the bike. No hidden messages appear.

When I walk the bike back, the conversation has moved away from Dad's hidden clues. Toph is questioning Dad.

"So she's a bit of a super-human, right? Have you figured out how her antibodies worked so fast?"

Dad smiles, gazing at me, while I keep fiddling. "Hard to know for sure. Until Lucy decides she wants her blood cells to be dissected under a microscope, we'll just refer to her as *gifted*. Another very telling test would be to use her blood to cure a separate Alzwell overdose case."

"You mean on Art," Toph clarifies.

I snort. "As much as I'd love to wake him up so he can coherently suffer through his sentence, there's something very comforting about knowing that a very evil part of him is gone, and only I have the combination to free it. Wait a second—the combination," I repeat, my brain waves spark with a fresh idea.

"Hear me out here, Doc," Toph continues to Dad. "I could use some superhuman genes myself here. I got second place last week during a preliminary meet. What can we do about that?"

I switch the gears down and roll my eyes at the absurdity of this conversation. I switch the gears back to third and sixth, bringing my ear close to the bike.

"Well, for starters, maybe you should lay off the red meats and fast food. Changing your diet might help," Dad answers. Toph nods and heads to the grill for seconds.

"Listen to this," I say, switching the gears again. Mom kneels on the grass next to me, bringing her head in close. "When I change the gears back to third and sixth, there's this light clicking noise. Do you hear that? I think the gears are a combination, and that click is unlocking something."

I don't want to bust the bike open. Besides its sentimental value, it's my main means of transportation around Eugene and campus. I have Mom switch the gears back and forth as I listen to each part of the bike to hear exactly where the click is coming from.

"It's the right hand grip," I say confidently. "There must be something in there." I notice a seam circling around the outer most end of the rubber handle, about a quarter inch from the end. With the gears on third and sixth, I wait for the click and attempt to twist the end. To my astonishment, the quarter inch piece of rubber separates from the rest of the handle, turning counter clockwise with each twist of my fingers. After two more turns, the end comes completely off.

A hush comes over the six of us. I send Dad a sly smile. Howie barks, breaking the silence.

Without looking, I stick my finger into the tube, conceding that it's not empty. I feel a thin piece of rolled up foam and pull it out. Rolled inside the foam is a scrap of paper, and inside the paper lies a key. I hold the key up, and read the number on the paper scrap.

"Twenty-five eighty." I glance up at Dad. "Twenty-five eighty Winding Knight Oaks? This is the address to your old office."

"And apparently, the key to that office," Toph says. "Man, that would have been nice to have!"

We laugh. "Well, Dad, I don't need this anymore. Maybe you should keep it, for memories' sake. Frame it and put it in your new office."

"Tell you what," he says. "Let's switch. I've got a different key that will be more useful to you."

Out of his pocket, he pulls a large black key and hands it to me.

On the center of the black key is the word *MINI* with wings sprouting out from either side.

"Dad," I start. "What is this?"

He checks his watch. "Just on time. Go look out front."

I drop everything and sprint around to the front of the house with Toph and Howie on my heels.

There, parked in my driveway is a gloriously bright red Mini Cooper. My yellow surfboard is attached to the rack on top. The sun's rays are beaming off it, giving it a celestial glow.

"You've got to be kidding me," I stammer. I start jumping up and down, screaming like an elated mad woman. When Mom and Dad make their way around front, I pounce into their arms, hugging them, still bouncing.

I try to not look at the tears in their eyes so I can hold it together myself. Dad wipes one off his cheek. "Finally," he says. "You deserve it."

Mom kisses my cheek. "And now you can come home and visit even more."

"Thank you," I sniffle, still shaking my head in disbelief. I hug them tightly one more time before opening the door and hopping into the driver's seat. Dad sits next to me on the passenger side.

"I forgot one thing." He reaches into his pocket and pulls out a silver engraved key chain. I hook it onto the new car key and read.

"Fortune favors the prepared mind. –Louis Pasteur"

"Fortune?" I say. "Does that mean we're through relying on chance?" I hug my locket against my chest.

"Fortune favors the brave, my girl. You have conquered chance."

I think about his words for a few seconds. "Dad, you sound like a fortune cookie."

"I have some experience with that."

"Well, if you ever decide to bag working on the Alzheimers cure, you have a backup profession."

Dad smiles. "Together, we will cure it."

"Sounds good," I say. "In the meantime, let's go eat cake."

ABOUT THE AUTHOR

Andi Hyldahl is a graduate of Utah State University with a degree in nursing. As much as she loves poking limbs and passing meds, her creative beast escapes during the quiet hours of night shifts, where she dreams up stories and scribbles plots in the margins of her *Drug Dosages* book. Andi lives in Northern Utah with her favorite people, her husband Scotty and three kids.

Made in the USA
Middletown, DE
02 April 2017